NO JUSTICE

Also available by JK Ellem

Stand Alone Novels

A Winter's Kill
Mill Point Road

No Justice Series

Book 1 – No Justice
Book 2 – Cold Justice
Book 3 – American Justice
Book 4 – Hidden Justice
Book 5 – Raw Justice – coming soon

Deadly Touch Series

Fast Read – Deadly Touch

Octagon Trilogy (DystopianThriller Series)

Prequel – Soldiers Field
Book 1 – Octagon
Book 2 – Infernum
Book 3 – Sky of Thorns – coming soon

NO JUSTICE

by JK Ellem

NO JUSTICE
Copyright © by 28th Street Multimedia Group
Copyright © by JK Ellem

No Justice is a work of fiction. All incidents, dialogue and all characters are products of the author's imagination and are not to be construed as real. Any resemblance to persons living or dead is entirely coincidental.

All rights reserved. In accordance with the U.S. Copyright Act of 1976, the scanning, uploading, and electronic sharing of any part of this book without the written permission of the publisher is unlawful piracy and theft of the author's intellectual property.

No part of this book may be reproduced, stored in a retrieval system or transmitted in any form or by any means, without the prior permission in writing of the publisher, nor to be otherwise circulated in any form of binding or cover other than that in which it is published without a similar condition, including this condition, being imposed on the subsequent purchaser.

Interior book design by Bob Houston eBook Formatting

Copyrighted Material

ONE

The Home Depot didn't sell plastic drums big enough to fit a body inside.

The sulfuric acid was sourced from a janitorial supply company out of Austin, Texas and they had plenty left over from last time. But all they had were the standard-sized drums and Linton was a tall guy, long-limbed and gangly. In the battle between femur and crowbar, crowbar won out. So they broke both his legs before they folded him into the drum, topped him off with the acid and sealed the heavy-duty plastic lid.

The three men wore disposable coveralls, long thick rubber aprons, rubber gloves, and full-face respirators.

It took two of them to load the drum onto the hand-truck then wheel him into the vault. The vault was a five by five room with plain concrete walls, and a smooth gray-painted floor that the rubber tires of the hand-truck squelched over as they slotted him between the other drums.

The vault room was in an old abandoned bank building the family owned. It was located on the fringe of the old town where the main commercial hub used to be until progress pulled the shoppers east to where new stores, a mall, and a small-business center were built. New homes sprouted up around the hub of stores and restaurants, and the town shifted a mile or so up the main road, leaving behind the rundown empty carcass of its former self. The old town was now just a desolate stretch of unkempt dirt blocks, cracked sidewalks, and empty stores boarded up with plywood. Like most Midwestern small towns there was always a previous version of itself, hiding on the fringe like an abandoned child sulking among the weeds and decay.

The bank had closed the branch soon after the GFC, the town too small to justify the expense of keeping the doors open. Men in suits sitting around a mahogany boardroom table in Charlotte, North Carolina made that decision as they watched their bonus payments disappear when the stock price tanked.

The three workers closed the heavy iron door of the vault room then changed out of their protective clothing, leaving the coveralls, aprons, and respirators hanging neatly in an empty side office.

It was close to 9:00 p.m. when they finally emerged from the back of the bank building and locked the door. One of the men did a final walk-through of the building just to make sure it was secure before they got into their pickup truck parked in the darkness of the dirt lot at the rear. They didn't turn on the headlights until they hit the main road and headed back toward downtown.

TWO

The Greyhound bus limped into the parking lot of the gas station, a mechanical rattling and a trail of smoke coming from its rear engine compartment. The driver did a tight turn and parked near the entrance of the workshop away from the gas bowsers and the mid-morning customers filling up their pickups and SUVs.

The bus settled with a hiss of its air brakes and the front doors swung open with a grind of hinges in need of lubrication.

Hesitantly at first, like visitors from another planet arriving on an unknown world, the first few passengers disembarked, and heads turned to look around at the unexpected stop in their travels. The first few spotted the diner adjacent to the gas station convenience store. Discontent and grumpiness gave way to the hope of hot coffee and calorie-dense food. Word made it back up the line of passengers and into the bus like a telegraph and the slow shuffle increased to a moderate walk off the bus and across the concrete apron like ants forming a determined line towards a crumb of food.

When nearly all the passengers had spilled out, the last passenger, a man, disembarked pausing on the last step, like he was contemplating if the ground below was concrete or quicksand. Sometimes it was good to be last, that way you could watch the mistakes of all those who had rushed before you. You could watch them from afar. Watch what they did well and watch what they got wrong. Then you could proceed knowing you could make a more informed decision.

It wasn't that the last man off the bus was slow, or tired or old. He preferred the back of the bus. From there you can see everyone and no one can really see you. More emergency exits were located near the back as well, especially on the older Greyhounds like this one. Life had taught him to know where the exits were and to always be close to them. Mayhem and suffering could often be avoided if you were a few feet closer to an unlocked door or window.

The man still paused. Assessing, not hesitating.

He preferred caution, not rashness.

Prudence in moments of total uncertainty was a trait the man considered to be of infinite value. He had learned that lesson the hard way. Lives had been lost. People he had cared about.

The man looked like nothing special, just someone who blended in. Definitely not a tourist. He was someone who preferred traveling across the ground and not through the air. Someone who didn't throw caution to the wind hoping that it wouldn't blow back in his face.

Just an average man of slightly average height and build. Lean, not thin. Strong-framed, but not gym-junkie bulky. He wore oil-tanned leather work boots, well-worn dark jeans, and a weathered leather jacket over a ubiquitous black T-shirt. Muted colors. Woodland colors. Like camouflage.

Blend in.

Ben Shaw finally stepped down, planted both feet on the ground and looked around some more, taking in the sights, the sounds, the smells.

The sky was a glorious expanse of clear blue that stretched upward forever, deepening in color and texture the higher it went. The air was cool and crisp, untainted and fresh. Nothing like you would get in the city until the fall.

They had come off I-70 west just after Salina. The driver had announced they were going to detour along the back roads because of road works ahead, but they should still get to Denver on time. It was just over six hundred miles, a nine-hour trip from Kansas City where Shaw boarded the Greyhound early that morning. He was looking forward to catching some shut-eye along the way or just letting his mind wander as the bus passed endless miles of open farm land of wheat, corn, and sorghum.

But then the bus burst a hose on the back road and the trip took a temporary halt as they made their way to the nearest gas station.

Shaw slung a small brown canvas backpack over his shoulder and made his way toward the diner.

A few drivers were bent over pumping gas, the sound of the dials clicking over on the old bowsers. Mainly rural vehicles, pickups carrying tools, planks of lumber, and bales of hay in the back, and the odd SUV with a roof box. Shaw made a mental note of faces, makes, models, and license plates as he passed by.

Old habits die hard.

The gas station was one of the older ones, a retro throwback to the sixties, but kept in perfect condition by a proprietor still proud about appearances. Neat, tidy, and clean on the outside with the promise of good old-fashioned customer service. Shaw preferred these establishments rather than the newer, larger franchises typically found every few miles along the main interstates. There was a certain look and feel to these traditional places that Shaw admired and respected, something that couldn't be replicated with bright plastic signage, corporate colors, or with inflatable air dancing tube men and food pre-made off site then trucked in to be reheated.

Shaw passed neat racks of propane gas bottles, plastic bags of cut logs, quarts of oil in plastic bottles and vertical stacks of tires at discount prices.

Next to the convenience store was a mechanics workshop, the gloomy front yawned wide open like a cave, shadows moved between oil-stained hoists, the sound of power ratchets and tools being dropped accompanied by a barrage of profanity.

Shaw reached the diner, pulled open the glass door and entered. The air was warm and cozy inside and smelled of coffee, fried food and pancakes. The floor was checkered in the black and white tile found in thousands of similar diners across the country. On the left past the cashier was the kitchen with a long rectangular serving opening where plates of food sat ready and steaming on the ledge, and yellow order slips hung from above. The sound of frying and the clattering of pots, pans, and kitchen utensils being put to good use, drifted through the opening.

A red laminate counter ran almost the entire length of the diner with a row of padded red top swivel stools in chrome plated steel. A scatter of people sat at the counter sipping coffee, eating breakfast, or reading the paper. On the right against the large floor-to-ceiling windows were booths made from the same padded red vinyl with red laminate tabletops.

Shaw took a seat in the far corner booth, back to the wall, near the fire exit, with a clear view of the diner in front and of the parking lot to his left through the glass.

Sit where you have an uninterrupted view of everyone and close to an exit. No matter where he was, it was always the same.

He placed his backpack beside him, took off his aviator sunglasses and placed them carefully on the table next to the condiments stand. Some of the bus passengers, retirees Shaw guessed, were milling around at the counter, menus in hand, deciding what to have as though it was their last supper. Maybe it was. An older Asian couple from the bus, dressed in brightly colored matching tracksuits, had taken a booth two up from Shaw and they scrutinized the menu too.

A young waitress came over carrying a glass coffee pot in one hand and a white cup and saucer in the other. Neat and tidy, crisp uniform, clean apron with just a hint of starch.

She was pretty. Very pretty. Too pretty for this place.

She smiled at Shaw, placed the cup and saucer on the table in front of him and poured steaming hot coffee.

"But I haven't ordered anything yet," Shaw said.

"You look like the coffee type," she said, her smile never leaving her face as she expertly poured the coffee. She placed the pot down on the table and pulled out an order pad from her front apron pocket and a pen from behind her ear. She'd decided to serve him first despite the others being there before him.

Good old fashioned pen and paper. Shaw liked that. He was in a bar a few days ago in Kansas City and the waitress had pulled out some fancy hand-held device and tapped his order into it. Nearly an hour later his meal came that was completely wrong and the woman expected a tip.

The menu was wedged between the ketchup and mustard on the condiments caddy, but he didn't need to look at it. Every diner had what he wanted and from the sound that had come from the engine bay of the bus, it was going to take more than a quick toilet-stop to fix whatever was wrong. So he ordered steel-cut oats, no brown sugar, just a little cinnamon, and some half and half for his coffee, no sugar, no sweetener.

"You from the bus?" the waitress asked, still smiling down at him, giving him the once over.

"Yes, I am. Don't know how long it will be," Shaw replied. Her name badge said *Callie*. She was slim, had dark brown hair pulled back in a bun, dark brown eyes, long eyelashes and a petite nose with a smattering of freckles. Shaw guessed she was around twenty-five, maybe slightly older.

"Don't worry, Merv will have it fixed in no time," she said, looking out the window.

"Merv?" Shaw asked.

"He's the mechanic. We don't get many buses or tourists coaches through here, but he can fix almost anything if it's got an engine in it," Callie replied. "You won't be stuck here too long. Pity." She was flirting with him. He was good-looking by any standard, not just by local standards.

"Where exactly is *here*?" Shaw asked, trying not to sound rude. Some small towns off the interstate didn't like visitors, while some folks especially the small business owners in the town and their staff relied on the itinerant patronage. The economy of small places lived and died off the back of visitors passing through, and Shaw was just passing through.

"Well, welcome to Martha's End," Callie said theatrically. "Population six thousand forty eight. Well, that's what the sign says a mile down the road, but they ain't changed it in years. People come and go. You never really know the true number."

"I must have missed the sign on the way in," Shaw replied.

Callie touched his arm. "Well, this place is easy to miss. Martha's End is that kind of town."

Shaw detected a note of sarcasm in her voice. She was young and probably had no ties or commitments, but was still there. Maybe she had grown up and spent her whole life there, and couldn't get out. Small towns often did that to people, trapped them like quicksand. Once you're in a small town, you can't seem to break free and leave.

"Downtown Martha's End is just two miles west of here along the old highway. And if you hooked back on to the interstate and continue west for about twenty miles you'll come to Hays. That's a lot bigger than here. Not as big as Salina that you probably passed on the bus, but still a lot bigger than here."

Shaw liked her. She had a mischievous smile that matched her sense of humor.

"I'm Ben, by the way," Shaw extended his hand.

Callie pocketed her order pad and took his hand.

Her hand was cool and soft, delicate fingers, real nails not fake, and well-kept. No colored nail polish, just clear. Tasteful.

"I'm Callie," she replied. "You don't sit behind a desk do you?" Callie held Shaw's hand in hers a moment longer, her fingers feeling the texture and shape of his palm. They were working hands, not ugly and calloused, but rough from manual labor. "You can tell a lot from a person's hands," Callie said slowly, like in a trance, still holding Shaw's hand, examining it.

Yes you can, Shaw thought. She had done the reverse on him, trying to pick up clues. *Very observant.*

"What kind of work do you do?" she asked.

Shaw shrugged. "I fix things. Mainly handyman work. I'm good with my hands."

"I bet you are," Callie replied, flirting some more.

"Maybe you can read my palm, tell me my future?" Shaw said, as he pulled back his hand.

Callie rolled her eyes. *This guy's got nice hands and a sense of humor. I like that.* "Well, if you stay in Martha's End too long you won't have a future. Believe me," she said, joking. "Stay right here and I'll go get your order."

Shaw watched her saunter off, admiring for a brief moment the waggle of her tight butt through the fabric of her uniform. She came back momentarily with a stainless steel flask and poured the half-milk, half-cream combo into his cup then left the flask on the table and was gone again, busily taking other orders in the diner.

Shaw sipped his coffee. It was excellent. Hot and freshly brewed, not the over-cooked swill from a pot sitting too long on the hot plate.

Through the window Shaw watched as a man in oil-stained overalls and a grubby red baseball cap emerged from the gloom of the workshop and hustled across the parking lot toward the bus. He carried a thick black hose in one hand and a battered toolbox in the other. The bus driver was at the rear of the bus and had the engine door up and latched back. He stared into the engine like he knew what to do.

Must be Merv, Shaw thought as he drank his coffee and watched the man in the overalls.

The steel-cut oats arrived and, like the coffee, were freshly made, not some reheated gruel made six hours ago.

Shaw finished them in minutes and polished off his third cup of coffee and on cue, Callie returned, topped him up and cleared away the bowl with a smile.

He unzipped his backpack and took out a worn, dog-eared book. The book bulged with old Greyhound and Amtrak boarding passes that bookmarked certain pages and important passages. It was like an eclectic travel diary, a roadmap of his past travels spelled out by boarding passes he had collected along the way by road and train. Never by air.

Outside he could see that Merv the mechanic had finished replacing the hose on the bus and was packing up his tools. Passengers, fueled up on food and coffee, were already starting to drift toward the bus, anxious to get going again, worried that they would be left behind in such an off-the-beaten-track place.

The Asian couple a few rows away were finishing up their meal and packing up a large map they had sprawled out on the table.

Shaw wasn't anxious or in a hurry. He didn't want to stay forever in Martha's End, but was enjoying the hospitality, the open space of the road and vibe of the diner that you just didn't get from the concrete, glass and steel of the big cities. There was no one waiting with excitement for him at the bus station in Denver, holding flowers or a sign that said *Shaw*. No relatives, no girlfriend, just endless possibilities.

Then everything changed.

THREE

The huge pickup truck tore across the apron of the gas station and past the bowsers, barely missing a driver who was walking back to their car after paying for the gas. The truck pulled abruptly into a parking space outside the convenience store. It was a ruby red Ford F-250 crew cab with tinted glass, a massive square nose and chrome grill, a light bar mounted across the roof with a row of halogen lights, suspension kit, and massive off-road tires.

Shaw watched as three young men climbed out and made their way towards the diner. All three were big, bulked-up from lifting weights rather than from hard labor and an honest day's work. Frat-boy tough rather than farmhand toughened. Shaw recognized the familiar swagger the three men had. He knew the type. Every small town or large neighborhood had them. Bullies who walked, talked, and acted like they owned the place. They didn't break the rules, because they acted as though rules didn't apply to them.

Shaw continued to watch them through the window of the diner without staring directly at them.

Watching without looking.

He took a long deliberate sip of his coffee, his eyes over the rim of the cup, tracking the three men as they approached, noting every detail about them. They were maybe the same age as the waitress, mid-twenties, two-thirty to two-forty pounds. They wore boots, clean jeans, belts with big buckles, and long-sleeve durable work shirts, more expensive cloth and a better cut than what you would find at your typical rural outfitters. The men disappeared around the front of the diner just as Callie returned from behind the counter with a fresh coffee pot in hand. She stopped at the booth where the Asian couple were packing up and placed the bill on their table, before she walked to where Shaw sat and topped up his coffee.

"I see Merv's fixed your bus," she said, nodding out the window.

Shaw glanced outside again. No sight of the men. The engine compartment cover on the bus had been closed and the passengers were beginning to form a line again, tickets in hand, the driver ready to check off names and get everyone back on board.

Forty feet from Shaw the glass door of the diner swung open just a fraction more vigorously than required and the three young men entered, the door slamming against the backstop.

Callie turned away from Shaw at the sound.

She froze, coffee pot in hand.

Shaw could see her physically tense as she stared at the three men.

The diner was practically empty now, the breakfast rush had gone and most of the bus passengers were lining up at the coach or were making their way over toward it. Shaw and the Asian couple were the only ones left.

Shaw could see one of the men grab a passing waitress by the elbow and say something to her. She pulled her arm away and said something, none too happy the man had grabbed her so hard. She gestured with a flick of her head toward the kitchen and walked on. The man who grabbed her nodded at his two companions and they started walking toward where Shaw sat, while the other man went around the other side of the counter and through the kitchen doors.

"Friends of yours?" Shaw said, packing his book into the backpack, but leaving the bus ticket on the table.

Callie glanced down at Shaw. "No friends of mine. The Morgan brothers. Their father owns the biggest cattle ranch around here. He owns a bunch of other stuff too, some of the buildings in town and a few equipment dealerships. Even this diner. Hal the chef just leases the place." She learned in close to Shaw, like she was pouring more coffee and whispered, "And he's behind in the rent too. Morgan Senior sends his sons to collect it and the like." Callie slipped the check from her order pad and placed it in front of Shaw, then walked away preferring to go the long way around back to the counter so she wouldn't have to pass the two brothers coming toward Shaw.

The two men approached. When they reached the Asian couple they paused, a look of disgust on their faces. "Hey Jed, didn't these ones bomb Pearl Harbor?" one sniggered to the other.

Jed? Figures, Shaw thought as he watched on.

"Hell yeah. They're all a bunch of sneaky bastards," the other one said. They sat down at a table across from the Asian couple, who hurriedly got up and left cash on the table with their bill before moving quickly out the door.

Shaw looked down at his bus ticket.

Kansas City to Denver, Colorado.

Nine hours along six hundred miles of I-70 West.

Raised voices came from the kitchen. Then the sound of pans being thrown.

Shaw tried not to look at the two brothers, but he could feel them looking at him. He pictured smirks on their faces, wanting him to look in their direction.

Just let it go, Shaw repeated to himself as he read the fine print on the ticket.

"Where's that sweet bit of ass Callie gone to?" Jed asked loudly. Shaw could hear clearly everything they were saying. He was sure they were being deliberately loud-mouthed, almost goading him to look up and say something. But he didn't. He just kept staring at the bus ticket.

"I dunno," Rory replied. "Maybe we should pay her a visit tonight, ya know, like that other girl Jessie you had last week." They giggled and snickered some more.

"Whatcha mean the girl I had last week? Hell, she squealed like wunna Bill's hogs when ya were on top of her. Weren't nothing left for me after you had done her."

They both burst out laughing.

"Maybe we should pay Daisy and her mom a visit. It's just the two of them on the ranch I hear. You can have the old bitch. She ain't had no poke since her old man died."

"I ain't doing no old bitch. Hell no. We can do the daughter together. What they call that? You on one end and me on the other. Pig on a spit like in them movies you got."

The laughter erupted again and Shaw could feel his anger rise.

More commotion came from the kitchen. Raised voices had become shouting. Shaw looked up and could see Callie and the other waitresses busying themselves behind the counter and around the tables, refilling the coffee machine, swapping out the breakfast menus for lunch ones, trying their best to ignore the heated argument coming from the kitchen.

Shaw looked out the window again. All the passengers were nearly onboard the bus, just the last few waiting.

He looked down at his ticket again then flipped it over, contemplating it. He read the words printed on it, thick black capital letters. *Not valid on other dates. Non-refundable.*

Pulling out his wallet, Shaw counted out some cash and left a ten-dollar tip. He got up and slung his backpack over his left shoulder, not his right shoulder. Deliberate. He would pass the two Morgan brothers on his right side when he walked out.

The kitchen doors swung open, again just a fraction more vigorously than required and the other brother, Billy, came out and stopped at the cash register. He punched a button, the drawer slid open, he flipped up the bill holders and began to empty the cash, stuffing the bills into a paper takeout bag he found behind the counter.

Shaw watched him.

Just let it go.

Shaw started toward the door, but then paused at the table where Jed and Rory Morgan were slouching. Both of them sat up a little straighter as they regarded Shaw almost like they were expecting trouble.

Shaw looked down at them and said, "They were Korean. Not Japanese."

The two brothers exchanged looks. "Excuse me?" Jed said, his face scrunched up in confusion.

Shaw sighed like it took an effort just to converse with these two idiots. "They weren't Japanese. The two Asians you made a wisecrack about. They were Korean. It was Japan who bombed Pearl Harbor, not Korea." Then he slid on his sunglasses and walked out of the diner into the sunshine without looking back.

****

Callie started wiping the table where Ben Shaw had sat and watched out the window as the bus pulled away in a funnel of dust, grit and fumes.

Damn shame, she thought. He was the best-looking thing she had seen roll into town for a long time.

She let out a deep breath as the bus crawled slowly on to the road and drove away. She looked away from the window and picked up the cash, seeing the tip left behind.

She smiled. *Good looking and generous too.*

She opened her order pad and slotted the ten-dollar bill into the plastic sleeve behind a wad of ones. The face of Alexander Hamilton was a much-welcomed addition to the many faces of George Washington that she only had as tips today. It looked like her tips for the week were going to be the only pay she was going to get. *Again.*

The Morgans got their rent money. They had cleared out the till save for the coins and had driven off in their pickup truck, laughing and backslapping like apes.

Pricks.

This was the second time this month it had happened, and she and the rest of the girls were still owed two weeks wages. Hal had come out of the kitchen all angry and cussing, and said he would make it up to them in their pay next week.

He promised.

Again.

Callie finished wiping down the table then heard the front door swing open.

"Christ, not them again," she muttered. She turned to see who it was and her heart skipped a beat.

FOUR

Shaw stood in the doorway and nodded at Callie. "Do you know a cheap motel where I can stay for a few days?" He walked in and sat down in the same booth.

"I thought you'd gone. I saw the bus leave. I thought you were on it," Callie replied, trying to contain her delight. She liked the look of him more the second time around. Older, maybe thirty. Quiet and unassuming. Dark brown hair, brown eyes, and a rather intense face. But there was something about him, Callie thought, his manner. How he walked into a room. How he moved. How his eyes took everything in. He had like a restrained confidence. Good looks were great. Manners were a bonus. But a man with confidence was like a magnet to her. And he had all three covered.

"I thought I'd stay for a few days," Shaw shrugged. "See the sights, as they say."

Callie smiled, "Believe me there's nothing to see." She stepped deliberately closer to him as if to say the sights to see are standing right in front of him.

"Is there a decent place to stay in Martha's End?"

She nodded out the window. "Hang a left and the town proper is about two miles that way, if you continue along the road. We're just on the outskirts here at the diner. There are a few motels along the road on the way into town."

Shaw still held the bus ticket in his hand, contemplating. He didn't want to bring up what had just happened in the diner, with the three men and how they had taken the money from the till. He wanted to stay clear of small town politics. He didn't want to get involved, yet somehow it played on his mind. Something pulled at him and made him not get back on the bus.

"But—" Callie's voice trailed off.

Shaw could see there was something on her mind. He could almost see the cogs inside her pretty little head turning and recalibrating.

She leaned in again, like she had before, but closer this time.

She smelled good. Not the sickly sweet smell of a cheap fragrance. More like spice and ocean freshness.

"You didn't hear this from me, but a few miles up the road, the other way, if you turn right, head east, you'll find the McAlister ranch and I know they're looking for ranch hands. You'll get room and board for an honest day's work."

Shaw frowned. Callie seemed uneasy telling him this, but he didn't push the point.

"I don't mind, as I said, I'm good with my hands."

Callie caught herself subconsciously twirling her hair like some churlish schoolgirl, her mind thinking about something else. Thinking about his hands.

She came back to reality, "Eh, well—I know they could do with the help," she stuttered and began straightening the menus on another table. "Daisy McAlister, that's the daughter, it's just her and her mother running the whole place now, and I know they've had trouble finding and keeping the help. Her father died a few years back and it's a big place. It's a lot to manage just between two women."

Shaw thought about it for a moment. "I'm not looking for anything long-term. It's just for a few days then I'll be gone."

The door opened and the first of the lunch crowd started to come in.

"You decide. But don't cross onto the Morgan's land if you do. Their ranch runs adjacent to the McAlister's. They don't take too kindly to strangers," Callie replied. She straightened her apron and tucked a loose strand of hair behind her ear. "If you do take up the offer I might see you around, back in here maybe," she said with a knowing smile, before turning and walking away.

****

The air was cool and clear, and the sun was climbing towards its apex. Shaw stood on the shoulder of the road, both feet on a battered gentle slope of gravel and dirt. The gas station and diner were at his back, a thick layer of blacktop in front, inches from his toes, its edges cracked and warped in places, a white line border down each side and a thick faded yellow line down the center. It stretched away in both directions.

To the left, the road fell away and in the distance he could see the township of Martha's End. A cluster of nondescript buildings at the center surrounded by a small urban sprawl with a red water tower poking up into the sky. Quaint. Scenic. Civilized.

To the right the road shrunk into a broad expanse of open landscape. Sparse. Raw. Unknown.

In his head he did a quick recap of the morning's events, then made up his mind.

Shaw hitched up his backpack, turned right and started walking along the road.

FIVE

Ranch hand wanted.

The sign was faded and scuffed. Scorching sun, harsh rain and cold wind had weathered it over the years such that Shaw could hardly make out the words on the metal sign that hung beside the road. He had been following what seemed like an endless fence line of post and wire for almost two miles along the old highway. It was warm and he had taken off his jacket, tying it loosely around his waist.

The fence line then cut inwards along a side dirt road that led to a ranch entrance. A double gate of rusted tubular steel was hinged on each side to a set of tall posts with a high cross-beam, the wood worn and dilapidated, split and cracked. A sign *Private Property Keep Out* was attached to the gate with twists of old fencing wire. A rusted metal cutout sign hung from the beam over the entrance that announced *McAlister Ranch*.

The whole place looked tired and rundown. Shaw was already beginning to regret his decision to turn right at the gas station and follow the road. Maybe he should have turned left and walked into town, and found some nice comfy small motel with air conditioning, hot showers, and cable TV. Maybe he should have just stayed on the bus, not broken the trip and been closer to Denver by now. With each step he seemed to be getting further and further away from his original destination.

But something had drawn him toward this direction. Things he had observed in the diner. Something that Callie the waitress had said. It could be nothing.

He shook his head, berating himself. *This is a bad idea.*

He turned and walked back to the main road, starting back toward the gas station. If he hurried he could make it into Martha's End before dusk, maybe grab a ride from a local farmer heading into town.

Shaw had only walked a hundred yards when he heard the throaty rumbling in the distance behind him.

He recognized the sound of a custom exhaust.

He kept walking. Probably a truck or sports sedan.

Then the pitch changed as the sound drew closer, higher and more drawn out like the vehicle was accelerating, the revs topping out before the driver shifted gear. Shaw stepped further to the side and back from the broken edge of the blacktop.

A blur of red tore past his shoulder, missing him by a few inches, a backwash of heat, grit, and exhaust fumes in its wake pulled him nearly off his feet.

"Damn it!" Shaw yelled.

The taillights flared as the driver hit the brakes and brought the pickup to a stop a hundred yards up the road.

Shaw straightened himself, dusting off the dirt that had washed over him, then looked to where the truck had pulled up, the big motor idling. The driver waiting.

Son of a bitch.

Crew cab, ruby red, tinted glass. The same pickup truck from the diner.

The driver had actually crossed over on to the opposite side, into the oncoming traffic lane just to brush past Shaw.

Shaw began to walk toward the truck.

Now he was pissed.

He didn't care how many of them were in the truck. The three brothers, their ten sisters, the entire Morgan clan. It made no difference to him.

The truck just stood there as he approached. Taillights illuminated, driver's foot on the brake pedal, fat twin exhausts emitting a low rumble.

Shaw got within thirty feet, then the truck lurched forward with a screech of tires and a burst of rubber smoke, and took off.

Shaw watched as it shrunk into the distance, before finally vanishing in a watery shimmer of heat and road.

Pricks. Shaw shook his head.

He stopped for a moment. Contemplating. Then he looked back over his shoulder.

Ranch hand wanted.

He turned and walked toward the McAlister ranch, his mind made up.

****

Unlocking the steel gate was simple. It was a chain and latch affair. He made sure he closed it securely behind him. He made it about half a mile before he saw a boil of brown dust in the distance rolling toward him.

Daisy McAlister reined in her horse in a cloud of dirt in front of Shaw.

He stood still, and studied her.

She was young, maybe the same age as Callie back at the diner. Sunflower blonde hair that spilled around her shoulders, loose strands across her face. She wore a red checked riding shirt, sleeves rolled up but a few buttons undone at the front, riding breeches that hugged her supple legs like a second skin, and riding boots through the stirrups. Shaw couldn't really see her face too well as she kept her distance, but what really got his attention was when she casually slid out a rifle from a leather saddle scabbard and rested it low on the pommel. She didn't aim it directly at Shaw, but her intention was obvious.

Shaw didn't move, hands by his sides, in clear sight. He didn't want to give the young woman any reason to aim the rifle at him. He definitely wasn't in Kansas City anymore.

"This is McAlister land, mister. State your business," she said, her voice had a certain twang to it, but it also had a depth of maturity and confidence that belied her young age.

Shaw said nothing, trying to make up his mind what to say. So he did the next best thing, he slowly raised his hands. "Sorry. I mean no trouble. I'll just turn around and go back through the gate," he said, his voice calm and slow.

The horse moved slightly and Shaw could see her correct it using just the slightest movement of her hips and knees pressed into the animal's flanks. She was good. Shaw knew little about horse riding, but he knew that the woman in front of him had a skilled bond with her horse. Something that came only from spending years in the saddle.

"Did the Morgans send you?" she said, her voice turned harsh. She angled the rifle slightly higher, aiming below Shaw's waist. "Because if you're from them I'll put a round into your leg and you can limp back and tell them to go to hell!"

The situation was escalating. Shaw could see the weapon better now and his threat assessment went up a notch. It was a Winchester lever action. Black walnut stock, polished, looked after, cared for. Iron sights, no red dot. A true shooter's carbine owned and held by someone who appreciated the weapon, and was skilled and proficient in its use. Not a tool, but an extension of themselves.

"No, the Morgans didn't send me," Shaw replied, holding his hands a little higher. "I don't know who they are, but I think they just tried to run me off the road a few moments ago."

The woman said nothing. She was still assessing him like a threat.

"Red pickup truck, looks new, big wheels, raised, loud exhaust?" Shaw offered, he could quote the license number, but he didn't want to go too far. The woman might think he was a cop. *"Don't tread on me* sticker on the bumper?" he continued.

The woman raised an eyebrow, but the gun was still trained on him.

He was sure she had recognized the vehicle, but she still wasn't convinced. He could see the skepticism in her face.

"If you just let me go, I'll turn around and walk back out the gate. I'm sorry for the intrusion."

She thought about this for the moment. "Are you from the bank?"

Shaw frowned and was thrown slightly by the question. *The bank? What bank?*

"Because if you are, I'll shoot you all the same. Bunch of thieving jackals," she spat.

Shaw was intrigued by the woman now. She certainly had spirit and balls. "Do I look like I'm from the bank?" he asked, a bemused smile on his face.

The woman's face softened slightly. No, he certainly didn't look like he was from the bank.

Shaw was making some headway at least in trying to diffuse the situation. "I saw the sign on the gate saying *ranch hand wanted*. That's all. I'm sorry if I made a mistake. I was just looking for work and a place to stay."

The woman lowered the rifle, but still had it pointed in Shaw's general direction. "What's in the bag?" she nodded.

Very slowly Shaw unslung his backpack and threw it midway between them. "See for yourself. No weapons. Just a book, some toiletries and a spare change of clothes. I travel light."

The woman looped the reins over the pommel, swung one leg over the neck of the horse and slid smoothly off while still holding the rifle in one hand. Her dismount looked like something she had done a million times before.

The horse stood perfectly still and waited.

She walked to the backpack and, without taking her eyes off Shaw, crouched down and unclipped the top flap of it and tipped the contents out. She patted down the side pockets until she was absolutely sure there was no gun or other weapon.

"See. I'm unarmed."

"Lose the jacket around your hips and turn around slowly for me," she said, standing up fully. She stepped closer to Shaw and now held the rifle in both hands, aiming it squarely at his head.

She is good, Shaw thought to himself. *Overly cautious, but for a reason.*

Shaw undid the arms of the jacket and tossed it to the side. With his hands back up he did a slow turn until he faced her again. "I'm not carrying a gun or anything," he repeated. "The waitress at the diner, Callie, said you're looking for ranch hands and that I'd get room and board for a day's work."

"I know," the woman said. She lowered the gun completely and her entire demeanor changed. "Callie sent me a text and said to keep an eye out for some guy who was looking for work."

Callie had gone into more detail in her text about how good-looking the man was, but Daisy didn't explain that.

Shaw lowered his hands, a little annoyed. He felt like he'd been pulled from the line at an airport and had been given a full body search for no reason at all. "So you knew?" he said incredulously.

"I didn't know *exactly* who you were. You can never be too careful. We get all types around here."

She stepped closer. "I'm Daisy, Daisy McAlister. I'm sorry, but Callie has a tendency to exaggerate everything." She looked Shaw slowly up and down. *But she got it right this time,* she thought.

Up close she had dazzling blue eyes, golden skin and a proud jaw. She was a real mid-western beauty. Slightly shorter than Shaw and with her shirt unbuttoned a little too low, without dropping his eyes and looking like a fool he could make out the white-laced curve of her bra. She certainly filled it out amply.

"So you've gone from pointing a gun at me to being hospitable?" Shaw bent down and started to refill his backpack.

"I'm sorry," Daisy said again. Shaw stood up and could see in her eyes that she was genuinely apologetic. He wondered what had been happening in her past that warranted such distrust and fear. People, even in rural areas, didn't greet everyone who turned up on their property with a pointed gun unless something really bad had happened in their past. It got Shaw's interest up and he wanted to know more.

He picked up his jacket, dusted it off and tied it around his waist again. "That's OK. I'm Ben, Ben Shaw."

"Ben as in Benjamin Franklin?"

"No, Ben as in Benedict Arnold."

"Wasn't he a traitor? Swapped sides and joined the British?"

Shaw just smiled. This was going to be an interesting day.

SIX

They walked the rest of the way to the main house. Daisy led the horse by the reins. It ambled behind her and Shaw carried his backpack. The sun was low off the trees and everything was golden and hazy. In the distance brown shapes moved in open paddocks and there was the occasional sorrowful bovine moan.

Daisy explained that they had close to three hundred acres, small compared to the Morgan's land that shared a boundary on the eastern side. They had over ten thousand acres, and they ran cattle and grew crops as well.

"We get ranch hands here on and off to help, but in the last six months they've been scarce. We had a few last month, but they just upped and left a few days later. No reason, no explanation. I came down to the bunkhouse one morning with breakfast and they had cleared out. They even missed a week's wages. It's not much, but it's still money," Daisy said.

Shaw was content to just listen, gather information. Casual labor was not loyal, but it was rare they would leave before getting paid.

"You said we?" he asked.

"It's just my mother and me. My father, Stan McAlister, died about two years back. An accident or so they say." Daisy's voice didn't falter or skip a beat, and she didn't expand further on her father's death. She was strong-willed and independent, and she kept her raw emotions under wraps. Shaw didn't press the point, but he could tell there was something below the surface as he watched her. He didn't know the woman and she didn't know him, but she seemed troubled.

Daisy stopped and turned to Shaw, the horse nuzzling at the back of her shoulder. "I don't care how long you can really stay. There's plenty of work as you'll see. I look after the cattle, but they're grazing now for the next few months. We've had to sell a lot of them. I just can't keep up with managing them. Callie said you seemed like an honest person."

"And you trust what she says? I could be a serial killer for all you know."

"We went to school together here. We're best friends and I trust her gut. She's a better judge of character than me. Besides, I sleep with a gun by my pillow just in case."

Shaw didn't doubt it.

Just for a brief moment Daisy looked weary. The stress, pressure, and workload had taken their toll and Shaw wanted to help, but he was just passing through. He would fix what he could, but he would be gone in the next few days. "I can't ride a horse, but I'm good with my hands."

"That's fine. This is an old-fashioned ranch, but we do have a few vehicles. My father's old Dodge is in the barn and we have an ATV. I don't use them much, only when I need to get into town or go to the grocery store. I much prefer horses." She stroked the muzzle of the horse.

"What's his name?" Shaw asked, trying to shift her thoughts to something more upbeat.

Daisy smiled and her eyes brightened, her look of weariness gone as fast as it had appeared. "You really don't know much about horses, or ranches or anything rural, do you?"

Shaw shrugged. "I'm not really the big-city type either. I can't stand crowds and traffic, and the mayhem."

"It's a she, the horse and her name is Jazz." The horse reached towards Shaw, he held out his hand and she nibbled at his fingers. Her head was huge, almost the entire length of his arm, but compared to police horses he had seen, Jazz was a small horse. "She's an Australian Stock Horse, fast, agile, and built for endurance. They breed them tough because of the harsh conditions there."

Shaw could now see the slight feminine traits in the horse's face, the eyes, the bone structure.

"Maybe I'll teach you to ride?"

Shaw thought for a moment. Having something large under him that he had no control over didn't really appeal to him. Especially when it could outrun a human. Looking up at the saddle it seemed like a long way to fall at full gallop. "Thanks, but I'm fine with my feet planted on the ground," he smiled.

They reached the top of the dirt road and the homestead came into view. It was all verandas, wooden siding, sash windows and a tin roof. Large and airy, but in desperate need of attention. Shaw guessed that the house was originally painted a mustard color, but years of sun had bleached away the pigment to a yellowish stain. The paint had peeled in places and there were large patches of raw lumber black with discoloration, the original oils and protective resins long since washed away or evaporated. The rain had done its damage. There were blotches of rot on some of the rails and on the pickets along the verandas.

A chimney of worn brickwork ran up one side of the house. In its prime the homestead would have been spectacular, but neglect, scorching summers and the harsh Kansas winters had taken its toll.

The main dirt road split into three smaller, narrow tracks. One curved past the front steps of the homestead and formed a circular driveway around a large cottonwood tree before rejoining the main dirt road. A second angled to the right and led to a large red barn. Beside the barn was a small structure that was a bunkhouse for the ranch hands and itinerant workers. There were stables further away, past the bunkhouse.

Another track ran behind and then past the back of the homestead to a large three-gable shed that housed farm machinery.

Daisy paused at the junction. "I think the Morgans ran them off. We've been trying to get help here, but it's been hard."

"Ran them off?" Shaw asked. They continued towards the bunkhouse, the horse still following.

"They've been wanting to buy this ranch for years now. When my father was alive, Jim Morgan, the patriarch of the Morgan family, kept hassling him to sell. He said he wanted to amalgamate his farm with ours and have more space to run his herds. But my father didn't trust him. So he dug his heels in and refused to sell.

"That's the bunkhouse where you can store your gear and stay. It's nothing special, but it's clean and tidy. It has a hot running shower, beds, and a wood stove. It can get pretty cold here at night. Dinner is at six and I'll bring it down to you. Same with breakfast, which I normally make around seven."

Shaw just nodded. Apart from the occasional moan of cattle the place was quiet, deserted. "And your mother? Does she help around the ranch?"

"No, not really. She's been sick for a while. She hardly leaves her bedroom, so she's always here," she said. "I'll bring you down some fresh linen after I take care of Jazz." Daisy headed off to the stables leaving Shaw standing by himself

He watched her for a few moments then looked back at the homestead expecting to see an old woman at a window, looking back at him, but there was no one there. Shaw turned and headed toward the bunkhouse.

SEVEN

It was dusk by the time Daisy finished her chores for the day around the ranch. The sky stretched upwards from the horizon in a canvas of burnt orange, then blue, and finally indigo.

Carrying clean sheets, a pillow, and some blankets, Daisy made her way down to the bunkhouse. The first stars were coming out in the evening sky and she could see a gray twist of smoke spiraling upwards from the bunkhouse chimney. Winter was still a few months away, but the September evenings had an unseasonal chill to them.

She climbed the front steps and paused. The door was wide open and the glass front of the wood stove in the middle of the room cast a warm glow onto the porch. She knocked on the doorframe, but there was no answer so she stepped inside. The bunkhouse was small but comfortable. It was an open plan with high raked ceilings, a small kitchenette with a bar fridge, a wooden table and chairs, six plain wooden beds and an old leather sofa. At the rear was a wall that separated the living and sleep area from the shower stall and toilet.

The amenities were spartan, but after a hard day mending fences and herding cattle most ranch hands just ate, crashed, and slept. Some of the more ambitious would catch a ride into Martha's End and hit the only bar there before either staggering or hitchhiking home. Daisy didn't care as long as they showed up for work the next day sober. But it had been years since she had a large crew like they had when her father was alive. Back then the bunkhouse was often full, but lately it had been just one or two people coming for a few days then leaving.

The air smelled of wood smoke and a few logs crackled in the wood stove. One of the bunks had Shaw's backpack on it, so she placed the sheets, pillow, and blankets at the foot of the mattress then turned to leave.

She stopped.

There was the faint sound of running water coming from the bathroom area.

Shaw was taking a shower.

Daisy shook it off and started for the door, then stopped again.

She turned around again and listened.

It was definitely someone having a shower. The sound of water splashing. Maybe someone humming? Yes, she heard that too.

She felt a hollow pang of guilt in her chest and her heart thumped a little harder. She was caught in two minds, but she gave in to her curiosity. She edged forward toward the sound, tip-toeing carefully across the worn floor, praying she wouldn't step on a creaky floorboard.

She reached the edge of the back wall then, taking a deep breath, she slowly craned her head around the wall and looked down the narrow corridor.

Her breath froze in her lungs.

At the end of the short hallway was an open shower stall. No door. No glass. Three waterproofed walls and rudimentary copper pipes bracketed to the wall.

Shaw stood, wet and glistening under the stream of hot water that fell like rain from the large showerhead. His back was to her, his hands occupied washing soap out of his hair, water running down his nakedness.

Daisy could feel her throat constrict and her face and chest flare with heat.

His body was wrapped in a haze of steam that drifted like clouds around a mountain peak of bronze granite.

She couldn't move. She wanted to turn and run, but she couldn't take her eyes of him, his torso, his body. Everything.

Strong powerful shoulders, sculpted tapered back and shoulder blades that rippled under his skin as he moved and washed. Still her eyes dropped lower. Water cascaded down his back, over perfect butt cheeks, down strong supple legs, and then over flared calves.

Shaw blindly reached for the soap, his eyes closed.

Her breath caught again, her eyes went wide, and she swallowed hard as heat spread across her abdomen, before seeping lower.

Between his legs, from behind, she could see something long and heavy swing like a pendulum as he moved under the stream of water.

Daisy turned and ran from the room.

Shaw stepped out of the shower, toweled himself off, then wrapped the towel around his waist. He walked out of the stall and back into the open area of the bunkhouse. Immediately he saw the sheets, pillow and blanket all neatly folded and placed at the foot of his bed. He went to the open door and looked out just in time to catch Daisy almost running back up the dirt road toward the homestead like she had left something burning on the stove.

He gave a wry smile.

EIGHT

The line of trees offered good cover from high on the ridge while still providing an uninterrupted view of the homestead and surrounding area below. The forlorn moan of cattle drifted up to where the woman stood, screened behind the row of trees. Darkness had fallen soon after dusk. The night vision binoculars she wore were military spec, unavailable over the counter. So was all the equipment and supplies she had, enough so that she could stay outdoors undetected for days, weeks if needed.

The landscape below was a wash of ghostly green, but she could pick out clearly some minor activity. The young woman had first left the main house carrying a bundle of something, blankets it looked like, and walked to the smaller building near the barn. The woman guessed it to be living quarters for the hired help and knew there was only one person in there.

The young woman had gone inside the quarters and remained inside for precisely four and a half minutes. She had watched her from the ridge, and didn't need to look at her watch to know. A career of sitting for hours and even days totally concealed in a dugout hole in the ground, or perched on a chair in an abandoned building watching out of a window, had taught her patience and the instinctive measure of time passing.

When the young woman emerged again she looked flustered, agitated, in a hurry. She kept turning and looking back over her shoulder as she moved quickly back toward the homestead.

Guilt.

The young woman's mannerisms and gait reeked of it, like she had stolen something and was hurriedly leaving the scene of a crime.

The woman on the ridge panned the binoculars back to the bunkhouse and waited, almost expecting the man to appear on the porch.

But he didn't.

Twenty-six minutes later the woman appeared on the veranda of the homestead carrying a tray of what looked like plated food. She walked cautiously along the path again, careful not to stumble or tip over the tray. She placed the tray on a small outside table on the bunkhouse porch. A man emerged and they both sat down. He ate and the woman sat pensively with her hands in her lap and watched him eat.

Nothing was happening here. The threat assessment would conclude that the new arrival was of low-risk, like all the other ranch hands who had turned up looking for work.

This new one proved nothing special.

Nothing out of the ordinary. The woman on the ridge would make the call to Dallas when she got back and that's what her report would say.

She was about to pack up her gear and retreat when something completely out of the ordinary happened.

After the man below had finished his meal, he stood and stretched. Nothing special about that.

He walked down the steps, stood on the road, then turned ninety degrees and in the darkness looked up to the tree line on the ridge.

The woman on the ridge stood perfectly still and watched through the binoculars as a ghostly-green face looked right back at her.

NINE

The air was cold and sharp, earthy, tinged with the dusty smell of wheat and the sourness of animal feces. The wood in the stove had reduced down to a glow of embers and powdery ash. The bunkhouse felt cold and empty, bled of the warmth and of conversation from the previous evening.

Shaw was up at dawn. He opened the wood stove and threw a few split logs onto the embers, and they soon rekindled into flame. He draped a blanket around himself and walked into the small kitchenette.

There was a coffee maker on the bench, commercial quality, stainless steel, solid with switches not buttons, proper glass pot, made in the USA not some cheap plastic import, a welcoming sight to see first thing in the morning.

There was rust on the corners. That was a good thing too.

He found a plentiful supply of ground coffee in the cupboard. He set the machine then watched it patiently as hot water filtered through the basket and coffee began filling up the glass coffee pot beneath. The aroma filled the bunkhouse. Best smell on earth. But Shaw still waited, arms folded, huddled under the blanket, it was a ritual, an awakening process that couldn't be rushed.

Shaw couldn't function in the morning without coffee. He just couldn't. Caffeine needed to be in his system, seeping through his DNA before he could get any semblance on the day ahead. Until the first cup went down, he would be a zombie.

Finally the pot was full and the hissing and gurgling stopped. Shaw eagerly poured a serving into a large heavy ceramic cup and drank it, savoring the richness and taste.

He showered, and slipped into a change of clothes, before pouring another cup of coffee and walking out onto the porch where he sat and drank it as he watched the first rays of sun stretch across the paddocks.

Cattle grazed and moaned, and in the distance the blades of a windmill turned lazily in a light breeze atop a rusted spindly frame.

The ridge rose behind the barn, tall and jagged, dotted with a line of trees along the top. Shaw thought back to the previous evening. Daisy had returned with his dinner and they sat on the porch together, surrounded by darkness with just the warm glow of the wood stove casting light through the open doorway.

He could tell immediately that her demeanor had changed. She was standoffish, hesitant, awkward. She kept looking out into the darkness or to anywhere so their eyes wouldn't meet. And when they finally did she seemed embarrassed and fidgety like she couldn't string two words together, before quickly looking away again.

When he finished eating dinner he got up to stretch and suddenly he could feel the hairs on the back of his neck rise.

Shaw knew when he was being watched. It was like a sixth sense. He had spent so much of his life learning to watch and observe others that he knew intimately when prying eyes were on him.

And last night, in the darkness, he could feel eyes looking down on him. From high above, on the crest of the ridge.

It was a cloudless night and he could see the outline of the ridge in the distance against the brighter backdrop of pale cold sky and stars.

There was someone up there. Someone observing him. He didn't know exactly where, so he just let his instincts lead his eyes to where he felt the highest concentration of unease.

Shaw shook the thought from his mind and sipped his coffee. He could feel the caffeine finally seep through him, waking his senses up.

There was no movement from the homestead, but the kitchen windows were open and he could faintly hear sounds coming from within.

He finished his coffee, his appetite satisfied for the moment and wandered down to the barn.

It was a typical barn of the like found all over the Midwest. But like everything else on the property it was in desperate need of attention. The paint was peeling, and some wooden planks were warped and broken.

The barns doors were wide open. Inside was parked an old Dodge pickup truck that looked like something out of the nineteen fifties. Shaw knew nothing about cars, but he could tell that someone had lovingly cared for this truck. It was all shining red paintwork, chrome, and sweeping fenders complete with whitewall tires.

The cavernous interior of the barn had layers of organization, a reflection of Stan McAlister and his personality.

Workbenches with plywood tops ran along one wall. A wide assortment of saws, hammers, planes and other carpentry tools hung neatly on a long pegboard above the benches, and above these were shelves made from rough, recycled planks that held a collection of glass jars and old rusty cans full of screws, nuts, bolts and every fastening imaginable. Off-cuts were neatly stacked according to size and purpose. Paint cans meticulously sealed and labeled were stored in rows.

Order and efficiency was everywhere.

A place for everything and everything in its place.

The floor was dirt in some places, plain concrete in others, poured rough and stained with a lifetime of hard work, dedication and the unbridled satisfaction you get from making things with your hands. Patterns of oil, grease, paint, sweat and maybe even blood when a saw bucked or a chisel slipped, or when a hammer missed the nail.

Shaw understood. He felt at home in this place. Centered. Grounded. Purposeful. He needed to get back to the basics himself. For too long he had lived in a world surrounded by politics, distrust and other people's agendas. That's why he had embarked on his road trip, leaving Washington D.C. behind and another life, heading east. He had no regrets, but it was time for a change.

Shaw walked deeper into the barn. Everything was covered in a layer of dust, except the truck. It was regularly used.

A red steel upright tool chest and trolley combination sat against the wall. At the back of the barn hay bales were stacked high, and there was a set of steps that led to a loft, too gloomy for Shaw to see what was up there.

It didn't take long for Shaw to find a large tool caddy that he filled with what he needed, then he walked back outside into the sunshine. An hour later he had replaced several rotting fence rails in the nearest paddock and had re-nailed the ones that had torn from the posts, but where the wooden rails were still good.

The sun had climbed in the clear blue sky and the caffeine had started to wear off. He could feel the first pangs of hunger beginning to gnaw at him. It felt good to work with his hands again. There was something about manual labor that gave him purpose, the satisfaction that came from building or fixing something yourself. Shaw liked to do things with his hands and he wasn't the type to sit behind a desk and answer phones or fill out reports.

He hammered in the last nail and stood back. A small group of cattle had drifted over to where he was working and were keeping a watchful eye on his progress. Maybe they were expecting food or were just curious about him. It was no problem just as long as there was a solid line of fence between him and them.

The smell of bacon drifted down. He dropped the hammer back into the tool caddy and went to a water trough to splash water on his face and head, washing away the sweat.

He heard the screen door of the homestead slam shut and Shaw looked up. Daisy was making her way toward him carrying a covered tray of food.

She had a certain saunter that he admired as he wiped his hands on an old rag. She wore cut-off denim shorts, ankle boots, and a checked unbuttoned work-shirt, but tied off at the front over a thin camisole.

Shaw's gazed lingered just a moment more than it should have and she caught him watching her. She smiled and took the food tray to the bunkhouse, putting it down as before on the outside table on the porch.

"You're up early," she said as Shaw arrived.

"Not much sense in sleeping in when there's work to be done," he replied, eyeing the tray. Whatever was under the cloth, it smelled amazing, but Shaw couldn't keep his eyes off Daisy.

Damn, she looked good. She seemed to have perked up since last night, more friendly.

Daisy lifted the cloth and Shaw's eyes nearly fell out of his head. There was a huge plate of pancakes, a side plate piled with bacon, eggs, and steak, and a small jug of maple syrup.

"Wow, this is enough food to feed an army," he said as he looked at the spread. "I hope you haven't eaten."

"No, I thought I'd join you and keep you company." Daisy went into the bunkhouse to make a fresh pot of coffee while he sat down at the table, not before turning his head unashamedly and watching the curves of her butt in the cut-offs as she walked past.

Maybe he should stay a few more days.

TEN

The drive into Martha's End was smooth and straight. Shaw had the window down of the old Dodge as he drove and the cool breeze ruffled his hair. The late morning sun filtered through the trees and the pickup hummed at a smooth fifty-five miles per hour, the reassuring feel of the tires on the blacktop and the dappled sun on his face. The traffic was light, mainly rural trucks and a few pickups towing horse trailers.

He slowed as he passed the gas station and diner. The parking lot had a few more cars on this Saturday morning than the typical midweek turnout. People giving themselves a treat, venturing out on the weekend for a late breakfast or early lunch.

Shaw pressed the gas pedal and accelerated past.

The road dipped slightly, and the small township of Martha's End appeared in the distance, the water tower rising into the sky like a real-life pin drop from Google maps marking the town.

Daisy had given him the keys to the Dodge so he could pick up a new irrigation pump. The old one had seized up and the flow of water to the cattle troughs in the outer pastures had dropped. He was surprised that she trusted him with her late father's pride and joy, but she was in an upbeat mood during breakfast, his company may have had something to do with it. But Shaw had still seen no sign of Daisy's mother and that puzzled him. The ranch, like Daisy herself, was proving to be an enigma. But she gave him the keys anyway as she didn't have time, telling him any damage would be at his cost. She was busy herding cattle, rotating them through the feedlots for grazing so that the other pastures could replenish the feed on the ground. He said he didn't mind. He wanted to see Martha's End anyway.

As he reached the town limits Shaw dropped his speed to forty-five and the scenery abruptly changed from rural to urban decay. Shaw felt a tinge of sadness as he drove through the outskirts. Abandoned warehouses, an old bank building, boarded-up workshops, rows of dull-gray cinderblock, faded business placards, cracked neon signs, parking lots overgrown with weeds. A place where things used to get made, where steel was shaped into things, lathes turned, metal was pressed and welds ran true, straight and lasted.

Often the new fast Interstate highway that ran parallel to the old highway would steal every reason people had for stopping by the old town. What was once a prosperous, vibrant community had been relegated to a siding alongside the main artery that linked the major towns and cities. It was a sad story that was often repeated across the country.

There were no Golden Arches, no In and Out, none of the large branded outlets or fashionable shopping malls. Those would be farther west.

He saw the township proper ahead as he eased off the gas.

It was set out in a typical grid pattern with the old highway forming the main street that bisected the town, before continuing west and heading back out onto the open road.

He drove onto the main street and spotted a café, filing its location away in his memory.

Stores lined each side. There was an automotive repair garage, a dollar store, a drug store, a small neighborhood grocery and a smattering of stores that had closed down. The façade of the main street looked tired and faded, like distant memories pressed into the cardboard pages of an old photo album. Time and progress had moved on, but Martha's End had refused to follow, preferring to maintain its quaint rural feel like so many other small towns. But Martha's End was still real, with real people, with old-fashioned values, proud of their heritage, where everyone knew everyone on a first name basis and where one could still feel safe walking the streets at night.

The hardware store was located at the end of the main street and Shaw turned into the dirt parking lot. There were a few other vehicles parked there and he checked them off. Old habits.

The front of the store was a wall of ladders, wheelbarrows, pallets of fertilizer and an assortment of hand tools. Shaw pushed open the door and a brass bell rang above his head. He smiled and stepped back in time. The air smelled of raw lumber, wood oil, and wax. The floor had seen a million feet over the years, the original stain worn back to a dirty olive smear. There was a long counter along one side of the store, and behind this was a tall wall with built-in pigeon holes crammed full of small tools, parts, cardboard cartons, small boxes and hardware bric-a-brac, all neatly and carefully stacked. A ladder on a slant ran along a rail halfway up the wall to gain access to the top where larger boxes were stacked, the print on the sides faded and their cardboard sagging with age. Every conceivable space taken, brimming with bits and pieces of hardware.

It was obvious that Daisy's father had spent a lot of time over the years in this exact store and judging from what Shaw had seen in the barn, Stan McAlister had almost single-handedly kept this hardware business afloat as its biggest customer over the years.

"Morning." An old man with thin hair and thick glasses shuffled out from a storeroom at the back. He wore an old-fashioned woodworking apron, checked shirt and looked like he had been born in sawdust.

Shaw unfolded a piece of paper and gave it to the old man. "I'm here to pick up a new pump for the McAlister Ranch," he said.

The old man squinted at Shaw, squinted at the order, then back at Shaw. His eyes behind the thick glasses registered an unfamiliar face, but he smiled.

"No problem. It's out back, I'll grab it for you." He returned to the storeroom and emerged moments later wheeling a box bound with plastic ties on a trolley. The side was stamped with the stars and stripes in red and blue, and the words *Made in the USA*.

"Took a while to source one of these. Not cheap either," the old man said, as he parked the box on the ground at Shaw's feet. "In fact, the previous model it's replacing went out of production back in the sixties," the old man crooned. "Ain't been no need. That's how good they are."

Says it all, Shaw thought, pleased that Daisy McAlister was staying true while everything around her was being sent offshore. The world had become such a disposable society.

"Not many companies make 'em like this. I told Daisy, but she insisted that she wanted something made here."

The more Shaw learned about Daisy McAlister, the more he liked her.

The old man rang up the sale on a huge cash register that looked as old as him. The numbers popped up on plastic strips in a narrow glass window. No LED digits or electronic sounds.

"It's on account. We'll send a statement at the end of the month."

Shaw knew "send" meant *mail* not *email,* and smiled again.

"But the account is quite overdue," the old man said, raising an eyebrow at Shaw.

"How much is the balance?" he asked.

Shaw carried the box outside and secured it in the flatbed of the Dodge with some rope. He started the truck and drove out of the parking lot, heading back along Main Street looking for the café he had seen before, his fingers drumming on the wheel to the radio tuned to a local music station. You could never have enough coffee.

ELEVEN

The café was located along a strip of stores on Main Street, sandwiched between the small office of a rural insurance broker and a women's hair salon that displayed in the window faded hairstyle posters from the seventies. Shaw parked the Dodge in a space in front. Any other place he would be worried someone would lift the pump out of the back of the Dodge and steal it. But for some reason the town didn't have that feel to it.

The café had a cozy and relaxed vibe, and the smell of coffee beans was enticing to Shaw. He ordered at the counter and took a seat on a high stool along a bench by the front window so he could keep an eye on the Dodge and the passing traffic.

His coffee arrived and he took a sip, watching the cars and towns folk pass by as they went about their business. People stopped to talk to one another, share some news, a smile, a wave. Different from Kansas City. Community. No "street zombies" walking in a trance, heads down, eyes and thumbs glued to smartphones, oblivious to the world unfolding around them. This was the preoccupation of most people in the larger towns or cities and it annoyed Shaw when he saw it. The folk of Martha's End seemed more friendly.

Everyone looked plain, unrecognizable.

All except one.

Across the street he saw Callie. She spotted the Dodge parked outside the café then looked up and saw Shaw sitting in the window. Instantly a smile spread across her face.

She came in and sat down beside him. "Fancy seeing you in town," she said. "I saw the Dodge and I thought it was Daisy who had driven in." She moved closer to Shaw and touched his arm. She looked different out of her work uniform, more relaxed. She wore straight jeans and a long sleeve T-shirt. Her hair was down and it fell around her shoulders. She looked even prettier dressed casually.

Shaw smiled. "I just came in to pick up a new pump for the ranch. I thought I'd stop by and grab a coffee before I headed back." He angled his body toward her. She smelled good too, fresh like the beach. Shaw ordered her an iced tea and they sat together in a relaxed fashion.

"I'm so glad you took my advice, helping Daisy out around the ranch. I know she really needs any help she can get," Callie said, stirring ice cubes with her straw.

"So tell me about Martha's End," Shaw asked, looking at her deep brown eyes and long lashes. They were dangerous eyes, eyes that a man could get lost in and forget his own name.

"Well, what would you like to know," she replied, taking a sip of her tea, running her tongue slowly and deliberately over her bottom lip.

"Let's start with the name 'Martha's End.' Where did the town get its name from?"

Callie gave a mischievous grin. "That's easy. It was named after the woman who opened the first brothel here back around eighteen seventy. The town of Hays was a pretty wild place back then. Plenty of drinking places almost like the Wild West. Old Martha came in to Hays one day to set up her own establishment. The local madams took offense at the new competition, so they banded together and drove her out of town. She headed a few miles east, away from Hays and set up here. It just became known as Martha's End."

"How do you know all this?" Shaw asked, fascinated by the backstory of old towns and the odd names they had.

Callie shrugged. "Just the local archives. I'm a local. Was born here. Went to school here. My parents are both dead, but I stayed. Daisy grew up here too. We were best friends in high school."

"Were?" Shaw asked.

"We still are, but she's on the ranch and I don't see her as much these days. A lot happened when her father died. There was no one else to help. She had bigger plans. She wanted to move to the city. Then her father died and she couldn't leave. She's an only child and it's just her and her mother now running the whole place. At first she was overwhelmed. We talked a lot back then and she cried a lot at first, but then she grew stronger. She toughened up. She had to."

"So why didn't you leave? Go to a bigger city, see other places. Move to Hays or someplace bigger?"

The smile left her eyes for a moment as regrets came to the surface. Shaw could see she was wrestling with her emotions. She had spent her whole life in a small town and she felt trapped. When you were born and grew up in a small town, it's hard to leave and the prospects of ever leaving evaporate over time.

Callie looked out the window. Cars slid slowly up and down the main street and people walked by, a constant passing of time and age. She spoke without looking back to Shaw. "I don't know. I guess I feel safe here. I know everyone and everyone knows me. I've been into Kansas City and I just didn't like it. I'm a small town girl."

Truth was Callie didn't have the courage to leave. She didn't want to be alone, in a new town or city, and a stranger among strangers. For all her outward confidence and street smarts she was still insecure.

She turned back to Shaw and her face brightened. "What about you? Tell me about yourself." She wanted to change the subject.

She moved the stool closer, their knees touching. Shaw could see a gleam of excitement return to her eyes, like he had some juicy bit of gossip that she wanted to extract out of him. But in reality it was just the thrill of a new person in town, someone from the outside, an unfamiliar face amongst a sea of sameness. Shaw was a brief distraction from the daily drudgery and routine that was her small-town life.

"I'm just passing through," he replied, non-committal. "I'm heading to Denver. I was in Kansas City."

"So you're from Kansas City?"

"No, I was in Kansas City."

"So where are you from? Where's your hometown? Where were you born?" The questions came thick and fast like a volley of shots and she was getting agitated with the ducking and weaving by Shaw. He wasn't forthcoming. Maybe he was shy. Maybe he was deeply private.

Callie pulled back, correcting herself. "Look, I'm sorry. I didn't mean to pry. It's none of my business."

Shaw looked at her for a moment. He couldn't tell her everything, but she seemed eager and in a way he felt sorry for her. He didn't mean it in a disrespectful way. He just did.

She was like a puppy wanting you to throw it a ball and was confused when you didn't.

Callie looked at her hands in her lap, fully aware of the awkwardness of the sudden silence.

"I'm from Indiana. A city called Terra Haute. I went to University of Maryland, but I dropped out after one semester. I'm thirty years old and I have an older sister. She is in law enforcement in Virginia. We don't really talk much or keep in touch. Both my parents are dead. I worked in Washington for a while up until last year."

"Are you a cop?" she asked, with a look of surprise.

"No, I'm not a cop, my sister is. She gets to carry a gun." Shaw did too, but in another capacity.

Callie paused a beat, her brain trying to process the sudden flood of information, trying to cross-reference it to the man who sat in front of her, the man she liked the look of the moment he walked into the diner, and liked even more from what small snippets of information he just divulged.

"Are you married?" Callie asked. Not that it had ever stopped her in the past.

"Do I look married?" Shaw cocked his head.

Callie narrowed her eyes, thinking as she studied him. "No. You look troubled."

"Troubled?" he laughed. Callie liked it when he laughed. His smile made her tingle in all the right places. It took him to a whole new level in her books. It was a rich, deep and throaty laugh, confident, self-assured and mature. But he still looked troubled, preoccupied. He must have been, because he hadn't picked up on any of her clues. Most of the guys around here still lived at home and wouldn't know what to do with a pretty woman if one stripped off and wrapped herself in nothing but a Christmas bow and lay provocatively under the tree on Christmas Eve—while his wife and kids slept upstairs.

Callie thought back to last Christmas and grimaced on the inside. It was a stupid thing to do, but he said he loved her and was going to leave his family for her.

Shaw leaned forward when he didn't get a response, "Callie?"

Callie snapped out of her trance, her mind a million miles away, reminiscing on the foolish act.

"Oh, sorry," she stuttered.

"That's pretty much it. I'm taking some time off before I decide what to do next, see where the road will take me. But let me assure you, I'm not troubled. Far from it. I'm the most relaxed I've been in ages."

"How long will you stay here, in Martha's End?" Callie pressed forward, determined, her hand touched his knee.

"Just a few days. I just want to fix a few things around Daisy's place."

"Can I give you a reason to stay longer? Some things need fixing at my place too," Callie replied. The offer hung there, plain as day, obvious.

Shaw looked down at her hand on his knee, then back to her eyes. There was a question there, behind the dilated pupils. She looked intoxicating with her small nose, a smattering of freckles, her lips parted slightly, a perfect row of white teeth, the tip of her tongue just visible. It was the freckles that did it for Shaw. They always did. An innocent look and infinite sex-appeal all rolled into one.

"Are you always this direct?" he raised an eyebrow. He watched as Callie's finger made circles around his knee.

She slid her tongue back and forth across her upper teeth. "Only when I see something I like and when time is against me."

Shaw reached for his coffee and took another sip. "Tell me about the Morgans. What do they do here in town? What are they like? Why do they want the McAlister land so badly?"

Callie sat back on her stool, a little taken back by the change of topic and the slight rejection. But she would persist, maybe later. "The Morgans are the Morgans. They and the McAlisters were among the first families to settle here back in the day. Their family history goes back more than a century."

"How many of them are there? The brothers, I mean, or whoever lives on their ranch."

"There are the three brothers and then there's Morgan Senior, Jim Morgan. They're a bunch of bullies, always have been. We all grew up together, went to school here, me, Daisy, Jed, Rory, and Billy. Billy's the eldest of the brothers, the other two just do what he tells them. They were bullies back then in school and they just grew into bigger bullies now."

"What about the father, Jim?"

Callie nodded, cradling her glass of tea, rubbing the cold moisture up and down the side. "As they say, 'the apple doesn't fall far from the tree.' The three brothers are just younger versions of the father. They follow his lead and do his dirty work around town."

"Work?" Shaw asked.

"You hardly see Jim Morgan around town. He stays most of the time on the Morgan ranch, holed up in that huge house up there. It's like a compound. Fences, security cameras, guard dogs, the whole nine yards. Just keep driving past the McAlister ranch, past the boundary fence for about another three miles and you'll get to the start of the Morgan property. Can't miss it."

Fences, security cameras, guard dogs? This certainly got Shaw's attention. Unusually high security measures for a rural setting, unless someone was protecting or hiding something significant.

Callie continued, "He gets his three sons to do his bidding around town. You know, debt collecting, rent collecting. You were in the diner when you saw them come in. Hal the chef is still fuming over it. When he gets behind in his rent the brothers come knocking. But it's Jim Morgan who pulls all the strings around here. He makes himself out to be a business man and an upstanding member of the community, but he manipulates people around here."

"You're not working today at the diner?"

"No, it's my day off, I've got Saturday and Sunday off. It's a bummer, because the weekends are usually good for tips. More people come in, more locals and more out-of-towners. And I need the money. Hal still owes me a few weeks pay, but the Morgans cleared out the till yesterday."

"What about the police?" Shaw knew the answer before he even asked the question. It was typical of a small town where one family flexed its money and influence over the locals.

Callie nearly choked on her tea. "The police?" she scoffed. "Hell, they're in Jim Morgan's pocket. We've got no police force here in Martha's End. There's a small department based in Hays and they usually come from there, if there's trouble. It's only a few miles away."

Shaw thought about it for a moment then decided to tell her. "Yesterday in the diner, the other two brothers, Jed and Rory said some pretty direct things about you."

"Yeah, they wish," she replied, but then she grew serious. "What sort of things?" Callie leaned in again, more intimate.

"You know, things they would do if they could get you alone. Just mouthing off. They also mentioned some girl called Jessie, like they had assaulted her in the past. They laughed it off like it was no big deal." Shaw felt uncomfortable mentioning it, but he wanted to know if there was more to it. He was worried for Callie and didn't want anything to happen to her.

"That's just small boys talking big, beating their chests, carrying on like apes. Billy's still probably sour at me from prom night years ago when he spent most of the night trying to get into my pants."

"Why, what happened?"

Callie shrugged. "Probably told his brothers afterwards how I rejected him, so Jed and Rory think it's their role to stand up for their older brother. Billy has always been keen on me, but he's got a mean jealous streak in him. Always had."

"Jealous of your boyfriend back then? The one you took to the prom?" This seemed logical to Shaw. He was interested in this, how high school feuds continued well into adulthood and even to the deathbed. Forgiveness was almost impossible when you were young, but got easier as you got older. Thinking back, there were even some of his own high school buddies that he hadn't seen since graduation, but if he crossed them in the street today he would punch them in the face. No words. No questions. Just retribution.

"God no!" Callie retorted like Shaw had insulted her. "I took a boy called Taylor Giles. He was the only half-decent prospect in the class. The rest were either apes or stooges for the Morgan brothers. Back then the Morgans were the cool kids. Their father had money then and he still is the richest person in Martha's End today."

"So why was Billy Morgan jealous?" Shaw pressed the point, glued to the conversation like it was a midday soap opera on the tube. In college, he once watched the Bold and the Beautiful while ironing a shirt one afternoon, and before he knew it he had a huge pile of clean, neatly ironed clothes, and an empty ironing basket, and two hours of his life he would never get back. He imagined all across the country, women, and a few men, were cutting through similar and otherwise boring home chores with ease thanks to TV shows like that.

"Billy didn't like the fact that I associated with Daisy. After all, she was a McAlister. The two families have been feuding for generations, goes back to the Civil War."

"Over what? Their land?"

"Land. Always land. The Morgans claim that the McAlisters stole a tract of land from them over a hundred years ago. Some great-grandfather of the McAlisters was prospecting up in the hills behind their ranch and convinced a surveyor in Hays to realign and forge the boundary line so that it became McAlister land, not Morgan land. He must have found something worthwhile up in those hills. Daisy told me all about it. Ever since then it's just snowballed through the generations, the same story passed down from father to son, made a little worse with each telling. The Morgans are a greedy bunch. They have more than enough land, cattle, everything. But it's never enough. It's personal. It's in their blood. If someone cheated a great uncle of theirs over a horse, or a bale of wheat, or in a card game in a saloon in Hays back in the day, they would never forget. It's like they keep a tally, goes into an old ledger for the grandson or great-grandson to inherit and make amends. Daisy will tell you."

Shaw looked out the window of the café. A police cruiser slid past, slowing, watching, like a great white shark. White Chevrolet Impala, black and gold decals. This was the second time it had gone past. Maybe it was doing Saturday morning loops around the town, just checking, keeping the peace. Maybe it was something else. Shaw turned his attention back to Callie.

She was proving to be a wealth of information about the town and its occupants. Eager to please. Maybe a little too eager. What did she want in return? Daisy would never have been this forthcoming with him. He was a complete stranger.

"You said you were best friends with Daisy."

"Still are. Billy hated that fact, still does. Thinks we must be lesbians, because we spent so much time together in high school and I rejected his advances, especially on prom night."

"But nothing bad happened back then with the Morgan brothers? They didn't break the law back in high school?"

Callie rolled her eyes. "Sure they broke the law. Nothing major though. High school stuff. Drunk-driving, a few bar fights. Maybe caught in possession. But when your father owns half of town and is a major contributor to the Mayor's re-election and is buddies with most of those who sit on Hays City Commission, things get wiped from the records, forgotten, excused."

Callie paused, like she was searching back through the recesses of her memory, then said slowly, "Come to think of it, there was this one girl. Stacy somebody. A local girl. A few years back she had gone around town claiming that Jed Morgan had raped her on a date. She went into Hays and told the police. She pressed charges and everything. A few months later, when it went to court she didn't front up. The whole Morgan clan showed up to court like a posse, had hired some hot-shot lawyer out of Kansas City, thousand bucks an hour they reckoned. But the girl just disappeared, vanished. So the charges were dropped. There were no other witnesses."

Shaw looked at his watch. "Look, it's time I was getting back, Daisy might wonder where I've got to." He could see the disappointment on Callie's face, almost a theatrical pout. It made her look even more cute, if that was even possible.

She leaned in again, so close for a moment he thought she was about to kiss him. She whispered, "Look, a few of us are going out tonight. There's a local bar and a band just up the block. Nothing spectacular, but it's the only place worthwhile around here on a Saturday night. How about you come too?"

Shaw shook his head and was about to protest, but Callie cut him off.

"No arguments. I won't hear of it," she said, poking Shaw in the ribs with her finger. "Daisy is coming too. We used to do it every Saturday night, like a pact, but with the ranch and everything I hardly see her anymore. She needs a break. It will do her good."

Shaw considered it for a moment. "Look, it's not really my style. Noise. Bars. Live bands. I've got a full afternoon mending fences and replacing things around the ranch. I'll be dead tired after I'm done."

"All the more reason to come out with us and relax, blow off a little steam, see where the evening takes you." Callie raised an eyebrow.

TWELVE

Callie left the café, saying she had to run some errands before tonight, and she really wanted Shaw to come. Shaw finished his coffee and watched as a police cruiser, the same one that had passed by before, pulled up across the street. The officer didn't get out.

Then things changed and Shaw felt his gut tighten.

The ruby red pickup truck pulled into the parking space next to the police cruiser and a man got out.

It was Billy Morgan.

For a moment Billy Morgan didn't look in the direction of the café. He walked around to the police cruiser and leaned down, resting his arms on the open window of the car and speaking to the driver.

He glanced in the direction of the café and spotted Daisy's Dodge parked out front. Shaw finished his coffee and walked outside. As Shaw opened the truck door he could see Billy Morgan hustle across the street toward him. He moved with purpose, not threatening, but Shaw swung open the door of the Dodge putting it between him and Billy. He wound down the window. No point in getting glass on yourself.

"Hi there," Billy called out.

"Morning," Shaw replied, non-committal, unsmiling, assessing the man. In a beat Shaw took in the rest of the street to see who else may be coming toward him as well, but it was just Billy Morgan. No one else. The police cruiser was still parked across the street, the cop still sitting inside.

"You must be the new ranch hand over at the McAlister place."

Billy was bigger than the other two brothers, and he talked and walked with too much confidence for Shaw, like someone who gave orders and threw his weight around to make sure they were carried out.

"I'm Billy Morgan, you must be new in town." Billy gave a nod, but didn't offer a handshake, his words spoken as though Shaw should have known who he was. Like he was famous.

Shaw nodded back, but said nothing. Give as little information as possible. Billy Morgan seemed friendly enough, but Shaw could tell his smile and friendly manner was a front.

"Yeah, I'm sure old Daisy could use the help and all," Morgan continued. "You don't look like the ranch hand type. You don't look like the others." Morgan kept the smile on his face as he looked at Shaw. He was assessing him too. Was he a drifter like the others? Or was he going to be a problem?

"I'm good with my hands. I thought I'd stay for a few days and help them out," Shaw replied, still holding the door between them.

"That's mighty hospitable of you, mister…?"

"Shaw, Ben Shaw."

"Well Ben, you seem like a nice guy, and Martha's End is a nice place. We don't get many visitors, most people who aren't locals are just passing through like yourself. They don't stay for long."

Shaw shrugged and decided to play along. "I might stay a few days, I might stay longer. Depends."

Billy his eyes narrowed. "Depends on what?" Annoyance started to seep into Billy Morgan's face, his smile changing into a smirk.

"Depends on what needs to be done," Shaw replied. "What help Daisy wants."

Billy paused, then looked at the ground and gave a small shake of his head like Shaw had given the wrong answer. He stepped closer. "Look, I know you mean well. But we don't like visitors to stay too long here. It upsets the ebb and flow of the place."

"What ebb and flow?" Shaw asked flatly.

Billy Morgan would have made a good politician. He had a way of telling you what to do without actually telling you what to do.

"You see Ben, my brothers and I keep the town peaceful, we like to keep the place running smoothly. We know everyone and everyone knows us, and that's how we like it."

Shaw nodded back past Billy toward the police cruiser. "Isn't that what the local police are for? Are you a police officer?"

Billy was starting to get impatient. His smile was completely gone, replaced by the thin line and cold eyes. The welcoming party was over.

But Shaw wasn't finished, wanting to turn it up a notch. He hated people who used bullying and intimidation to get their way. "So it's like you and your brothers have been deputized? Like you have authority around here, like the police, or are you just doing your civic duty?"

Billy frowned. None of the other hired help of the McAlister's had spoken to him like this before, when he had given them their first talking-to. He didn't like this guy. He didn't like his own authority being questioned, especially from some out-of-towner who knew nothing about the place or the Morgan name.

"Listen, we don't want no trouble here. There's nothing much in this town to keep you here. I know someone like you would prefer the bright lights and excitement of those bigger places. More women, more fun." The smile had returned.

Shaw knew the tactics Billy was using, wanting to be everyone's best friend, making out they've known each other for years.

"Look, you probably aren't getting paid that much by Daisy. They don't have much money, so it's almost like charity what you're doing, and I can understand that. So I'll tell you what I'll do."

Here it comes, like you're doing me a favor.

"I'll give you a thousand dollars if you're out of town by sundown today. No strings attached, just leave by then. Hell, I'll even drive you to the bus station in Hays so you don't have to walk or nothing."

Now it was Shaw's turn to smile. "You'll give me a grand just to leave town? Just for getting on a bus today and going?"

Billy nodded, glad that Shaw was finally coming around to his way of thinking. "I sure will, no problem. A bit of cash in your pocket to enjoy yourself in the next town or city. Maybe hook-up with a few girls, spread a bit of love—you know." Billy grinned and nodded like they had a secret male-only understanding.

But Shaw was wired differently. A lot differently.

Shaw made to look like he was thinking about the offer. He slipped into the seat of the Dodge, shut the door of the truck. If his mind wasn't made up before, Billy Morgan had certainly made that decision for him now.

Billy seemed quite pleased with himself, rocking back and forth on his heels, another drifter taken care of.

Shaw started the engine and glanced up through the window at Billy Morgan. "That's a nice rig you've got there," Shaw said, nodding at the pickup parked across the street, chrome and deep metallic paint glistening under the midday sun.

Billy turned and looked back over his shoulder, then back at Shaw, his grin even wider. "Yep, she sure is a beauty. You like it?" Billy replied, puffing out his chest slightly. He liked it when people complimented him: on his truck, on how sharp he dressed, on how good he was in the sack after he roughed up the girl first, like he was doing her a favor having sex with them.

Shaw nodded. "Is it to compensate for the small dicks you and your brothers have?"

Billy Morgan balked, like his brain needed time to digest the words, but Shaw gave him no time.

"The next time you decide to run me off the road, I'll beat you senseless and mount you on the hood of your truck like a deer."

Shaw hit the gas and pulled out of the parking space leaving Billy Morgan gaping after him.

THIRTEEN

The town was an illusion. On the surface everything appeared normal, but something was hiding below the surface. Moving deep within the fabric, a different pattern had been woven. A threat of retribution or implied violence that shifted under the veneer of an otherwise ordinary rural community. It made Shaw naturally curious and wanting to find out more.

Good town, bad people.

The needle on the speedometer on the Dodge hovered at an even fifty-five miles per hour. Endless fields of yellow stretched to the horizon on either side of the road, the air a dusty haze with the smell of wheat and chaff. Everything looked normal, peaceful, serene. Yet Shaw could feel the strong undercurrent of dread in his gut. He trusted his instincts. It had saved his life a few times, but had got him into trouble as well.

"Never trust what you see. Trust what you feel. Use your eyes to see only what was coming next." That's what someone told him once. "Words to live by in this game, otherwise you won't last long."

Shaw could feel something coming. He felt it in the diner the day before. He felt it sitting in the café, looking out on the street. He felt it when he looked in the rearview mirror.

Before he pulled out of town, he had found the car details in the glove box and he placed it on the seat beside him together with his driver's license.

See what was coming next.

A couple of miles outside the town limits of Martha's End the police cruiser tucked in behind Shaw and slowly grew in his rearview mirror.

The police cruiser edged closer, its light bar flickered, the headlights flashed, wanting him to pull over. Shaw eased off the gas, indicated and pulled over onto the rough shoulder of the road, a funnel of dust kicking up as the tires crunched over the loose gravel.

The police cruiser parked behind Shaw and he watched as a cop got out, adjusted his belt, smoothed his pants and made his way over to the driver's side of the Dodge. Shaw kept both hands on the steering wheel and looked up at the cop. Behind the glint of the aviator sunglasses, the cop seemed just a kid, like he should still be in college, he had that baby-face look. Red hair, fair skin, gangly limbs and still growing. Black starched shirt, tan pants, two-way microphone clipped to his shoulder and a badge on his shirt that said "Giles", and a black handgun on his hip holster that said he was in charge.

"Yes, Officer, can I help you?" Shaw asked, squinting into the sunlight, hands still on the wheel. That was important. The cop had one hand on his duty belt, and the other hand closed around the grip of the gun. Typical stance and protocol for a routine traffic stop. But this was going to be anything but a routine traffic stop in Shaw's mind.

"Sir, is this your vehicle?" the cop asked. No arrogance, just a deadpan face, but the tilt of the head and the eyes behind the aviator glasses said otherwise.

Shaw kept both his hands on the wheel. He knew the procedure well. When you get pulled over by a cop, best keep your hands on the wheel where they can be seen. Not in your lap and certainly don't reach for anything without asking permission, making it clear first your intention. No sudden movements. Shaw had seen too many twitchy law enforcement graduates during routine traffic stops draw their weapon because the driver was just reaching for their license or cell phone, or coffee cup without thinking. And Kansas was a concealed-carry state.

"No, this is not my vehicle, but I have permission to use it," Shaw replied, not offering more.

"Then sir, I'm going to have to see proof of registration and your driver's license," the cop replied. Shaw noted the slight tensing of the kid's posture. Nothing major, just moving to another level of the threat assessment.

Standard procedure.

"I have no weapons on me or in the car. The registration and my license are on the seat beside me. Is it OK if I grab them?"

The cop bent in slightly so he could get a better view of the inside of the cabin, one hand still firmly on his gun. "No problem," he replied.

Shaw reached over and passed the cop the registration and his license through the open window.

The cop took his time scrutinizing them both, then finally said, "It says this vehicle is registered to a Miss Daisy McAlister."

Shaw nodded, "Yes, that's correct, Officer." Being polite and respecting his title was important to the kid with the gun. It established the line of authority, and maintained control of the situation. "But you already knew that," Shaw added. "Before you pulled me over."

The eyes flickered behind the aviators, the cop unsure for a moment. Was he being asked or told?

"It says here on your license that you reside in Washington D.C. Are you here on business or just passing through?" the cop asked, ignoring the comment, remaining in charge.

Shaw smiled, playing the game. "Not sure yet. The people seem so nice here that I might just stay for a while."

Surely this couldn't be Taylor Giles, the guy Callie had mentioned back at the café, the one she had taken to the prom in high school? The name badge matched. Maybe he was stuck in a small town just like her. The place had the gravity of a black hole. You can't break free.

The cop did a slow loop of the Dodge, noting the pump box in the bed, then nodded to Shaw, pausing to look at the face on the license one more time like remembering Shaw's personal details was important. "We don't like strangers around here." His hand rested again on his holstered handgun, the threat obvious. "Can I give you some advice?"

Shaw didn't want advice, but went along. "Sure."

"I'd be leaving town today. There isn't much here to see." He handed back the driver's license and registration. "It'll be best for everyone."

Everyone?

Shaw took the license and paperwork, and placed it back on the seat. He wasn't angry at the kid, but it was two veiled threats in one day to leave town. He must be doing something right. Time to turn the tables like he had done on a few inexperienced young cops before.

"Am I free to go, Officer Giles?"

"Leave town, Mr. Shaw. Just some friendly advice."

Shaw nodded like he agreed to the advice, put the truck in gear then paused, his foot hovering over the gas pedal, his arm on the doorsill.

The cop turned, his job done, and headed back to the cruiser.

Shaw hung his head out the window. "Hey, can I ask you something?" he said, like he was asking for directions.

Taylor Giles stopped, turned and stood where he was, his sunglasses glinting, hands on his hips. "Sure, go ahead."

"How much does a police officer make in Hays?"

Giles seemed taken back for a moment, unsure, his face scrunched in confusion. "Excuse me?" he replied, as he slowly walked back to the Dodge.

"You know. How much does a cop make around here? Like how much does he get paid?"

Giles shrugged, "Why?"

Just let it go. Just drive away, the voice inside Shaw was telling him, the voice of logic, reason and commonsense.

But Shaw was riled now. It was a free country and he didn't like being told what to do or where he could or couldn't go. Not especially by one of the minions who was probably on the payroll of the Morgans. This cop, this kid with a gun, was just reinforcing the message Billy Morgan had made outside the café.

Shaw smiled, "Well, you see I was thinking about joining up, you know, becoming one."

Giles shuffled awkwardly on his feet, unsure if it was a serious question or if the man was joking with him.

But Shaw didn't give him a chance to answer. Shaw nodded at him. "You must get paid a decent amount right?"

Giles said nothing, but he was getting aggravated, tossing up whether the guy was being a public nuisance or not. "It's OK, I guess." Giles replied, not knowing where this was going.

Shaw never forgot a face. He had filed away in his memory so many faces over the years from his past, a past that still haunted him.

His brain was like one huge depository of faces, places, and what people would consider minor, insignificant and easily forgotten details. What people were wearing, how they were behaving, their facial expressions, and more importantly the look in their eyes. It was always the eyes that gave them away. It wasn't where they were looking that gave them away, it was where they *weren't* looking; at Shaw when he was looking directly back at them in a crowd, at a demonstration, or just filling up their brand new expensive car at a gas station. And Shaw had filed away in one of the many filing cabinets in his brain the details of Police Officer Taylor Giles when he first saw him yesterday filling up his car at the diner.

"Well, it must be better than OK, the pay I mean," Shaw added, turning the tables, the kid was out of his depth. "Was that the six-point-two liter V8 you had? You know, the fast one?"

Suddenly it dawned on Giles and the color drained from his face. He told his friends and work colleagues that it was paid for from an inheritance from an aunt who died last year in Topeka. He told them she had left him a lump of money in her Will. But Giles was too young and dumb to see the error, especially when Jim Morgan owned the Chevrolet dealership in downtown Hays. The untrained eye would have missed it, but Shaw hadn't. Maybe he should have bought a Dodge instead.

"Man, that was a nice car I saw you filling up at the gas station yesterday. Brand new Chevy Camaro. Nightfall gray metallic, I think they call it. Black center stripe, twenty-inch machined-finished wheels, two-tone leather seats. I saw the interior when you opened the door and got out." Shaw gave a short whistle. "They must be paying you cops in Hays a pretty packet for you to be driving a fully-optioned beauty like that."

Shaw turned back to the road ahead, and pressed down on the gas. The tires on the Dodge slid then bit and threw up a stream of gravel and dust as he swerved off the shoulder and back onto the blacktop at speed, leaving Officer Giles staring after him in his wake.

FOURTEEN

The bar was a small establishment set back off Main Street. It had rough brick walls, polished wooden floorboards, soft lighting and a gleaming length of mahogany bar that was all brass fittings and taps. The beer was cold and the music loud, and people pulsed in waves to country music from the live band as waitresses navigated between patrons, delivering drinks and food to tables.

People also jostled at the bar and the crowd was a mix of locals and workers swapping their weekly wages for a good time.

Shaw had spent the afternoon replacing the old water pump. Then he worked on the windmill, twisting off rusted bolts and lubricating bearings and gears as he watched Daisy work Jazz through the cattle, shifting them between paddocks.

They had driven into town in the Dodge, Daisy content just to sit with her thoughts in the passenger seat while Shaw drove. She hadn't been forthcoming with conversation and when Shaw had asked her how her day was she just replied in one-word answers, preoccupied with looking out the window at the fields of orange and brown as the sun slowly sank.

Callie had met them in the parking lot of the bar and she was quick to remind Shaw with a whisper in his ear that her place was just a short walk away.

Inside the bar they found a quieter booth away from the throng of noise and people.

Callie had slid right next to Shaw on the vinyl seats and straight away her hand found the inside of his thigh under the table.

Discrete, but direct.

Daisy had sat diminutively, and didn't say much all evening while Callie just bubbled with chatter, being playful and full of excitement. Daisy had a certain confidence about her, but didn't need to be the center of attention. Shaw had seen it in the way she went about running the ranch. But there were cracks in her façade, a sign of growing up too fast, the vulnerable girl living beneath the skin of a young woman. Shaw was always attracted to the most vulnerable. No chemistry or physiology could explain his compulsion, and that's what made him vulnerable too, a need to help those who needed helping. The Morgan brothers turning up to the diner was the reason he hadn't got back on the bus, and Daisy McAlister was the reason he decided to stay a few more days.

Daisy sat across from him drinking a beer straight from the bottle, her eyes watching Callie who was spinning and dancing with some guy on the dance floor. It had taken Shaw some effort to convince Callie that he didn't want to dance, so she gave up and grabbed the nearest eligible guy and pulled him up instead to dance with her.

"Is everything OK?" Shaw asked.

Daisy turned back from watching Callie dancing. "She likes you," she replied, taking another sip from her beer, her eyes avoiding his, peeling the label on the bottle obviously more interesting than looking at Shaw's face.

Shaw smiled. "I think she likes everyone. She seems like a fun person." Shaw's eyes lingered over Daisy while she was looking down at her beer.

Might as well get an eye-full, he thought.

She looked good, natural beauty, minimal makeup, her skin and face had a healthy glow, she looked different out of her work clothes, but she looked good in them too. She wore tight jeans, boots and a low-buttoned sleeveless check shirt with a lace bra underneath, the frill and tiny bow in the center just visible when she leaned forward.

Attractiveness came in many forms and Shaw never fell for the most obvious, the prettiest, or those who were the center of attention in the room, those women who men seemed to gravitate to like dogs in heat. He preferred the dark horse, the less obvious, those who hovered in the background and didn't flaunt themselves. Daisy McAlister was all of these and that's what made her all the more alluring.

"Just don't hurt her," Daisy said, finally looking up, catching Shaw watching her, and gave him a quizzical look.

Shaw shook his head, "How would I hurt her?"

"You're not staying, she'll fall for you and next thing you'll be gone. She deserves better. I've seen her get involved with too many guys who just blow through here. They use her and she lets them."

"I can't help that," Shaw replied. "It's her choice, she a grown-up, like you. She's an adult. She can make her own decisions." Then Shaw tried a different tack. "Maybe I'm not interested in her. I'm just looking for some peace and quiet. I'm not interested in getting involved with anyone."

Daisy cocked her head. "Then you better tell her that and don't lead her on." Daisy could feel her anger rising.

Shaw looked at her in disbelief. "I'm not leading her on," he said a little too loud. A few people on other tables turned and looked in their direction like they were a couple having an argument.

Daisy snapped back, the heat building in her cheeks, "Well, she seems to be all over you like a rash. She told me you had a very cozy little talk in town today. I thought you went to just get the pump, not meet with her like it was some kind of rendezvous."

"I didn't know I had to punch a time-clock," Shaw replied in a calm voice.

Daisy said nothing and went back to peeling the label off her beer bottle, leaving a small pile of confetti on the table.

Shaw rolled his eyes. "So this is what this is about? You're jealous."

"You're kidding me, aren't you? Jealous over a blow-through ranch hand like you?"

Shaw gave a smirk. "You *are* jealous aren't you?"

Daisy slammed down her bottle, spilling some on the table, beer frothing from the neck. Now she was furious. She hated the way he was grinning at her across the table, like he saw and knew everything.

Smug bastard.

Daisy placed her arms on the table, leaned forward and hissed, "You know nothing about me or what I've had to do." It all came pouring out. "You sit here like some know-it-all, but mister, you know nothing!"

Shaw just sat back and let her take out her frustration on him. She needed to take it out on somebody for the last few years, so it might as well be him.

"I've had to run that ranch almost single-handedly since my father died. My mother did what she could. We had no money left to us. There was no life insurance, nothing! He died and left us just the farm and the cattle." Her eyes flared as she spoke. "The bills are piling up. The bank has threatened to foreclose and we'll lose the place in a fire-sale if that happens, I've got the Morgans breathing down my neck wanting to drive us off our own land and I don't need some out-of-town city hick like you telling me *you know me* or any of the shit my mother and I have had to put up with over the last few years."

Daisy looked away and took a swig from her beer, conscious of the tears in her eyes, not wanting to seem weak to anyone. She wasn't looking for pity either. Life had dealt her a rough hand, but she had to deal with it and suck it up. She didn't have the liberty like Callie or most people to walk out of the door at the end of the day and forget about their worries. For her it never ended at five pm. Running a business, especially a farming business, was a twenty-four-hour-a-day gig. It was constant and never-ending, and the stress and responsibility had taken its toll on her.

She couldn't remember the last time she had worn a dress, or put on some makeup, or bought a new pair of shoes or had been asked out on a date. Callie had all these and more and maybe, just maybe, Daisy was a bit jealous of her lifestyle.

But Daisy was too proud to ask for help, or money, or for a hand. Maybe too stubborn as well. Selling the ranch was not an option, yet everyone had said it was the best thing to do after her father died. It had been in the family for generations, but with modern farming these days it was all about herd consolidation, organic feedlots, artificial insemination and the like. She didn't have the know-how or money to change. Bigger players and government lobbying were pushing the smaller landowners to the brink of bankruptcy.

Shaw felt bad. "Look, I'm sorry if I've upset you. I'm—"

"Forget it," Daisy said, still looking everywhere but at him. "This was a bad idea coming out tonight. It's probably just as well you're not staying anyway and will be gone in a few days." She pushed her chair out, got up and glared at Shaw. "I'm going. You can catch a ride with someone else. Or maybe you can spend the night at Callie's place." She walked away through the crowd and headed towards the exit.

****

The parking lot sat adjacent to the bar, and was cracked concrete, dim lighting and pickups squeezed in side-by-side off a narrow driveway that ran from the street.

The Dodge was parked away from the bar, close to the street at the front of the lot. Shaw burst through the exit door, hoping to catch up to Daisy before she drove off. He saw the silhouette of several shapes clustered in the middle of the lot.

Shaw quickened his pace. As he closed the distance the dark shapes split into four people: three male, one female.

The three men had formed a triangle with the woman in the middle. One of the men had the woman by her arm. She jerked and fought, but couldn't break free from the man's grip.

"Take your damn hands off me," she yelled.

"Can I help you?" Shaw stopped a few feet away.

Four heads turned in unison toward him.

Billy Morgan had Daisy by the arm while the other two brothers, Jed and Rory stood watching, hands on hips, enjoying the show.

"Well, what do we have here? The new ranch hand." Billy Morgan smirked at Shaw. "You should have gotten on that bus like I said. Now you just keep moving on. None of this concerns you. It's just a little private conversation between the young woman and me."

Shaw could see Daisy wasn't afraid, but Billy held her arm tight, his fingers digging into her flesh, her face twisted in pain. Billy looked back at Daisy. "Now you stop your fretting. I ain't going to hurt you."

"Let her go, Billy," Shaw stepped closer, angles, distances, and fist combinations running through his head. He could definitely drop Billy Morgan, maybe Jed too if he came at him at the same time. But all three at once would be a problem. Not impossible, but not preferred.

Billy Morgan let out a belching laugh and shook his head at Shaw. "I told you this ain't none of your business. You should have taken that bus ride like I said and left town. Could've been in Colorado by now banging some sweet piece of ass, instead of wasting your time on this frigid bitch."

Jed and Rory let out a roar of laughter.

"I didn't want your money," Shaw replied.

Daisy looked at Shaw in surprise.

"Maybe Billy, you should give Daisy a little taste of what she ain't had for a while," Jed chuckled. "You know, let her see what a piece of real grain-feed meat feels like."

Jed and Rory grinned like fools.

"Would you like that, Daisy?" Billy said, pulling her closer to him, twisting her arm up. He stunk of alcohol and sweat. "You ain't got no prize-bull on your ranch like me, honey. Hell, I'll even do both holes if you like? Would you like that?"

"I'll get on the bus, if you let her go," Shaw edged forward. There was no one else in the parking lot.

Billy Morgan seemed to contemplate this for a moment. He lowered Daisy's arm slightly. "Well, you see that's the problem right there," he said, smiling at Shaw. "That ride is long gone now." Billy was relishing the moment, wanting to drag it out as long as he could. His eyes narrowed, the smile gone, replaced by a cold sadistic stare. "So you see, the only choice left for you now is leaving town in an ambulance. That's the only ride I'm offering."

FIFTEEN

"It's a fair enough trade isn't it? I let her go, but you get to stay with us." Billy Morgan still had a hold of Daisy's arm. Jed and Rory moved closer to Shaw.

Three against one. Bad odds for one person. Better odds, if you knew how to handle multiple attackers.

The Morgan brothers were big, heavy with muscle, but that usually meant they were slow, with poor reaction times and a lack of agility. But they could do some damage, especially if all three ganged up or if the fight went to the ground. The ground was the worst place to be when you had multiple attackers. The brutality doubled. On the ground six fists became six boots and the scale of damage that could be inflicted suddenly went off the charts. Skulls, spleens, kidneys and livers didn't like being kicked.

There were no CCTV cameras on poles, no cop cars nearby, no bystanders to witness the one-sided beating. But then the brothers knew this. The spot they had chosen was deliberate. They had seen Shaw, Daisy, and Callie go inside the bar. Better to hang in the shadows of the parking lot and wait. There was no one coming to help Shaw, and Daisy would just be a burden in a fist-fight.

Shaw looked at the three brothers.

Dogs and bullies hunted in packs.

"OK," Shaw said.

"OK, what?" Billy asked.

"Let's get this done. I'm tired and I want to go to bed," Shaw replied.

"Hospital bed more like it," Rory sniggered.

Billy let go of Daisy and pushed her toward Shaw.

"Take her, you can have her. She ain't nothing special," Billy laughed.

"Get in the truck Daisy and wait for me," Shaw said, without taking his eyes off the three brothers. Daisy looked confused.

"They'll hurt you." Daisy turned back to Billy. "You're pathetic. So you've been paying off my workers so they don't come back?" she snarled, fury in her eyes.

Billy said nothing, just smiled at the ground.

"You're scum. All of you are scum!"

Shaw said again in a calm voice, "Daisy, please just get in the truck." Shaw didn't want the situation to get out of control. He could mitigate some of the damage, but Daisy was the unknown variable. He needed to remove her from the equation otherwise her distraction could get him killed.

Daisy turned to Shaw and he nodded. He saw something change in her face. An understanding, a respect for him, almost appreciative.

She walked toward the Dodge, unlocked the door, and got in.

Shaw looked after her, then turned back to the three brothers. They closed in around him. "OK," he said. "It's just us."

Jed came first, dumb and predictable, all wide-eyed throwing a haymaker like he was pitching at Fenway Park. Shaw stepped in, blocked the punch then drove his elbow into his jaw dropping him like the sack of shit he was. Shaw stepped back and pivoted just as Rory rolled toward him throwing wild punches. Shaw switched stance then drove the top of his foot up and out in a compact front kick, driving it deep and hard into Rory's groin, cutting the man's sperm-count in half permanently. Rory screamed and collapsed in a tangle of pain, tears and expletives.

Shaw stepped back and surveyed the damage. Street-fighting was never clean, choreographed, or precise like the movies. Martial arts taught you technique, survival and fear taught you adaptive brutality.

Billy hadn't moved. He never did. He preferred to watch as his brothers did the dirty work for him. But now both were curled up, writhing on the ground.

"So now it's just you and me." Shaw looked at him.

"Well, see that's where you're wrong again." Billy Morgan jerked his head and gave a short whistle through his teeth, and things got a whole lot worse for Shaw.

Something big detached itself from the shadows between two cars and moved toward them.

The man was huge, well over six feet and built like a locomotive. He wore a singlet, soiled and stained, rough jeans and massive work boots. He lumbered forward toward Shaw like Frankenstein. His head was a huge bald cannonball, raked with scar-tissue and pitted like the moon. His face was pushed in, like it was made from clay by uncaring hands, a nose flat from being broken numerous times. He had crooked yellowed teeth and drool dripped from the corners of thick lips that were twisted in a cruel smile.

His arms hung like a gorilla, the skin bulging, vascular and corded. He flexed massive hands that were knotted and calloused like old tree roots. He was as huge and as ugly as a troll from some child's nightmare, given birth to in a boiler, raised in the backwoods by apes, kept in a cage with attack dogs until he was called upon when needed.

Billy nodded at Shaw then turned to the giant. "This is Ox. Ox, meet the guy you're going to put into the intensive care unit for a very, very long time."

The giant made a deep guttural sound, in between a hideous laugh and dog-like snarl.

Shaw stepped back, keeping his distance as the giant closed on him.

Then he heard a sound that he had heard a million times before, the sound of smooth oiled metal.

The sound a handgun makes when you rack the slide and cycle a round into the chamber.

They all turned, even the giant.

Daisy McAlister appeared out of the gloom. In her outstretched hands she held a Glock 9mm handgun pointed directly at Billy Morgan's head.

"Don't move," she said through gritted teeth. "If one of you so much as blinks I'll shoot you. Do you understand me?"

Billy Morgan raised his hands. Jed Morgan staggered to his feet, groggy and rubbing his jaw. Rory was still in pain on the ground, but he looked up at Shaw. "I'm going to kill you," he wheezed.

"I said don't fucking move!" Daisy pressed forward, the barrel of the gun sweeping between the three brothers and the giant who just stood looking at her like a halfwit.

"Now come on Daisy, we were just having some fun," Billy replied. He wasn't too concerned with Jed and Rory, they would live.

Daisy ignored him and motioned to Shaw. "Let's go," she said, keeping the gun trained on the group.

Shaw ducked past Billy Morgan and stood beside Daisy. "The key's in the ignition, start it up," she said, her eyes never leaving the group.

Shaw nodded, jogged a few yards to the Dodge parked near the entrance of the lot. He slid into the driver's seat, fired up the engine, backed out of the slot and reversed all the way back to where Daisy stood, lining up the passenger door with her shoulder. He reached across and pushed open the passenger door so she could slide in quickly.

Daisy backed up while covering all three brothers with the gun until she could feel the car door against her butt, then she moved around to the opening without looking behind her. She glared at Billy Morgan and settled the gun on his face. "Stay away from my ranch. Stay away from my family. Stay away from anyone I employ." She slid fast into the seat, pulled her legs in, and slammed the door.

Shaw hit the gas hard. The Dodge leapt forward, skidding before fish-tailing out of a hard turn onto the street then accelerated away.

****

For about a mile Shaw said nothing. He kept checking the rearview mirror as they sped out of town, the darkness the only thing following them.

He turned to Daisy. The gun was in her hands on her lap, her finger off the trigger. She was ashen-faced and her shoulders were trembling. It had taken every ounce of courage for her to do what she had done. She had carried her Winchester around the ranch only as a deterrent to strangers like Shaw. Shooting vermin or putting down a sick cow on a farm was different to pointing a loaded handgun at another human being with the intent of pulling the trigger. She just faced the very possibility of shooting a person tonight, in self-defense she could later claim.

Shaw had seen guys who were crack shots on the combat range unload a full magazine in seconds and hit dead-center with every round. But they would freeze when they had to draw their weapon for the first time for real on the street. Their hands would tremble, their aim would waver and they would break out in a cold sweat from fear. Shooting paper targets was one thing. Shooting living flesh and blood was something completely different.

"Jesus, I didn't know you carried a gun," Shaw said, keeping the truck on the speed limit. Dark hemmed in all around them, the headlights kept a steady beam on the blacktop.

"I keep it under the driver's seat, as protection. It's all legal. I have a permit." Her voice was distant and hollow. She stared straight ahead out the windshield.

Shaw squirmed in the seat realizing that he had been sitting on a loaded gun all the time he had been driving around town today. He hadn't told Daisy about being pulled over by the police either. He shook his head. He had told the cop there were no weapons in the car. If the cop had done a search Shaw would probably be spending the night in the jail right now.

"Daisy, I'm going to reach for the gun. I just want to put it away. Is that OK?"

Daisy said nothing for a moment, then she nodded.

Shaw took one hand off the wheel and slowly reached across her thigh and took the gun off her lap. "That's good." He said reassuringly. "We're doing fine."

They passed the gas station and the diner, the bright neon lights punctured the night, a welcoming sign that they were nearly home. The diner was open, a few cars were parked out front. Shaw could see people sitting inside and waitresses shuffling back and forth.

Callie! Damn!

They had just up and left her back at the bar.

"She'll be fine," Daisy said, reading Shaw's thoughts as they passed the diner.

I know, but will you be?

SIXTEEN

"I'm sorry."

"For what?"

They sat in the bunkhouse, the fire crackled and threw warm orange across their faces. Daisy was perched on the old sofa in front of the wood stove, a blanket thrown over her shoulders, knees drawn under her. Shaw sat on the rug across from her. They had not stopped driving until they reached the ranch. It was nearly midnight. While Daisy was checking that the homestead and the stables were secure, Shaw had stripped the Glock she had given him and reassembled it.

Old habits.

It was perfectly clean and oiled, like it had never been fired.

Now it sat on the kitchenette counter, all fifteen rounds in the magazine, magazine reinserted, but no round in the chamber. Civilian ready, how he preferred. Next to it was his book, the bus ticket sticking out marking a page, Colorado looking more distant.

"I've never pointed a handgun at anyone, let alone one of the Morgans," she replied, her eyes watching the flames as they danced and flickered. It was best to let her talk. Shaw wanted to know more, a lot more now that things had happened like they had. It was important to let someone talk. Let them control the flow of information rather than turn this into an interrogation.

Daisy had gotten a text from Callie wondering where they had gone. Daisy replied, telling her she had suddenly fallen ill and asked Shaw to take her home. Callie replied with a sad-faced emoji and said they would catch-up tomorrow, and to tell Shaw she had found another guy to have fun with and for Shaw not to be too heart-broken.

He wasn't.

Daisy looked at Shaw. "I'm sorry for what happened. Really."

"Nothing happened, thanks to you. I didn't fancy fighting some ape anyway. It's not your fault."

"I've never had anyone for a long time stand up for me. No one. It has always been just me and my mother, like against the world."

"What did Billy Morgan want?" Shaw asked.

"Just the usual crap he goes on with. He told me that I should reconsider his father's offer on the ranch and that I shouldn't be holding out for a better one."

"Can I ask how much?"

"No amount of money will be enough," she replied harshly, her anger flaring again. She could turn from an apologetic young woman, in shock from pointing a gun at a man's head, to a wild woman full of rage when the subject involved her family or the ranch. Such grounded values were rare today. She was extremely protective of tradition and the family's heritage. She had opened up on the drive home, telling Shaw of the feud between the Morgans and the McAlisters, covering the same ground that Callie had, but he didn't tell her that.

"Thank you," she said again. A smile this time. She was slowly getting back to her old self and Shaw liked it when she smiled.

"For what?"

"For coming after me when I took off out of the bar. For stepping in when you saw Billy Morgan had my arm. You were outnumbered. You didn't need to step in. No one around here would have done a goddamn thing. They would have kept out, walked on by, done nothing because it was the Morgans."

Shaw got up, opened the door on the wood stove and threw in another log. More heat radiated into the room. He had all the doors and windows locked and secured. He came back and sat on the sofa next to Daisy.

"What do you think they will do?" she asked.

"Bullies typically retreat, go to ground for a while to lick their wounds then regroup, work out a way to retaliate. That's the way they think."

"I didn't mean to pull you into this," she turned to Shaw, her thigh touching his, crossing that space people usually reserved for intimacy. Shaw didn't move or flinch, he just looked into her eyes.

"Stay," she whispered, then she stretched her neck and kissed him, full on the mouth, slowly at first, testing the waters, judging the response.

Soft lips on his. Her gentle inhale drawing his breath into her mouth.

She pushed forward, the blanket slipping from her shoulders, her arms and hands coming forward around Shaw's neck, pulling him closer.

He could feel the hardness of her breasts crushed against his chest. There was a hunger there, in her mouth, her tongue, her teeth. An appetite that had been starved for years now rising to the surface.

But he didn't kiss back.

"What's wrong?" Daisy pulled back momentarily.

"You don't have to thank me like this, Daisy. I don't expect anything from you," he said quietly.

"I need this," she said. *God, how I really need this.*

She reached for him again, this time harder, more aggressive and he responded. She undid her belt and buttons at the front of her jeans, took his hand and slid it down the front, under her panties. She guided his fingers downward through a narrow bed of tight bristles until his fingertips came to a fleshy crease that he parted with one finger and delved deeper into a channel of warm slipperiness.

Daisy groaned hungrily for more. With her own fingers she traced the outline of something large and throbbing along the inside of his thigh. Stroking back and forth, coaxing a lengthening mass that swelled and stretched under the tight denim like it would split the material, some powerful force beneath struggling to be unleashed. She could feel him squirm and she rubbed harder, kneading it like a length of dough, its size growing even more.

She couldn't take it any longer, a furnace building from within her own body as her skin rippled and scorched with desire.

She stood abruptly, pulling him up by the front of his belt with her, toward the heat of the stove, their mouths still locked together, hands working with deliberate urgency, pulling, tugging, unbuttoning. A blanket was hastily thrown on the floor together with a scatter of cushions, the heat enveloping their newfound nakedness.

She paused for a moment and stepped back, her heart thumping like a racehorse. She just wanted to see him completely.

My god!

His shoulders, his chest, arms, all interlocked in a beautiful puzzle of muscle and sinew. Not bulky like some steroid-induced gym junkie, but natural, lean, toned, athletic, honed from functional physical work.

Her eyes lingered longer, moving downward across a mosaic of cobbled abdominals, perfectly woven.

Her gaze was drawn inexplicably downward some more.

Then her eyes found it. They had to, its size was beyond reason, yet perfect as she stared.

He was hard and hungry, swollen beyond pain, a rod of granite, thick and engorged.

Curiosity gave way to yearning. She had to touch it, hold it, feel its weight and hardness in her hand.

She gasped as she took it, a thick rod freshly forged from the fire, once molten now iron-hard. She started rubbing its length, tight skin moving back and forth over solid vascular flesh, her fingers unable to coil around it completely.

His hands worked her torso, rough and gentle at the same time, her breasts swollen and hard like cement as he gripped each in turn. He slipped his other arm behind her waist and arched her torso back until she was almost on tiptoes, still holding him like a thick tree branch as though she was teetering over the edge of an abyss.

But he held her firmly as he ravaged her breasts with his mouth, his tongue, teeth and lips, biting and sucking at her tender nipples, dark, swollen and skyward, her hand pulling him harder like a stubborn tree root, her other free hand pulling his head down. He worked from one breast to the other, leaving a trail of hot wetness over her skin.

He laid her down carefully on the cushions, her legs wide, pink petals unfurled and glistening, and drove into her.

SEVENTEEN

Daisy McAlister was a changed person. Like a desert flower, buried below the sand and dirt for years, waiting for the quenching rains to come so she could drink long and hard, and revitalize herself. Now she felt stronger, in bloom, full of vitality. For too long she had remained sheltered, withdrawn, below the surface, in hibernation like that flower.

And now, from what had happened last night, Ben Shaw had been that quenching rain. But she wanted more. She wanted a monsoon.

Sunlight streamed through the kitchen windows as she busied herself. Fresh coffee was on, steak and eggs were cooking in the pan, and she had set the table out on the veranda. She wanted Shaw to come up to the homestead and eat his meals here from now on. But her mind wasn't completely made up about him moving up from the bunkhouse. Caution was how she had run her life lately, and she certainly wasn't going to start throwing it to the wind just yet.

She stood over the sink and looked out the window. She could see him making his way up the path. She wiped her hands on a dishcloth, checked the eggs and went through the open veranda doors carrying a coffee pot and a jug of cream.

"You were gone when I woke," Shaw said as he climbed the stairs, pausing when he saw the round table and two chairs set up near the railing and the effort she had made. White linen tablecloth, nice cutlery, plates with floral designs, cloth napkins folded neatly.

Placing the coffee pot in the middle of the table, she said, "Don't worry, I'm not asking you to marry me, it's just breakfast and I want you to eat up here from now on. You're not like the other ranch hands I've had—I mean employed," Daisy said, quickly correcting herself.

Shaw smiled, enjoying seeing her cheeks momentarily flush. "I know what you mean."

"No strings attached. No commitments. That's what we said last night," Daisy said. Shaw nodded as he sat down, "That's right." Daisy went back into the kitchen and returned with a large serving dish heaped with eggs, steak and toast. She placed it on the table and sat down.

"No one is going to die of hunger working around here," Shaw said, as he looked at the pile of food in front of him.

They ate and talked, enjoying each other's company. There wasn't the usual awkwardness or stunted conversation that typically followed intimacy between two strangers. The conversation was free and flowing, natural not forced.

She touched his wrist. "What's this?" There was a small tattoo on the inside of Shaw's wrist, a wreath of antlers encircling the letter V. "I saw it last night." Daisy had seen a great many things last night.

Shaw put down his fork. "It's my own design, had it done a while ago. It means *Virtus*. It's from ancient Rome, it means doing what is right."

Daisy nodded with approval. She liked guys with tattoos. Not too many, just a few here and there. It was an expression of themselves, a certain uniqueness. She was keen to discover if Shaw had any more on his body. Last night was a blur, but she still felt the heat inside her, leaving her warm and glowing all over. She felt different, more open to him, and he enjoyed listening to her. It was like she hadn't had someone to talk to for a very long time and she needed to get out everything that had been bottled up inside.

She spoke more about the ranch and the McAlister family history, and Shaw was just content to sit back after he had eaten, enjoy his coffee and the uninterrupted view of the landscape from the veranda. Cattle moved in the distance and the sky was a wide expanse of light blue.

She smiled when she told Shaw about her father. But there was still sadness behind her smile as she reminisced.

"So he fell from his horse up on the ridge," her voice petered off as she took a sip of coffee.

"Who found him?" Shaw asked. He didn't want to pry, but questioning everything was his profession and he could extract information subtly without the person even knowing.

"I did."

Shaw waited.

"When he didn't return, I rode up there. I found his horse grazing halfway up along a track. "

"Was an autopsy done? Did they say how he died?"

"The police said he had fallen, probably from his horse. I found him at the bottom of a ravine. Neck broken. They say his horse maybe got spooked and reared up, and he toppled off." Daisy gripped the cup, her knuckles white. She never believed the explanation she was given by the police or by the Medical Examiners office.

"But he was an expert rider, grew up with horses. Felt more at home on one than behind the wheel of his Dodge."

Shaw leaned forward. "Had he been there before, on that part of the ridge?"

Daisy nodded. "Many times. There wasn't any part of this land he hadn't ridden, staked-out, measured or walked. This place has been in the family for generations. It was in his blood. The soil was always under his fingernails. But…"

"But what?" Shaw asked.

"He'd been going there a lot before the accident, like he was preoccupied. He would go for days sometimes, camp overnight, take a pack, a bedroll and just his horse. Sleep out under the stars. My mother asked him and made a joke saying that he was meeting another woman up there. But he said he was just scouting out some of the land, making sure of the boundaries."

"Is it far from here?"

"No, just a few hours ride, we could be up and back easily in a day." Daisy turned to Shaw. He had a questioning look on his face, his head tilted.

"What now? We go today?" Daisy asked.

Shaw shrugged. "I'd like to take a look. See some of the property. You could give me a tour."

"But there's work to be done. I need to move cattle from one of the paddocks and drop some feed. And you need to start fixing the fencing along the eastern boundary."

"That can wait. Come on. I'd really like to take a look up there. Plus it would be good to get away for the day. We're not really going anywhere, we'll still be on the ranch."

Daisy smiled. "Technically, yes."

"What do you mean *technically*?" He looked across the landscape and up to the ridge. It rose up behind the bunkhouse, rugged in places, dotted with pockets of trees and vegetation, rimmed at the top by a forest.

"It's a fairly easy ride, but some parts can be steep. But the best trail cuts across a tract of land that's shared with the Morgans. It runs right along the boundary between our two properties."

"Look, if you don't want to, that's fine. But if we went, you'd have to teach me how to ride and we'd need to go slow."

Daisy thought for a moment. She hadn't been up to the ridge since her father died.

EIGHTEEN

It was gloomy inside the house and it smelled of dust, dead flowers and age. Shaw stood at the start of a long narrow hallway just inside the front screen door. He looked up as floorboards creaked overhead. It was Daisy getting ready and she said she wanted to check on her mother before they rode up to the ridge.

While Daisy had cleaned up after breakfast then went upstairs, Shaw walked the perimeter of the homestead checking that everything was secure.

Old habits.

He started with the outbuildings, the sheds, stables, barn and gradually he moved closer until finally he arrived at the exterior of the house itself, all the time he felt like he was being watched, observed, from afar. Not close, but close enough.

He was amazed at how open and unlocked everything was. Country folk were certainly more trusting and open with their property and possessions than city people. People living in the cities had layers of security around their homes and apartments, like CCTV, triple-locks on doors, panic alarms and guard dogs.

Urban paranoia that was justified. But Daisy had none of these safeguards, except a gun she said she kept by her bed.

Maybe it was a matter of being more trusting in the country. Leaving your doors and windows open thinking it was safe. Shaw preferred everything to be locked, secured and squared away.

He had made a quick sweep of all the doors and windows from the outside and was amazed to find no window locks and some of the doors had old, flimsy locks that could easily be breached with little or no effort. He made a mental note to fix these when he got back.

He stood in the hallway waiting. To his right was a staircase leading to the second floor, the ornate balustrade was worn with age and the faded carpet was secured with brass carpet rods that were tarnished.

Against the wall near the front door there was an old mahogany hallstand with an arch-shaped mirror, turned legs and a small drawer with a brass handle. The mirror was warped and dulled with age like everything else in the house. Time and neglect were winning the war.

He slid open the small drawer, but it was empty. He would have had the handgun in this drawer, close to the front door where most unwelcomed confrontations happened and where a weapon close to hand would be handy. He had put Daisy's handgun back under the seat of the Dodge. That's where she had it, so that's where he had returned it.

Off the narrow corridor there were a series of doors on each side. The house was laid out in typical fashion for its era, a central hallway that ran from front door to back door with rooms on either side.

He paused in the hallway, in two minds whether to have a look around or wait for Daisy to come downstairs. Somewhere deep inside the house a clock ticked.

He decided to have a quick look around, but not stray too far in case she caught him snooping. He walked along the hallway, his steps softened by the tattered and frayed hall runner that stretched into the murky distance.

The first door he came to, he tried the doorknob. It turned and the hinges protested as he pushed the door open cautiously. Inside was more gloom, curtains drawn shut across large windows. Dark bulky shapes squatted in the corners of the room, covered with sheets, gray with dust, the air stale and musty. Dead flowers brittle and dry sat in glass vases.

Nothing interesting in here.

He quietly closed the door and looked back at the rectangle of light from the front door, making sure he was still alone. It was as though he was descending into a train tunnel, the farther he went, the more isolated and distant he was from fresh air and sunshine. He could feel the old house pressing in around him, the walls moving a little closer, the shadows folding toward him. It was eerily quiet except for the mechanical ticking of the clock somewhere in the house.

Shaw saw something move at the other end of the corridor, toward the back of the house, a ripple in the gloom like someone had walked across the corridor. He paused, his eyes squinting, trying to see beyond the shadows.

Maybe it was just his imagination, an optical illusion of being in a narrow, confined space that was poorly lit.

He continued his search.

On the other side was another door, the wooden stain peeling and cracked. This door had a large sturdy lock, the kind he imagined would take a large brass key. He tried the doorknob.

No luck. It was locked tight.

"That's my father's study."

Shaw jumped in fright and whirled around.

Daisy stood behind him, just a few feet away, hands by her sides, the light at her back, her shape a dark outline, her face obscured.

"Sorry, I was just looking for the bathroom," he said. "All that coffee. Thought I'd better to go before I get on that horse."

For the first time in a long while Shaw felt uneasy.

Daisy just stood there, perfectly still.

Shaw couldn't see her face clearly with the light behind her, but he could sense she was looking directly at him with an intensity that felt like the air had stood still. Her posture was one of contemplation, making up her mind if he was telling the truth or not.

Shaw walked toward her until the shadows washed away and her face gradually came into focus, cold and hard.

Then a smile broke across her face and all the menace evaporated in an instant. "Come on, I'll show you. It's just off the kitchen," she said, her voice light and upbeat.

****

After two hours in the saddle Shaw finally felt the first physical signs that he was not made for riding a horse. They had taken it slow, Daisy leading on Jazz and Shaw on probably the most docile horse she could find for him in the stables. He had settled into the rhythm in his hips as the animal moved under him, but his butt and lower back were sore. He was regretting suggesting they ride up to the ridge, maybe he should have taken the ATV that was in the shed back at the ranch.

Despite this, they had made good time as Shaw urged the horse on with the occasional nudge in its flanks as Daisy had showed him in the quick tutorial she had given him when they had saddled up in the stables.

Rather than confront Daisy about her sudden mood swing back at the homestead, he thought he would just watch her, look for little changes to her demeanor or her posture. The eyes and the facial expression always gave it away before the mood change surfaced. But in a way he was still glad she was cautious with him and hadn't let her guard down completely. He was still a stranger to her, no matter what had happened in the bunkhouse the night before. Maybe she just felt vulnerable, just in that moment, her system flushed with adrenalin from the confrontation with the Morgans in the parking lot. Maybe she just needed a release. She seemed to turn on a dime from being all sweet and hospitable, to sudden hostility and aggression. There was an underlying current to her, something dark and sinister below the surface. She was certainly an intriguing woman.

They passed through foothills dotted with small boulders, scrub and low vegetation, and as they ascended up the trail the air cooled, a slight reprieve from the beating sun. It was late morning by the time they reached the top of the ridge and they paused by a small stream to water the horses and let them graze for a while.

Shaw grimaced as he gingerly slid out of the saddle, thankful for the rest stop. His rear was almost numb and he could feel each vertebra in his back creak and groan.

Daisy smiled, amused at his discomfort. "You've been in the cities too long, sitting your ass in trendy cafes and sports bars. You need to spend more time out here away from things like that, get in the saddle more." She opened a saddlebag and pulled out a pair of binoculars as Shaw stretched and arched his back.

"I don't sit in cafes or sports bars," he replied, wincing at his discomfort. He slowly hobbled away from the horses and looked out at the spectacular view. Nestled in the valley below was the ranch. From up here it looked like a child's toy farm set. The red barn, the homestead, the sheds, and he could make out the bunkhouse. Cattle moved slowly, brown dots against a pale backdrop, and he had an appreciation for the beautiful and vast landscape. There were hills in the distance and he could just see the town of Martha's End with the red water tower.

Daisy walked and stood beside him. Pointing below and to her left she said, "That line is where the Morgan's land starts, just on the other side of the fence line. If you follow the edge of the forest there, it takes you straight to their boundary between us and them." She handed Shaw the binoculars and he followed where she was pointing. The ridge fell away abruptly on the opposite side into a sea of fractured rock and deep furrows where wind and rain had gouged the soil. At the bottom there was a wooded spread of cottonwoods, thick and wide. Beyond that a narrow dirt road curved around the cottonwoods and ran parallel to a fence made of rough posts and barbed wire.

"What's that road, the dirt one down there? Where does it lead to?" Shaw asked, without lowering the binoculars and without sounding like he really cared.

"That used to be an old cattle trail, but it was graded by my father more than twenty years ago. It eventually runs to some old cattle yards on our land on the other side of the ridge. There's nothing there, just a few rusted-out sheds and outhouses. I think my great-grandfather built them and used to brand cattle there. There's an old coal mine hole there as well. My grandfather did a little prospecting a long time ago, dug it out. It flooded a few years back, I think."

Shaw followed the dirt track back toward the McAlister ranch, and he could see where it joined the main road past the paddocks until it ran through a series of cattle gates then up past the barn.

"So where is the Morgan homestead?"

"It's more like a compound. You can't see it from here. It's on the other side of that line of hills. Three, maybe four miles away. Too close to this side of the boundary for my liking."

Shaw raised his point of focus. In the distance a series of low hills rippled in the haze. Nothing difficult to traverse. The forest of cottonwoods on this side of the dirt road would provide good cover, especially at night.

He pulled his focus closer.

The road branched off toward the Morgan boundary fence, then stopped a few feet before an old hinged cattle gate but didn't continue further. Obviously it was once used as a property entrance for cattle to pass through, but now the trail was overgrown with grass.

He panned slightly to the right, then the left. As far as he could tell there were no surveillance measures along the fence line or on the open ground beyond. No visible structures at least. But once he left the cover of the cottonwoods, crossed back over the dirt road and the fence, he would be out in the open, exposed. A vehicle with half-decent headlights or spotters would light him up like daylight. If they knew he was there. There were just a few rocky mounds, but nothing substantial to provide cover. It was no man's land. The place he didn't want to get caught.

He would have to move fast. But he could, when he needed to.

"So where to now?" He handed back the binoculars to Daisy. They walked back to where the horses were grazing, taking care to stay away from the edge.

"It's not far, we just cut across the top here through the trees. The trail runs along one side."

She passed him a canteen and some food from her saddlebag. Her Winchester sat snuggly in its saddle sheath.

Shaw wandered back to the edge on the opposite side to get the best view of the ranch below as he ate, while Daisy readied the horses again. There was a line of trees a few feet back from the cliff edge. He looked down toward the ranch then backed up slowly, one foot at a time, keeping the ranch in view until he felt the first row of tree trunks at his back. Low branches fell around him as he retreated a few more steps then stopped. He still had a clear line of sight to the homestead below and all the main structures including the bunkhouse. The trees provided a quick cover, if someone needed to pull back and hide while still keeping an eye on the ranch.

It was the perfect spot. A spot he would have chosen, if he wanted to watch the bunkhouse below and not be seen.

He looked around on the ground. The dirt, bracken, and scrub were undisturbed. Nothing to suggest someone had been here recently. When someone stood for a while, even for just a few minutes, they tended to shift their weight on their feet, kicking up the soil and dirt, even get bored and nudge stones and rocks aside with their toes. But not this person. Their movement was minimal, and what footprints or marks they may have made, they had covered them up, walking backward, retracing their steps typically with a branch sweeping the ground in front of them as they retreated.

They were good, Shaw thought. Really good.

Almost as good as him.

NINETEEN

It was a straight drop. No trees, no bushes, no ledges to break someone's fall. Nothing. Just a vertical plummet onto the jagged rocks that covered the bottom of the ravine two hundred feet below.

Shaw squatted for a moment longer examining the crumbling edge. A few loose stones and soil broke off and fell, and he prodded the edge with a stick. One wrong foot and he would end up down there like Daisy's father. The path around the side of the ravine was only a few feet wide, barely enough for the two of them and certainly not wide enough for a horse. Yet Daisy had said Stan McAlister was thrown from his horse, or at least that's what the investigation concluded.

He stood up. Daisy was standing back from the edge, behind Shaw, almost pressed up against the rock face. She didn't want to see the bottom of the ravine.

Bad memories.

The last time she was in this exact spot she had looked down and seen her father's body, broken, twisted and bloody at the bottom, flesh and bone smashed against hard rock.

She didn't want to relive it again.

The track was too narrow here, too dangerous on horseback, so they left the horses tethered to a cottonwood just before the path branched away from the main trail and started to elevate and curve around the outer edge of the cliff side. Shaw imagined the path was once wider, but in time, wind and rain had worn it away.

On the opposite side it was just a sheer cliff face of jagged shale just like the side they were standing on, but without any path or obvious way to traverse across the mountainside.

"Is this the spot?" Shaw asked.

Daisy just nodded, her face pale, her eyes filled with sadness. It hadn't changed much in the years. It was a lonely spot, and being here now brought back all the raw emotions she had felt on that day. She remembered stumbling back to her horse, just fragments of memory as she rode back to the ranch to tell her mother to call the police, but that was all. She couldn't remember much else. Shock had numbed her memory of the day.

The police came from Hays. It had taken them a long time to get here. The place was isolated, remote, off the track. Then a police search and rescue team came up and recovered the body, winching it up on a hard stretcher and carrying it down the ridge to a waiting ambulance.

Shaw looked around. It was a desolate place, away from the main ridge, almost hidden. "Where does the path lead?" he asked.

Daisy didn't move. "I don't know," she replied, "It's not on any map, this trail." To get here they had to cross a shared boundary between the two properties. "It's still McAlister land, but I've only been up here twice."

Shaw nodded. There was nothing here, no animals, no clues, nothing.

It was eerily quiet too and colder, like the ravine walls had absorbed all the sun's heat, but refused to give anything back.

"I don't know what my father was doing up here. I don't know why he spent so much time up here."

Shaw looked at the path. It curved around the side and out of sight. There was something beyond there. Something that had held Stan McAlister's interest.

Maybe the answer was where the path led. Maybe there was nothing on the other side, just more shale and rock. Maybe Daisy's father just came here for the solitude to get away from the ranch and his troubles. But he could have picked a more scenic spot, something with a view. This place was dead. It reminded Shaw of an old abandoned quarry.

But one thing was for certain.

He didn't fall off his horse to his death in the ravine below.

He was on foot and either he slipped and fell as he was making his way along the path, or something much worse.

TWENTY

It was mid-afternoon by the time they had rode back down the ridge and had made it to the foothills again. Shaw was more confident on his horse and he rode alongside Daisy. With each footfall away from the ravine her mood brightened. At first when they set off on the return journey she was withdrawn, silent, just focusing on steering Jazz through the rocky terrain, and guiding Shaw and his horse.

Instead of forcing the conversation Shaw thought it was best to leave her to her own thoughts. The only thing she had said when they had saddled up was *I don't want to ever come back here again.*

But her mood brightened the closer they got back to the ranch. She wanted to see Callie tonight, call her up and get her over for dinner, like how it used to be, spend more time with her friends. She had neglected them over the years, had been preoccupied with the ranch, but that would change. She would get the help she needed to run the place. Somehow she would find the money, perhaps sell some more cattle, then restock when things were better.

Ahead Shaw could see the gate of another shared tract of land. Daisy dismounted and slid the chain over the post and swung open the gate. Shaw nudged his horse forward and Daisy walked Jazz through then closed the gate.

They had only gone a few hundred yards when Shaw heard the sound, the high-pitched revving of engines.

To the left, cutting a fast line toward them came two Polaris ATVs. They were the racing turbo-charged variants. Side-by-side, two occupants in each caged cockpit, driving hard, their engines in high gear, punching out one hundred sixty eight horsepower as they flew across the ground, the big tires tearing up dirt in their wake, suspension struts bouncing up and down as they raced toward Shaw and Daisy.

Daisy pulled up Jazz, slid her Winchester out and held it across her saddle. Shaw pulled up beside her and watched as the ATVs hammered toward them.

The lead vehicle cut a sharp turn in front of them, and skidded to a violent halt in a hail of stones and dirt, blocking their path. The other ATV pulled up alongside the first.

Jazz and Shaw's horse were well trained, they didn't spook at the noise or the sudden movement of the two machines.

Four men climbed out, two from each vehicle.

One was Billy Morgan, but Shaw didn't recognize the other three men, and they didn't look like ranch hands or grunt-employees. They were dressed in black drill pants and polo shirts, with baseball caps pulled tight and purposeful over their heads and military boots. They all looked lean, fit and hardened.

All three men carried compact assault rifles slung across their chests, holographic optics, handguns on their hips as a secondary weapon. None of them had touched their rifles, they just let them dangle in front of them, supremely confident.

Daisy held her reins in one hand and her Winchester in the other, not pointed at anyone. "I'll handle this," she said.

It was a strange sight, Shaw thought. Old-school versus modern. Horse and Winchester lever-action with iron-sights up against modern ATVs and hi-tech assault rifles with holographic sights. Skill and experience versus laziness and technology.

Billy Morgan walked over in a slow relaxed manner like he was walking into church on Sunday. The three other men held back, but slowly fanned out. One in particular took a keen interest in Shaw, even though it was Daisy who was cradling the rifle.

The man had already assessed Shaw as the real threat, not the girl with the gun.

This man seemed in-charge of the other two, he had an air of authority, older, gray hair under his cap, and a poise that spoke of a quiet confidence that came from a wealth of disciplined hard-earned experience.

"This is a shared boundary, Billy. We are permitted through here. You know that."

Billy Morgan smiled, but he was looking at Shaw as well.

"This ain't Morgan land," Daisy said, adjusting her hips, Jazz moved slightly under her, the horse's ears were laid back and she snorted at the man standing in her way. Even the horse didn't like Billy Morgan.

Billy hooked his thumbs through his belt, cocky and sure. "Not for much longer."

Daisy tilted her head. "What do you mean?"

Billy shrugged. "Put an application into the Hays City Commission asking them to grant exclusive rights of this tract of land to us, not you. Our ranch is bigger, more important, of more commercial significance than yours. I'm sure they'll come around to my way of thinking."

"You mean, after you have paid them off first," Daisy spat.

"Now, now Daisy don't get all conspiracy theory and political on me. I put in a proper planning application like anyone can, and it'll run its due process. I'm just a tax-paying citizen like everyone else here, entitled to a fair chance."

"You Morgans are anything but fair. You've bribed, cheated, and bought your way to where you are today." Daisy said. She could feel her anger rise and the heat prickle her neck. The trip to the ravine had given her a bitter edge. She felt like she had been cornered again, but she wasn't going to just lie down and play dead. Jazz snorted again and stomped her front leg.

"Nice horse," Billy said, still keeping his distance.

"Why don't you come closer so she can kick you in the ass?" Daisy replied.

Shaw rolled his eyes. He wanted Daisy to diffuse the situation, not escalate it, but it was important he didn't get involved unless he had to. This was her land, her family heritage. She needed to establish she was in charge, not him. That would be important to her. Also he didn't want to draw the attention of the three goons Billy had brought with him. He preferred to stay in the background, act like the subservient employee.

Shaw tried to look nowhere in particular, but he had all three men in black in front of him clocked: ex-military, all tanned and fit, probably saw recent time in Iraq or Afghanistan. Now retired from the service, but making a bucket load more money as private security contractors for the rich and influential like the Morgan family.

"What's with the goons, Billy? You scared of me? One little old girl against three armed men?"

Shaw shrank a bit further in the saddle, slumped his shoulders, trying to look timid. If he dismounted it could be seen as an act of aggression, and the three goons would no doubt bring their weapons up. Then it could all go to hell fast.

"You pulled a gun on me, Daisy. Last night, if you remember." Billy glared at her. Gone was all the cockiness and showboating, his eyes glazed over with pure menace.

"That was self-defense. I used reasonable force in the face of great bodily harm."

Shaw looked at Daisy and felt somewhat surprised at her comment. She knew her rights in Kansas almost to the letter.

She continued, "We weren't doing anything illegal, like we're not right now. You and your brothers and that *thing* you brought with you last night were going to attack me and my employee, Mr. Shaw here."

"You pulled a damn gun on me!" Billy Morgan yelled, stepping toward Daisy.

Then three things happened simultaneously.

Shaw slid off his horse.

The three goons brought their weapons up.

And Daisy McAlister brought her Winchester up and overlaid the front sight on Billy Morgan's forehead, her finger on the trigger.

"Just like now, Billy," she replied, hunched behind the rifle, staring down the barrel. "Reasonable force. I'm standing my ground. Four of you against two of us, and one of us isn't even armed, Billy. Looks bad for you."

No one moved. One red dot on Daisy, one on Shaw, one on the horse.

"But you'll be dead," Billy replied, his face turning red with rage. He didn't like having a gun pointed at him—now twice in less than twenty-four hours by the same bitch. He was the one who threatened people. No one threatened him.

"Yeh, but you'll be dead first. Take your head clean off at this range."

It went quiet. No one said a word for what seemed like a few minutes.

Shaw didn't move, couldn't, he had no weapon and they were outnumbered.

Again.

The girl's definitely got balls, he thought. Wouldn't back down from anything when it involved the family name.

Billy Morgan seemed to be contemplating. Then he slowly nodded, turned to the three men in black and told them to lower their guns. He turned back to Daisy and smiled, but behind the smile his brain melted white hot with rage, but he contained it. Barely.

"This isn't going to end well, this feuding between us. Between our families. It can be resolved another way."

Daisy lowered her rifle. "I ain't selling the ranch." Her reply was definite.

Billy looked at Shaw, his eyes appraising him, wondering what the man was doing here. "Mr. Shaw?" he said, his voice dripping with sarcasm. "Mr. Shaw doesn't seem to say or do much, just take orders from a woman." Billy sneered. The three men in black sniggered to themselves.

Shaw just shrugged. "She's the boss. I just do what she says."

"Are you going to move or not?" Daisy said impatiently. She wanted to get back to the ranch and the cattle.

Billy pointed his finger at Daisy. "You'd better watch yourself, Daisy." Then he pointed it at Shaw. "You too. I ain't done with you either. You'll see." Then he turned and stomped back to his ATV, signaling to his men to follow. Two of the security men turned and slid back in to their ATVs, but one didn't move at all, his eyes locked on Shaw, the same guy who had taken an interest in him before.

He nodded at Shaw, "You're no ranch hand, son. There's something about you. Something I don't like. I'm going to keep a special eye out for you, if you come my way." With that the man turned, walked back to his ATV.

The ATVs growled to life, spun in opposite circles of dust and dirt, and sped off back up the hill.

Shaw watched them until they dropped over the lip of the hill and disappeared.

TWENTY-ONE

The sun was starting to dip below the trees by the time they had finished the work for the day.

After returning to the ranch Daisy tended to the horses, then stabled them. Then she jumped on the ATV and dropped feed bales to the various paddocks. She was upbeat after the encounter with Billy Morgan and his men. She drew strength from the courage she had shown, and she knew somewhere above in the late afternoon sky her father was looking down at her smiling, proud of his daughter. *Don't give an inch to those Morgan bastards!* she could almost hear him say. She drew strength from his words as she always had, but words didn't pay the bills.

The day started with sadness for her, but had ended with a kindled courage and determination that no one was going to bully her or her ranch. Having Ben around was a good thing, it had bolstered her resolve.

She swung past the barn just in time to see him emerge wiping his hands on a dirty rag. He had spent what remaining light there was fixing the locks on all the sheds and external doors around the house. He'd found a box of parts in the barn.

"You nearly done?" Daisy said as she straddled the ATV, the engine idling.

Shaw nodded. "Just for the day. I don't think I'll ever be done even if I spend an entire year here."

Daisy smiled. She wished he would stay for a year. It was only a few days, but she was already getting used to having him around. There was something about him that Daisy just found damn attractive. She hated guys who were arrogant and full of themselves. But Shaw had an understated confidence about him. He was sure of himself, but outwardly he rarely showed it. But it was there, like he didn't want to show too much of himself. She owed a lot to him. Just being here for a few short days had meant a lot, just his company and the reassurance of him being around. She was going to miss him when he was gone, and she felt a sudden sadness in the pit of her stomach.

Then there was the other thing, the other night in the bunkhouse. She had never felt so alive as a woman in all her life.

She looked up at him and he just stood there, his dark brown eyes looking at her. He had given her a lot of confidence in the last few days and she wanted more.

"I've texted Callie, she'll be over by seven. She just finished work and wants to get freshened up before coming over. She'll bring the pizza and I'll provide the beer, if that's OK with you?"

"Fine by me." Shaw replied. He didn't own a cell phone anymore, had gotten rid of it before he started his road trip. Didn't see much use for one anymore. He had no one to call and he didn't want anyone to know where he was. He was "off the grid" and he intended to stay like that for a very long time.

"She wanted to know if you were still here. I said yes. So she definitely wanted to come by."

Shaw raised a questioning eyebrow.

"I better set her straight when she comes," Daisy said with a mischievous little grin. Then she dropped her eyes to the front of his dusty jeans, cursing herself for the momentary lapse. There was an outline behind the denim of his jeans, near the crotch and she felt her throat contract.

"Set her straight about what?" Shaw asked, already knowing.

Daisy looked up, her cheeks flushed. "Did you mean what you said today?" she asked, ignoring his question. "About me being your boss? About doing what I say?"

Shaw nodded, "I work for you. That makes you my boss, I guess."

Daisy paused for a moment, looking at Shaw from top to bottom then back again. They had about an hour before Callie would arrive. "Good, now that we've got that settled I want you to strip out of those filthy clothes and wait in the shower for me."

Daisy revved the engine and skidded off in a cloud of dust, leaving Shaw looking on, a faint smile across his lips.

****

Steam enveloped them, strands of white condensation that moved, formed then broke apart again.

Daisy stood behind Shaw, a stream of scorching water falling like a monsoon on both of their bodies as she soaped and lathered him. She was fascinated by it. It felt like a thick rod in her soapy hand as she reached around him to stroke it back and forth, a colorful emulsion of froth and suds coating it as she rubbed harder.

"It's not a toy," Shaw said, as he gave a slight wince. Daisy tended to be slightly aggressive with it. "Be gentle," he said over his shoulder.

"Shut up, I'm the boss."

Daisy rubbed harder, longer strokes, ignoring his discomfort, enjoying watching his buttock tense in painful pleasure. She knew he was trying to hold back from her teasing. She wanted to see what would happen. She had never seen a man ejaculate before and she was curious. She had felt his release deep inside her last night, hot and copious like lava that filled her. But now she wanted to see more.

"Well, if it's not a toy you'd better start using it," she replied with a coy grin. But she didn't let go. "Hold still," she ordered, increasing the speed, tightening her grip, focusing on the head of the huge shaft, building the intensity with each stroke.

Shaw moaned, and placed a hand against the shower wall like he was about to pass out. His body tensed and this only made Daisy go faster, harder with her hand, her breath coming in short bursts, wrapped in the heat of her own arousal. She was in control and she liked it.

Shaw arched his spine and threw his head back, his eyes squeezed tightly shut. Daisy's hand now a blur, back and forth, rubbing the head hard, almost pulling the appendage from his body. She felt it swell even bigger in her hand, the climax building.

Then it burst.

Shaw convulsed. Hot strands of ropy creaminess pumped endlessly from him. Daisy kept milking him for a good minute after the final spurt until every last drop was expelled.

Shaw hung his head, giddy on his feet. "My god, that was amazing," he said, his voice hoarse.

Daisy smiled, enjoying her dominance. She was in control, not him.

She still held him in her hand, amazed that he was still rock-hard, unspent, still capable of more.

She didn't ask, she just told him. "Now me."

He turned and took her by the shoulders, pivoting her around so she was pressed up against one wall of the shower. She arched her back, pushing her buttocks back toward him, widened her stance, lifting herself up on her toes, improving the upward angle he had from behind.

Water cascaded down her neck and back, her breasts hard, her nipples raked against the rough shower wall. Shaw pushed her further forward, parted her tight round buttocks, splitting her open, her engorged lips parted like a flower, viscous in her natural arousal. It was about her, not him. What she had just done was for her benefit.

"Fuck me," she groaned over her shoulder. "Do it now." She was unable to wait any longer, the anticipation driving her crazy. She wanted to wash away the filth and grime, the anger and sadness she had felt today in a wave of sexual ecstasy.

He eased slowly into her, allowing her juices to coat him properly before he slid in fully to the hilt. He fell into a rhythm, slowly at first, then increasing the intensity. He lifted her cheeks wider, opening her up fully to him, going deeper, increasing the speed of his thrusts. Daisy responded instantly, leaving a heavy waxen sheen on him as he thrust in and out, the water running off his hardness.

"Fuck me harder." It was a command, not a request. Her fingers curled around the cold water pipe, knuckles white. Her other hand bracing against the wall, allowing her to push back against him, forcing him to drive deeper into her. His balls swung back and forth, low and heavy like two rugby socks with a cricket ball in each.

It was purely instinctual to Daisy, her movements, her needs, her body and she gave in to whatever it wanted.

For too long she had trekked across the dry and barren desert without reprieve, while having to endure watching her friends find their own oasis of pleasure. For years she had lived this nomadic, lonely existence. But now she had discovered her own oasis. It had appeared before her, bigger, wider and deeper than any of those her friends had bragged about.

And it was all hers. She wasn't going to share it with anyone. She wanted to dive deep into its waters, drink long and hard to make up for all those years of nothing when her cup was dry and empty. Now it was full to the point of overflowing, she was beyond taking little sips to make up from lost time.

She wanted to drown in it

And if she drowned? So be it. It was a beautiful way to die, she thought to herself.

Daisy could feel him tense behind her, she could feel him thickening inside her, her own heat building, a fire starting to burn and grow from the cold ashes of years of loneliness and regret.

Then a deep throaty growl from behind her, not in anger, but animalistic, primitive. A torrent was forming deep within the oasis, a wave slowly building below the surface, approaching the shore, rising higher and harder as it approached, more powerful with each thrust.

Fingers, hard and sharp dug into the flesh of her shoulders, the pain exquisite. She arched her back further and gritted her teeth like she was going to split. A bow pulled back too far, a spring stretched beyond recovery, a delicate vessel too small and fragile for what was being forced into it.

Daisy felt like her flesh was being pulled from the bone the harder and faster he went, like a machine, her own heat in unison with his growing hardness. It swelled and bulged like birth.

She screamed as she climaxed, tears not water ran down her cheeks, her fist beat the wall as her body convulsed in waves of ecstasy expelling her own release from her insides.

Then his wave broke.

The shores of her oasis were swamped by liquid fire that scorched her insides, overfilling her.

Smaller, less violent waves followed behind the bigger one until eventually the swell subsided and the surface of the oasis was tranquil once again.

Daisy let go of the water pipe, the metal brackets holding it in place almost torn from the wall. Her whole body alive and every nerve ending tingling with tiny pulses of electricity that throbbed.

The drought had been truly broken.

TWENTY-TWO

"That's strange?" Daisy glanced down at her phone on the bench in the kitchenette of the bunkhouse. She had a towel wrapped around her body and one wrapped around her hair, a few loose strands hanging down.

"What's up?" Shaw sat on the end of the bunk, pulling on socks and getting dressed. Despite the wood burning stove and all the doors and windows being closed, there was a chill in the air. He got up, opened the door of the burner and stoked it with a few more logs.

Daisy picked up her phone and read the screen. "It's Callie. She says she can't make it, she has car problems, she says sorry and will catch up soon."

Shaw walked over and looked at the screen. "Then we'll have to try and rustle up some food."

"No, that's fine, I've got some steaks in the fridge up at the house." Daisy held the phone, still staring at the screen, her mind elsewhere. "I was looking forward to seeing her. It has been a while. We text each other almost daily, but it's not the same." She turned to Shaw. "Looks like it's just you and me tonight."

Shaw was dead tired. It had been a long and interesting day, but it was far from over.

"First you'd better get dressed. I'll walk you up. I just want to check around the outside of the homestead and buildings."

She smiled. "Why? Everything is fine. I don't expect Billy to be snooping around in the dark. He wouldn't be game after today."

Shaw shrugged. "That's OK. Just habit. We'd better go."

****

The sky was inky black with a smear of stars that stretched as far as the eye could see. Daisy insisted she cook the steaks, not Shaw. So she stoked the grill on the front veranda, lit it then busied herself in the kitchen making a salad and setting the table outside while Shaw did the rounds of the property.

For too long she had remained hidden like a hermit on the property and now she didn't care. She had always been confident and protective of her family ranch, but Ben had brought something else out in her in the last few days. She enjoyed his company, but she also enjoyed the sex. Why shouldn't she? She didn't feel ashamed with herself. He was still a stranger, but she liked him. A lot. She was still in control, but she wanted sex, not commitment. She wanted plain old fashioned stress-relieving sex and she felt liberated now that she was having it. She was a young woman who had foregone so much over the years to run the ranch and help her father. She had no resentment, but now it was her time, her turn.

It was time maybe to be selfish, think about her own needs and desires for once, she thought as she placed cutlery and plates on the table on the veranda, watching Shaw.

She wanted him to stay for longer, but she knew he would eventually leave. But until then she was buoyant and going to take full advantage of him.

No crime in that.

Shaw came out of the barn and could see Daisy on the veranda. The air was cold and laced with the smoky scent of hickory and grilling meat. The homestead was lit up like a Christmas tree. Daisy wanted all the house lights on, to make a statement, not to hide anymore.

Shaw could have eaten a horse, but he thought he should check on them first.

He had found a small but powerful LED flashlight in the barn that he slipped into his pocket. He headed across the yard toward the stables. The yard lights cast pools of yellow light, but the darkness still pressed in around him as walked. He preferred the dark, felt he could move better without being seen.

The horses shuffled when he went inside and walked down the center of the isle. It was a small stable, only eight boxes on each side and a small tack-room at the front. A few horses poked their heads out of the stalls, turning their inquisitive eyes toward him as he walked by. There were six horses in all, but room for sixteen. Shaw imagined the stables full when the ranch was fully stocked with cattle and there was more staff to help mustering. Now, like the cattle, their numbers had also diminished, a sign of a place in decline. It was a shame. Daisy would have to give in to the fact that even with less cattle, she still couldn't cope. The ranch took a lot to keep it going and maybe selling to the Morgans was her only option.

Jazz poked her head out at Shaw and he patted her, awkwardly like he would pat a dog, unsure of where on the animal's massive head was best. "You did good today, girl," he said, and she nuzzled his hand. He could see clearly the female features and facial lines. He used to think all horses looked the same, unable to believe you could tell male from female. But now, up close there was a clear distinction.

Shaw pulled out a carrot from his jacket pocket. He had ducked into the kitchen and swiped a few from the fridge when Daisy was outside lighting the grill. Jazz chomped through the carrot with her big teeth like a mulching machine chewing up a branch.

"Now, you are familiar with the saying *don't bite the hand that feeds you?*" Shaw said with a questioning look at Jazz. He thought he saw her give a short nod as she gobbled up the carrot.

"Well, just remember this carrot and who gave it to you, OK?"

Horses were clever and intelligent creatures, and sometimes people didn't realize how much they were almost like humans. "Just keep her safe," he said, as he patted her head again.

Shaw moved on to the next stall and saw a familiar face and shape loom toward him. It was the horse he had ridden today. The chalkboard sign that hung from the stable door said *Freddy*. "You did good today too, my friend." The horse sniffed Shaw's fingers then gave them a quick appreciative nibble. Shaw gave Freddy a carrot as well and he made quick work of it. A few other horses, hearing the chewing sound poked their heads out from their stalls, wondering where their treat was.

Shaw looked at them and held up his hands "Sorry guys, I could only steal so many. Next time I'll bring a few for you as well."

Shaw exited the stables and looked to the east to where he imagined the Morgan compound was, nestled behind dark rows of open hills in the distance. It was a cloudless night, the big disc of the moon shone down bathing the landscape in ghostly shades. It would provide some natural light and that would help him later.

Daisy called out to him from the veranda, waving him in. Dinner was ready.

Shaw started walking then stopped. At first Shaw thought it was piece of twisted fence wire, or maybe part of a plastic soda bottle discarded by one of the past ranch hands. He lifted his foot, shone his flashlight on the ground, then picked it up.

He turned the object over in his hand. Eight inches, black thin twisted material, molded like a blade into a deliberate symmetrical shape. The object wasn't plastic, but precision engineered from some type of lightweight composite material. Most people would have mistaken it for a piece off a toy, but Shaw recognized it instantly. The object in his hand was commercial quality or better, not designed for or readily available for the recreational market.

Shaw looked up, straight into the dark sky.

There was no movement, no ghosting or ripple in the darkness, no telltale signs. It would be near impossible to see it at night, but it could see him.

He saw nothing.

He slipped the object into his pocket, looked around, then started to walk toward the homestead.

Daisy was on the veranda plating food off the grill.

He would have to tell her soon, about the object he had found. About everything else as well.

TWENTY-THREE

The mist was getting closer. It crept toward Shaw like a living thing with no distinct features, edges or end to it. Just a wall of ghostly white.

Shaw pulled his leather jacket closer around him, the collar turned up against the frigid air. It had been warm during the day, but the temperature dropped soon after the sun had gone down. Now it was cold and brittle.

It would be midnight soon. He had waited for nearly an hour in the warmth of the bunkhouse after dinner before he ventured out, making sure Daisy had gone to bed and the ranch had settled in for the night. He then left the bunkhouse and made his way past the barn and followed the dirt road that he had seen that afternoon with Daisy. He navigated in the darkness from memory and by moonlight. The cold landscape was a palette of ghostly grays, dark shapes, blurred outlines and silhouettes. He was either totally alone, or surrounded by hundreds of faceless monsters.

Every once and a while he searched the sky to see if anything moved against the cold starry backdrop. But he could see nothing.

He had made good time, his pace quick and determined, constantly checking all the angles including the road in front and behind for the signs of car headlights. The ground was flat and offered no cover whatsoever.

Eventually he came to the forest of cottonwoods, and plunged thankfully into the mass of trees.

He knelt behind a thick tree trunk, its surface ragged with deep fissures and blotchy with moss. He was glad to be off the dirt road. He would move faster now, his shape hidden by low-hanging branches and diamond-shaped leaves.

He set off again, skirting the edge of the forest, staying a few rows in but keeping the dirt road visible to his right as a reference point. He could just make out the line of the boundary fence on the other side. He could always duck behind a large tree trunk, if a car came along the dirt road.

The cottonwoods pressed in around him as he threaded his way through the forest, the mist seeping between the trunks in seductive swirls that reached out to Shaw like hands wanting to hold him back. He kept checking the fence line to his right, waiting to spot the old hinged cattle gate. A few moments later its dark outline broke the regular pattern of the wire and post fence.

Looking both ways first, Shaw left the cover of the forest, scuttled across the road and slid quickly between the tubular frame of the cattle gate then immediately went to ground. He crouched low in a shallow ditch on the other side. The ground was dirt with loose stones, bare except for a few tufts of wild and unkempt grass. He knew this part of the property was rarely used for cattle. When he was up on the ridge he could see no herds, which meant he had an uninterrupted line to traverse through the hills without the chances of spooking cattle and alerting anyone.

But he was now in no man's land.

He had no cover to screen his approach, natural or otherwise, except the odd rock formation scattered nearer the foothills farther away. He needed to move fast, hoping there was no surveillance measures in place to trigger his approach.

Shaw took off at a slow jog in a straight line as best he could judge.

The moon was high and it painted the terrain in front of him in a million shades of gray and black. Shaw had changed back at the bunkhouse into the darkest clothes he carried with him. Dark jeans, black T-shirt, and his faithful leather jacket. It helped camouflage him as he sped across the open fields, but he still felt hopelessly exposed. He stopped once or twice, immediately going to ground, lying flat on his stomach among the grass and weeds, thinking he heard something, like the cry of an animal. But after a moment of waiting he moved on. It was nothing.

He came to a stretch of ground, bare and scalped of all vegetation, rough and littered with stones, and rutted in places like it had been once plowed then forgotten. It was an old wheat field, no longer used. He pressed on, following the straight line of a furrow, his footing slipping at times on the dry crumbling earth.

A square shape loomed to his right. An old building, maybe a pump shed used for irrigation, he thought. He crept slowly toward it, watching for any movement. It was small with corrugated iron sides, pitched roof, pale and rusted out, crooked with age, two windows, both broken, just a carcass of an old tin shed long abandoned. The door was just a single thin sheet of iron screwed to a simple frame with a bolt, but no chain or padlock. He looked around then pulled open the door. It groaned on old dry hinges.

He turned on his flashlight, covering the lens with his palm, suppressing the light. A dull red from his hand threw shadows around him. Inside it was dirt floor, wood frame and reeked of oil and diesel fumes. A block of machinery stood in the middle of the floor, scaled with rust, seized with age, old and dead. Pipes led out from the base of the machine to a hole cut in the corrugated wall. It was an old irrigation pump, maybe hooked up to pump groundwater to crops that no longer grew.

There was nothing else here. The place was creepy, and had a sinister feel to it. Shaw turned to leave then stopped.

A glint of something came from the dirt floor, just a wink, nothing bright but something shiny enough to catch the suppressed light as Shaw turned around, the flashlight pointed downward.

He crouched down and held the flashlight an inch above the brown dirt, a small intense circle of light formed, the object within its corona.

It was a small silver identity bracelet, oval nametag, clasp broken and hanging from each side. Shaw turned it over and squinted at the tag.

Annie.

A woman's name, engraved in small neat letters, upper and lower case with a tiny love heart at the end.

Shaw pressed the flashlight against his thigh and stood up, the tiny bracelet in his hand, and looked around the shed again.

He slipped the bracelet into his pocket, then squatted down again. Careful not to wave the flashlight around he searched the immediate area around where he had found the bracelet, allowing some of the light to spill through his fingers.

Then his heart skipped a beat. Something small, cubic, white with a yellow tinge lay in the dirt.

It was a tooth.

Leaving the tin shed, Shaw continued his direct line over the next set of hills. But with each step he could feel like he was approaching something malevolent, like it was drawing him in, pulling him across the darkened landscape toward its core. Another mile farther he felt the cold seeping in to his gut and he could see the horizon lighten around the edges of the hills in the distance.

He was getting close.

He reached a larger hill, steeper than the others, like a natural wall. It was harder getting up it too, and a few times he lost his footing and slid backward through a river of loose stones, rocks and dirt as he went. But he kept going, determined to reach the top and see what was on the other side.

He could feel the atmosphere change as he crawled the last few feet, on his stomach, his hands and knees dragging him up the slope toward the summit.

Fragments of sound drifted down toward him. Laughter, voices and a brightening glow that rimmed the jagged edge above him.

He squeezed between two large rocks at the top and found himself on a narrow ridge with just a few feet of scrub before it dropped away on the other side. He crawled slowly toward the edge on the opposite side, pausing behind a low rock formation.

Below was a wide expanse of flat land. The surrounding hills formed a natural horseshoe shape around it like a crater, screening it, protecting it as a natural fortification. Nestled at one end, nearest to Shaw was a huge complex of buildings, like a mini city, brightly lit and in the middle of nowhere.

A ribbon of blacktop lit by light poles led to a main entrance where there was a formidable-looking guardhouse and barrier gate. The road snaked away from the entrance back toward the main highway. The complex was a series of buildings, large machinery sheds, open-style workshops, storage areas, and a large solar panel array. There were roads and pathways linking everything and sheds that housed an assortment of vehicles all lined up in neat rows under floodlights. There were ATVs, various pickup trucks, and a few loaders. A high perimeter fence of mesh ringed the entire place with tall light towers spaced evenly, throwing pools of light.

Callie was wrong in her description. It wasn't a compound or homestead. It was a small city, and it reminded Shaw of an arctic base camp only much bigger. Totally self-sufficient in the desolate landscape. He could see huge generators for backup power, a refueling station with large diesel tanks housed on frames, and a cluster of satellite dishes next to a row of portable site buildings that looked like barracks or offices. The place gave off enough light that it seemed like the sun in the middle of a well-organized and laid out solar system.

Shaw pulled out the compact binoculars he had brought.

On an opposite hill, a series of lights snaked up a steep driveway and, perched at the top, overlooking the entire complex, was a wide sprawling house of stone, wood, glass and steel. Even in the dark with the exterior lights on, the house looked massive, its architecture modern but rustic, designed to incorporate elements of the surrounding terrain. It looked like a resort-style hunting lodge, but on a more opulent scale.

But there were no obvious cattle yards, livestock pens or any traces that a typical ranch would have. Maybe the main working ranch was located somewhere else. Daisy had said that the Morgans owned tens of thousands of acres. To Shaw, the complex looked like the nerve-center of the entire Morgan operation.

Shaw did another slow pan of the area. There were no security cameras as far as he could tell. But that didn't mean there wasn't any. The best surveillance was the one you couldn't see. Most CCTV cameras were set up for the public to notice, to act as a deterrent. But here the lack of any obvious cameras made Shaw feel uneasy. The operation looked too slick, too modern, too expensive to leave security as an afterthought.

****

"Where is he?" The man with the short gray hair said. He sat in a small office surrounded by screens and keyboards, and spoke into a headset mike.

His ear buzzed with a reply. "He's on the west ridge, just near the edge, about two hundred feet up and about three hundred feet out from the perimeter. He's watching through a pair of binoculars, not night-vision. We've got eyes on him from the air, about three hundred feet behind him on the diagonal. At this point he's still blind on that. It will hold that position, but we'll follow him in if he moves."

The man with the gray hair hit the mute button. He eyes were cold, hard and gray like granite, and focused on the image of the man on the screen. He could see the 'intruder', as they had designated him, on the screen in front of him, a ghostly shape outlined in the green wash of the night-vision camera. "You've either got balls son or you're extremely stupid," the man said to the mass of pixels on the screen.

He couldn't clearly make out the intruder's face, but the man with the gray hair knew who it was. It was the same person who was with the girl today, the two of them on horseback they had stopped. Some people called it gut instinct or intuition. He preferred to call it a career built on hunting and killing people like this.

He took his mike off mute. "If he gets to the fence, shoot him."

TWENTY-FOUR

As he saw it, he had two choices: either turn around and go back to the warmth of the bunkhouse and catch some much-needed sleep. Or take a closer look at the sprawling complex below.

But Shaw had spent most of his life not choosing the comfortable, warm, conservative option. He much preferred taking the risk, taking the option that was often uncomfortable, cold and more challenging. And that had made all the difference in his life. A better difference.

He tucked the binoculars back into his jacket pocket and slithered over the edge, head first, down the slope toward the fence. He wanted to take a closer look. Just a look. Nothing more.

Maybe.

He took his time, careful not to dislodge rocks and stones, following a zig-zag pattern as he descended, crouching all the way, the dark fading to gray the closer he got. He came off the hill and crouched behind a large boulder, taking a moment to assess.

He figured the distance to the fence was still another two hundred yards or so. There were wide patches of semi-darkness where the fence lights didn't reach and that's where he intended to make for.

There was another reason as well. There was a row of shipping containers, big boxy shapes of corrugated steel with faded paint and hinged doors, lined up neatly on the inside of the fence. They would provide good cover as he approached, if anyone was looking in his direction from inside the fence.

To get to the fence there was another stretch of no man's land. No cover. No trees, No rocks. Just flat dry ground with sparse knee-high scrub. But it was still fairly dark where the shipping containers had thrown tall shadows towards his direction.

There were voices beyond the fence, gruff and deep, that carried through the cold air, workmen banter coming from the front of a nearby building that looked like a temporary site office.

A forklift went past on the inside of the fence, its lights bobbing up and down, an empty pallet on its forks.

Shaw edged forward, crouching as he moved, gravel crunching under his boots, the fence looming toward him. He could see some of the buildings in more detail, but his vision narrowed as the shape of the shipping containers grew. He angled slightly to the right, wanting to get a clearer view of the two men who were talking near the site office. They wore hardhats, bright yellow.

It was a cattle ranch, so why the hard hats? Why all the machinery and trucks and sheds? The closer Shaw got, the more he realized the place looked like a construction site, not a cattle ranch. Maybe he had gotten lost. Maybe this wasn't the Morgan's ranch. Maybe he had followed a wrong line as he crossed the hills and ended up somehow on an adjacent property.

He kept moving forward, toward the fence, his eyes on the men. There was something strange about them, something out of place.

Then he stopped, the fence twenty feet away, the hard edge of a shipping container shielding him. He crabbed sideways, still crouching, wanting to get a better view of the men. They stood near a white pickup in front of the office. There was a corporate logo on the side of the pickup, but it was too dark and too far away to see it clearly. It looked like a triangle with diagonal lines in the middle.

It was too late when Shaw heard the sound.

Then that moment of dread when the brain registered the sound. It came from above, like a large angry wasp.

Then the soft sound of feet on dirt.

Shaw turned.

Three men stood behind him, dressed head-to-toe in black fatigues, night vision goggles, weaponry trained on him.

Shaw did the only logical thing and raised his hands.

One man stepped forward, swiveled his assault rifle to his side on a sling, drew a handgun from a drop-leg holster in one smooth motion and shot Shaw dead-center in the chest.

****

Shaw was dead. He could feel it. They had buried him in the ground. No flowers. No speeches. A few people had come to pay their respects, but they offered no sympathy. He could see them, blurred and out of arm's reach, they hovered above him, ghostly images that moved under the insides of his eye lids.

His body felt crushed under tons of dirt, soil and rock. Deep down in his tomb. He couldn't breathe, the pressure around him too much to move his diaphragm, like his lungs had forgotten how to draw air. Every fiber of every muscle, every strand of every nerve-ending ached like his body had been fed through the rollers of some machine, and he had come out the other end flattened.

The ground shook as a hand burrowed its way through the dirt and soil above, and down to where his corpse lay in the darkness. The ground above parted slightly, letting in some light and slowly the insides of his eyelids warmed red. More light came and his chest moved. He sucked in air through clenched teeth, his jaw and head aching.

A hand found then gripped his shoulder. Then a voice from far away.

"Mr. Shaw."

His name, calling to him.

Then again, "Mr. Shaw. Wake up."

He opened his eyes and came awake in a flurry, sucking in deep breaths.

Slowly his surroundings came into focus.

A woman, small-framed, old but with kind eyes of concern stood in front of him, one hand still on his shoulder, either to settle him or restrain him, he couldn't tell. He wanted to snap her neck because he needed to. Someone had to pay for how he felt and she was the nearest person.

She smiled at him, a paper cup in her hand, which she offered. She guided the lip of the cup toward his mouth like he was a child, not capable of his own biomechanics. Water passed over his numb lips and a little dribbled down the side of his mouth. He was reduced to a child, numb, dribbling and reliant.

"What have you done to me?" he croaked. He drank some more.

Slowly his senses; sight, smell, touch, and feeling began to recalibrate back to normal, but he knew he would be far from normal for a few hours yet.

Then he realized what had happened.

"You tasered me?" Shaw asked her. The nurse stepped back as if to say *not me*.

The room came into focus, and he looked beyond her.

"It was necessary, Mr. Shaw. You were trespassing." A man stepped around from behind a huge ornate desk. The room was a cavernous affair of high ceilings with exposed beams, walls of stone and hewn wood, plush leather sofas, thick woven rugs, a massive fireplace encased in a heath of mortared river rock, logs thick and flaming within, floor to ceiling bookcases of dark heavy wood housed rows of leather books. Chandeliers shaped like antlers hung from the ceiling on thick links of black chain.

The room dripped of authority and refinement, a reflection of the man who now stood in front of Shaw.

"I was worried for your safety, Mr. Shaw. I didn't want any harm to come to you."

Shaw rubbed his neck concerned that his head might fall off. He felt like he had gone ten rounds with Mike Tyson, Evander Holyfield and Lennox Lewis all at the same time.

"You shocked me?" he asked again, as he shifted on the leather sofa, not confident that he could stand up. He felt sick, he felt sore, but most of all he felt livid.

The man stepped closer, "Please accept my apologies, Mr. Shaw. My name is James Morgan. But everybody calls me Jim."

Shaw felt like calling him something else, a word starting with the letter 'C' came to mind, but held the urge.

Jim Morgan didn't offer his hand to shake and if he had, Shaw would have broken it.

Jim Morgan was a big man. Impressive and powerful, matching the room they were in. His face weathered with age and experience, short-cropped gray hair, and intelligent brown eyes capable of extracting the truth from anyone. He had a manner that was warm, but authoritative. He was a man used to getting whatever he wanted.

"It was that or shoot you dead," Jim Morgan said, looking over his shoulder. The man with the gray hair stood off to one side in the room, like a tiger waiting to pounce, one hand on the grip of his handgun, eyes intent on Shaw.

"Mr. Cole here wanted a more—permanent solution to your presence," Jim Morgan said, a slight smile across his face. "I have the safety of my staff to think about. We can't have strangers just coming on to our property and allow them to just wander around."

"So what, I'm now your prisoner?"

Jim Morgan threw back his head and laughed, deep and resonating. "Oh no, Mr. Shaw. Definitely not. I consider you to be my guest."

The response seemed genuine, but there was something below the surface of the man's face that made Shaw feel anything but a guest.

Jim Morgan nodded, and the nurse stepped forward and took Shaw's pulse. "You will be sore for a few hours, but the effects will wear off," she said, her small, delicate fingers on his wrist. Her demeanor sounded as though he just had a mild headache and that it was an everyday occurrence to zap guests with fifty thousand volts.

The nurse gave a nod to Jim Morgan and left the room.

Shaw pushed himself up on the sofa, but hated that he couldn't stand, his legs all jelly. Jim Morgan was standing. He wanted to stand in front of him. Look him in the eye on equal terms, but Shaw was at a distinct disadvantage. He was incapacitated and he didn't like it one bit. He once had taken a 40 caliber round to the chest with full body armor on, and was winded for a few minutes. This was worse.

Jim Morgan lowered his large frame into a wing-backed chair across from Shaw. For a large man he moved with grace and poise, and he spoke like a politician, always saying what people wanted to hear while the true design of his machinations remained hidden behind his eyes.

"Now Mr. Shaw, can I offer you a drink? Maybe a scotch? I have a single malt that I bring in especially from Scotland, from a distillery just north of Inverness." Morgan rose again without waiting for a response and went to a sideboard that was stacked with every conceivable bottle of liquor. He poured a generous measure of liquor into two heavy glass tumblers, then returned and offered one to Shaw. "If you don't drink scotch, Mr. Shaw, then we're not going to get along."

Shaw looked at the glass. It was thick and heavy, and the amber liquid swirled. No ice. No water. He could take the glass and in a split-second bury it into Jim Morgan's throat. He would bleed out in under thirty seconds and make a real mess of the Indian Cherokee rug.

As if reading his mind Jim Morgan raised an eyebrow. "Let's just put our differences aside for a moment and share a drink like civilized men. I don't want Mr. Cole to have his way with you after all. He took a lot of convincing not to kill you." Jim Morgan proffered the glass again and Shaw took it.

Slowly he raised it to his lips and took a sip.

Christ, it tasted good. Immediately the scotch spread down his throat and began to bring life back into his body.

Jim Morgan saw his expression. "Yes, it's the best medicine money can buy." Morgan sat down again and Cole remained standing in the background, his eyes never leaving Shaw like it was a battle of wills.

"Now, I have a favor to ask you Mr. Shaw, or can I call you Ben?"

Shaw knew the drill. He had used it a thousand times before during interrogations. First you make the suspect feel comfortable, unthreatened, then you ask them a favor like you were indebted to them. But then that would be reversed eventually until they felt obligated to tell you everything. If they didn't comply, then the favor would turn into threats. Not threats of violence, but the usual threats of incarceration, like how many years did they want to spend in a federal prison? Ten? Twenty? It was up to them. It was their fault. They weren't going to get a lawyer. The Patriot Act wouldn't allow it. So start talking or you'll never see the light of day. Somehow Shaw knew that Jim Morgan would offer violence, like his sons, if he didn't get what he wanted. Shaw was looking at a master of reverse manipulation, the tutor of his sons. The apple never fell far from the tree.

"How do you know my name?"

Jim Morgan smiled like it was a stupid question. "I know everyone and everything that goes on in this town, in this county, Ben." He said his name like they were long lost buddies. All part of the mind games. It may work on the local hardware store owner or the new cop in town, but Shaw was immune to such psychological warfare. Under it all he knew Jim Morgan was another bully, the head bully of the Morgan clan who had raised and nurtured his three sons to follow in his footsteps. The man would slip a hundred-dollar bill into the church collection plate on a Sunday, then that very same day take a pair of pliers to a storekeeper's hand if he was late with the rent.

Shaw could feel the heat from the scotch in his gut, but another kind of heat was building in his head, an intense dislike for the confident and articulate man who sat across from him with the silver tongue and aura of false empathy.

"You and Mr. Cole are very much alike," Jim Morgan nodded at Cole. "Cut from the same cloth even."

"I'm nothing like any of your hired goons. Why do you need ex-military contractors on a cattle ranch in Kansas anyway?"

"To stop people like you."

"I'm just passing through, helping a neighbor of yours out," Shaw shrugged. "No harm in that."

Jim Morgan took a sip of his drink, holding the scotch on the middle of his tongue, savoring it for a moment as he studied the liquid in the tumbler. He swallowed then said, "But you're here. You came across onto my land. I have to take precautions. I can't have people stumbling in here of their own free will, can I?"

"It's overkill, don't you think? Assault rifles, night vision cameras, your own private army of contractors. Why?" Shaw kept quiet about the other thing he had discovered, didn't want to give away too much to the man.

"You can never be too careful these days, Ben, with all these terrorists and the like. I have many business interests that I run from here. Cattle and agriculture is just one of them."

Jim Morgan stood up and poured himself another drink. "Look, I want us to be friends, not enemies," he said over his shoulder. He returned and sat down again. "I think we can help each other, don't you think?"

"I don't need your money."

"Oh, I know that. It was stupid of my son Billy to offer you money to leave. He just made a bad judgment call about your character, that's all. Money doesn't interest you. If it did, you wouldn't have made a career of doing what you were doing in Washington." Jim Morgan smiled. "Don't get me wrong, Washington is full of rich elitist politicians, lobbyists, advocates, government contractors, all bleeding Uncle Sam dry like vultures. But you don't seem like the K Street type."

Shaw felt the first glimmer of concern. It was becoming obvious that Jim Morgan had done some research on him. The man was resourceful, cunning and didn't leave anything to chance.

"Look, I just want a favor. That's all." Jim Morgan leaned forward to emphasize the point. "That's all. Just a favor."

For men like Jim Morgan it was never just a favor. It always escalated into something more until eventually you found yourself forever a slave to their whims.

"And in return?" Shaw asked.

"In return you will keep your anonymity. I'm sure Daisy McAlister would change her opinion of you, if she found out exactly who you really are."

"That's in my past. I've done nothing wrong."

Jim Morgan seemed to contemplate this for a moment, the cogs in his head turning. "Then why are they looking for you, Ben?"

TWENTY-FIVE

"Who is looking for me?" He already knew the answer, but wanted to call Jim Morgan's bluff.

"Who? Your last employer, Ben. I agree you've done nothing wrong. You've broken no laws, you've kept a low profile, flown below the radar as they say. There's no manhunt going on for you. You're a free man, not a criminal. But I imagine that with your last place of employment you never really leave, do you? I'm sure they would be interested in your whereabouts. Just in case." Jim Morgan smiled like a man holding a royal flush and Shaw had only two of a kind.

Shaw just wanted to be left alone. Stay off the grid. Fade into the periphery. But now all this was at risk from a man he hardly knew, who seemed to know a lot about him. A man who was proving to be thorough, resourceful and who never left anything to chance, especially a potential threat like Shaw. It was the qualities Shaw had in himself, but he now realized he had underestimated it in Jim Morgan. He was a shrewd, calculating businessman, not some small-town hustler who had got lucky by bullying people.

"It does make for interesting reading, Ben, your career doesn't it?" Jim Morgan let the words sink in, enjoying the bewildered look on Shaw's face. "I can't imagine what you listed on your Form 1040 each year as your occupation?" he continued. "All I want you to do is help me, help Daisy McAlister. That's all."

Help me help her. This was a pathological liar talking. Maybe Jim Morgan was more suited to Washington.

Shaw smiled at the spin Jim Morgan had put on the request, like the phone company calling you up to tell you how you could reduce your phone bills, if you just shifted to a new plan they were offering. It was all sleight of hand, trickery and lies. He could have run for political office, maybe that's where his true aspirations lay.

"How could you possibly help Daisy McAlister? Your sons have done nothing but threaten and intimidate her," Shaw said, flicking a glance at Cole.

"Look, my sons can be a bit harsh in their methods, blunt with their approach."

Yeh, I wonder where they get that from? Shaw thought.

"They can be a bit eager. They still need to learn a lot. I apologize for their indiscretions."

The apology seemed genuine to Shaw, but he imagined that Jim Morgan and the entire Morgan family still bulldozed their way through people with very little real regard for the consequences unless it benefited the Morgan name.

Jim Morgan continued, "Her ranch is slowly slipping into bankruptcy. Ever since her father died in that tragic horse riding accident it has been one unfolding tragedy after the next. Her mother died soon after and then it all became too much for poor Daisy. She's had to sell cattle just to keep the place afloat. Pretty soon the bank will foreclose and it will be a fire-sale."

Shaw held his thoughts and kept his expression deadpan. But the revelation had been like a punch to his gut. Not many people around town knew Daisy's mother was dead as well. Daisy had managed to keep that fact private. But Jim Morgan made it his business to know everything about everyone. Not even his own sons knew the old woman had died.

"I've made her a very good offer for her land, well above market value and it's the best offer she is going to get. I really want you, Ben, to make her see the light. Please make her see that there are no other options. If you care about her then you'll make her see this."

"Why is the land so important to you? Why do you want it?"

"It makes good business sense, Ben. Geographically it's well suited to our expansion plans here. We want to expand our cattle holdings and having the McAlister land adjacent to ours is the best option. You can't prevent progress, Ben." Jim Morgan sounded like he was on the campaign trail, giving a speech to win an election.

"She is very set in her ways. It's about the family legacy more than the value of the ranch. If she sells, then she believes she will be ending the McAlister legacy, letting down her father," Shaw replied.

Jim Morgan took another ritualistic sip from his glass. "Look, I totally see her point of view. I understand all about family traditions and bloodline succession. One day you and I will just be dust under trampling hooves. We all want to live forever, but we can't. So we try and build a legacy to pass on to the next generation."

Shaw felt that the next Morgan generation was as tainted as the first.

"But if Daisy doesn't take my offer, there'll be nothing left to pass on. She's a young woman. She may want kids of her own someday, but they'll have a very hard future without money."

There was some truth in what Jim Morgan was saying. Maybe Daisy McAlister needed to swallow her pride and not be so stubborn. Too many owners held on too long to loss-making ranches only for their selfish desires to continue the family name. The McAlister name would go on, but maybe not as how Daisy's father intended.

"I will talk to her." That's all Shaw said, but his mind was working overtime processing all the information.

"Good. I knew, Ben, you were a fair man." Jim Morgan rose and extended his hand.

Shaw drained the glass of scotch. No point in wasting something that sat in a barrel for the last thirty years waiting to be drunk. He set aside the glass on a side table and got to his feet, the strength returning to his legs.

He took Jim Morgan's hand, the grip firm, his hand rough and calloused, a testament to his heritage. The man was charismatic, charming, and extremely convincing.

"Thanks again, Ben."

Jim Morgan turned to Cole. "Mr. Cole will see you out. The least we could do is run you back."

A clock on the sideboard said it was 2:00 a.m. "It's getting late for both of us," Jim Morgan said.

Shaw nodded and made for the door. He had no intention of sleeping. There was too much to be done, if he was going to save Daisy McAlister from a criminal like Jim Morgan.

****

Three armed men marched Shaw to a waiting black SUV that was parked under the portico of the homestead. Shaw was unconscious on the drive in, but he was very conscious on the car ride out.

They pushed him into the back seat and two men got in the back as well, one on either side, sandwiching him in. Cole sat in the passenger seat and gave a nod to the waiting driver who pressed the gas and the large car glided off down the side of the hill, a hiss of its tires on the smooth driveway.

Shaw hoped he was going to get an opportunity to see more of the compound up close as they drove through it to the main gate. But in a deliberate move the SUV did a sharp right turn at the bottom of the driveway and, instead of driving along the main road through the complex, it exited via a rear gate with a key code, onto a dirt track and into the darkness.

The trip back was a lot faster, warmer and more comfortable than the trip in for Shaw. The big SUV drove at speed, its soft suspension making it feel like they were driving on a smooth road. The beam of headlights dipped and bobbed illuminating the harsh landscape ahead. Shaw looked out of the window, but it was pitch black.

Instead of taking him back along the main road and to the main entrance of the ranch. They pulled up in front of the tubular gate that Shaw had slid through hours before. In the dark he had missed the dirt road they had driven him back on. They seemed to know the road well.

The men slid out, the headlights lit up the gate in front in a brilliant glare. Shaw got out and one of the men handed Shaw a zip lock bag. Inside it were his possessions including the flashlight and binoculars. Shaw noted its other contents and made a mental note for later.

They pushed him forward. Cole got out and walked around to Shaw, his hand firmly on the grip of the handgun snug on his thigh.

"If you come back again without an invite from Mr. Morgan, we won't taser you again. I'll personally put a bullet in your brain like I've done many times to people like you."

Shaw turned and faced Cole, the other men forming up behind the chief of security.

The two men looked at each other, both unblinking, both committing the detail of each other's face to memory.

Seconds passed then Shaw just turned and, without saying a word, walked away toward the gate.

TWENTY-SIX

It was only after his third cup of coffee that Shaw started to feel normal again. Tiredness he could deal with. Long hours, little or no sleep, and the need to be totally alert and aware were no strangers to him in a previous life. A life or occupation that he wanted to put behind him, but Jim Morgan was going to drag it up all over again. If Shaw let him.

Shaw stood on the porch. The sun had only been up for an hour and he had sat warming himself by the wood stove in the pre-dawn darkness, alone with his thoughts.

Packing up his few belongings into his backpack and catching the first bus out of town or hitching a ride was not an option. Not his style. Plus what information he had gained in the early hours of this morning had answered a lot of the questions bouncing around in his head since he first arrived.

Up at the main house, Daisy was setting the table for breakfast. She waved and smiled. Shaw waved back then grimaced, his chest still had residual soreness, but it was slowly fading. He had taken a shower as soon as he returned and discovered a small puncture mark in his sternum and another larger one on his right buttock. He knew he was not feeling the after-effects of just being shot with a taser gun. Normally the effects would wear off after five or ten minutes. He had been knocked out cold and awoke on the sofa in Jim Morgan's study, feeling like a zombie. There had to be another reason.

Now he knew why.

While he was on the ground in spasms from having fifty-thousand volts surge through his body, they had also shot him with a tranquilizer gun in the butt. They weren't taking any chances. They saw him as a clear and present danger, and took him down as such.

The fact that they brought him back to the gate where he crossed onto the Morgan ranch meant he was doomed from the start. They had tracked him from the moment he set foot on Morgan soil. He may as well have painted a fluorescent target on his back.

The old tin shed was a separate issue. Maybe it wasn't important to Jim Morgan. Maybe it meant nothing that Shaw went inside, they didn't care. The shed was something else that Shaw didn't know the answer to—yet.

He slipped his hand into his pocket, pulled out the silver identity bracelet and looked at the name engraved on it again.

Annie?

More questions than answers.

He'd left the tooth in the zip lock bag in a drawer in the kitchenette, hiding it under old and faded instruction manuals for appliances that had long been thrown out. It wasn't the kind of memento he wanted to carry around with him, he wasn't the tooth-fairy.

In his other pocket he had the other object he had found, another answer to a nagging question. He had made some progress in finding the answers.

He pushed off the porch and made his way up the path to the homestead.

Time to come clean.

****

Daisy sat still and didn't say a word while Shaw described what happened the night before. He told her everything—well, almost everything. He left out the part about finding the tooth and silver identity bracelet in the tin shed. He didn't want to complicate things. He had no idea if the two items were related or who was Annie.

He explained to Daisy how he had ventured onto the Morgan property, been shot with a taser, then tranquilized, and the cozy little chat with Jim Morgan. When Shaw finished, she asked him why he had gone onto the Morgan property without telling her. She wasn't angry, just confused.

"I wanted to know what they were up to. I wanted to see for myself. I didn't want you involved. I was just protecting you, that's all. You're the boss. I'm just a humble employee. There's less risk, if I got caught."

Daisy smiled, thinking back to last evening in the shower. She liked being the boss with him. It gave her certain privileges that made her pulse rise just thinking about it. In her mind the kitchen table was going to be next.

"Don't you think it's strange, all the security they have? It's like a prison, not a ranch."

"I know they have a lot of interests, not just cattle," she replied. "And their land holdings are scattered across Kansas." Daisy went on to explain that she had never actually set foot on their property, ever, even though it was right next door. But she had spoken to other people over the years, other ranch hands who had worked there and people in town. It was around the time her father died that things seemed to change with the Morgans. They became more insular. People stopped seeing Jim Morgan in public, and his three sons became more visible around town. Rumors went around that the security was being beefed up at the ranch. Fences with razor wire started to go up and security cameras were installed along the main road entrance. Townsfolk who were previously employed were let go, replaced by staff and contractors brought in from out of state. Everything became very secretive.

"I didn't see one head of cattle, no feed lots, nothing that would make me think the place was a working cattle ranch," Shaw said.

Daisy just nodded.

"Daisy, I need to know why the Morgans want your land so badly. There must be something more than just using it for expansion. As you said, they have land all over Kansas. OK, so your ranch is adjacent to theirs and it makes sense to want your land, but I don't think running more cattle on it is what they are truly interested in."

Shaw could see she was thinking. Now was a good time to tell her the rest.

So he did.

"Oh, by the way."

Daisy looked up at him.

He continued, "Just to let you know. You, your home, this ranch has been under surveillance. Someone has been watching you probably for a while now. Maybe a week, but I'd say longer, during the day and at night too. Recording you coming and going, your daily routines, what time you get up in the morning, what time you go to bed, your movements around the ranch. They know your habits."

Daisy's eyes went wide. She was stunned. "Who? Who the hell is watching me?" she demanded.

Shaw shook his head, "I don't know. But I bet they have even been here when you weren't, probably walked right into this house, gone through your stuff, opened your drawers and cupboards, looked inside, touched your personal effects and such. Maybe even been inside your house while you were here, when you were asleep. Maybe even walked straight into your bedroom, walked right up to your bed and watched you sleep."

Daisy could feel her anger rise and the blood drain from her face at the same time.

Shaw gave a slow nod. "And they're probably watching us right now."

Daisy looked confused, so he slipped the object from his pocket and put it on the table.

"What is it?" Daisy stared down at it. It was the blade-like object he had found the previous night in the yard, a few hundred feet from where they now sat.

"It's a propeller from a commercial drone," Shaw said. "It's been flying over your property for some time now, I imagine. Probably hit a power line or something and threw one of its propellers." Shaw picked it up and twisted it in his fingers. "They're designed to come off so the drone doesn't get hitched or caught on something in flight."

"Where did you find it?" she demanded.

"Just near the house. Found it last night when I was doing the rounds of the stables and sheds. Stood on it."

Daisy took the propeller from Shaw. "So they've been watching me. Spying on me all this time?" She knew some ranches were using drones to monitor cattle movement and check on pumps and water flow in more remote parts of their property. But she had never actually seen one for real.

Shaw could see fire in her eyes.

"Who? Who is *they* you keep saying?" she yelled.

"I don't know, but I'd say the Morgans or someone working for them. This type of drone is hi-spec, commercial and maybe even military quality." He didn't tell her that despite the drone being hi-spec, it still only had a short range, maybe five miles at the most. That meant it could be remote piloted from the Morgan's complex, but more than likely someone close by was operating it. From inside the McAlister property.

The perfect spot was up on the ridge behind the barn where they were yesterday. High, clear access. From up there the person piloting it would have an uninterrupted view down onto the homestead and all the outbuildings, and the signal would be stronger. If Shaw was setting up a surveillance grid, that's where he would have chosen to pilot the drone and keep an eye on Daisy.

"How do you know all this? I mean it could be from a kid's toy, like a remote controlled plane or something that just strayed onto my property." Daisy looked at Shaw questioningly. Now he felt like he was being interrogated.

"I've seen these before," he replied. "I know a few things about surveillance and security." Shaw didn't want to say anymore.

Daisy looked away out across the brown landscape. She felt violated, her privacy, her space, her domain. It was like someone had come onto her land like a peeping-tom, a voyeur, a pervert. She could deal with someone, a stranger in the flesh, if they were trespassing. She could shoot them. Protect herself. But a machine high in the sky, beyond her reach? How could she deal with that? It made her skin crawl.

Shaw tried to put it gently. "You need to tell me what's going on. If I am to help you, you need to trust me. Please."

She turned back, relief in her eyes. "You'll help me? You know about these things. I don't."

"Of course. I don't trust the Morgans as far as I can throw them." Shaw had done enough interrogations to know when the person sitting across from him was lying. And as skilled and as smooth as Jim Morgan's words were in his study, he was lying to Shaw. Jim Morgan had no interest whatsoever in helping Daisy Morgan. His words were hollow.

She smiled. Shaw liked it when she smiled, but he knew it wouldn't last long. He had to ask.

"Tell me about your mother."

Instantly Daisy's smiled faded.

He knows, she thought.

At first Shaw thought tears would well up. But she was strong, and she fought them back.

"I'm sorry," she stammered. "I didn't mean to lie." There was pain in her eyes. Pain and a little fear. "She died not long after my father. She couldn't cope with the loss."

"Daisy, please understand I'm not judging you, and you haven't lied to me."

"But she's dead. She's not here. There's no sick woman upstairs. It was a ruse, a lie."

Daisy had been running the ranch practically by herself since her father had died. Her mother went into deep depression and died soon after.

She explained to Shaw that she lied only to the ranch hands she employed. She needed the help, but didn't want them to know it was just her, all alone. She lied for her own safety.

"Who else knows about this?" Shaw asked. "What about Callie? Does she know?"

"My mother died soon after my father. The land passed from him to her, then to me, so it's all mine. But it was only the strangers, the drifters who were looking for temporary work, who I told a different story. It was Callie's idea. At first she helped me out as much as she could on her days off, but she has her own life to lead. So she came up with a plan to keep an eye out at the diner and around town for people who were just passing through looking for work. It was our secret. She said it was a sensible thing to do. At first I thought it was just being dishonest, saying it was me and my mother on the ranch, but I had no choice. I needed help, but I didn't want strangers to think I was all alone. It was dangerous, but I was desperate."

Shaw felt awful, sick in the gut. He felt sorry for Daisy. He couldn't imagine what she must have gone through over the last few years.

Shaw put his hand on hers and looked into her eyes. "You're not alone. We'll get through this. I promise."

Daisy reached across and wrapped her arms around Shaw. He felt a few hot tears on his neck, no words. None were needed.

Daisy pulled back and laughed, wiping her eyes with a napkin. "Sometimes Callie would pretend to be my sister, she lived here for a time and I enjoyed the company," her voice trailed off, remembering sadder, lonely days of recent.

Then she brightened up, like a huge weight had been lifted from her chest. She pulled out her cell phone. "I tried texting her again this morning, but she hasn't replied."

Shaw sat back, poured another cup of coffee and said nothing for a moment, just looking at Daisy. She was a strong, determined woman, but he didn't know how much longer she could live a life like this. No matter how independent and strong-willed a person was, loneliness was a hidden disease that crept up on you slowly, and would eat away at your mind, your confidence, your personality.

"What do we do now?" Daisy asked, putting the cell away.

"I need to know what your father had been doing in those months leading up to his death, what was he working on, what was occupying his mind."

Daisy nodded reluctantly. She knew what she needed to do.

Shaw continued, "You said he was spending a lot of time up on the ridge and beyond, camping out, staying overnight. Do you know where he went while he was away? What he was doing?"

Daisy thought for a moment. "I have no idea. He never told me or my mother. He did become very reclusive. He didn't neglect the ranch, but at night he would spend hours in his study—doing what? I don't know."

"Daisy, I need to look in his study. The answers we are looking for could be in there."

It wasn't something Daisy wanted to do, but she understood that if they were going to get answers then she needed to swallow her feelings. She hadn't ventured into her father's study since he'd died. She and her mother had left it exactly as it was, like a shrine, something untouched, memories they wanted to preserve and not disturb.

She nodded.

"But first I need to ask you a question. How good a shot are you with that Winchester of yours?"

"I'm very good," Daisy smiled, all signs of sadness gone.

"Good enough to hit a flying object, the size of a manhole cover, maybe at about a hundred yards away and moving at speed?"

Daisy knew where Shaw was going. She could think of nothing better than to shoot down the thing that had been spying on her.

"Hell no. I couldn't hit that with my Winchester."

Shaw felt his hopes sink.

Daisy grinned mischievously. "I've got something much better to take down that bastard thing."

TWENTY-SEVEN

It was beautiful. There was no other way to describe it. A motif of ducks and pheasants engraved on the silver side plates, polished walnut stock, under and over barrels, perfectly balanced. Shaw rotated the hunting shotgun in his hand, the cold lethal gleam of metal under the lights of the basement.

"It was my father's." Daisy stood beside him, the doors of the gun cabinet open. "He used to shoot ring-necked pheasant during the season. Plenty of them around."

Shaw wasn't a hunter. Many people were, but he couldn't imagine shooting something feathered or furry that had no chance in fighting back. High-powered rifle, telescopic scope, and lead projectiles traveling a high velocity versus teeth and claws, hundreds of yards away just foraging for food to survive, it hardly seemed sporting.

But a threat carrying a gun or knife, or wearing a suicide vest strapped to their body, walking into a crowded bar, sports stadium or shopping mall wanting to harm innocent people, then that was another situation altogether. He could easily shoot someone like that. And he had. Dead.

The gun cabinet was dark wood with heavy hinges and double locked. Rows of other rifles, some hunting, others more suited for home defence, were all secured upright, snug in mounts. Below these were cardboard boxes of ammunition, all different sizes and grains printed on the sides. A large stars and stripes hung from a rafter, dull and dusty with age, but timeless in what it represented. Shaw recalled that a similar one hung in the barn. More remnants of Stan McAlister. More reasons to like the man if they had met. His style, his values, his patriotism, all the things that were being eroded in modern America.

"You can hit it with this?" Shaw asked, as he handed the shotgun back to Daisy. She broke the breach of the gun and hung it casually over her shoulder. She selected two boxes of ammunition then closed the cabinet and locked the heavy doors, slipping the key back into her pocket. "If it gets within range, yes, I'll hit it. I've been shooting pheasant since I was a kid. My father taught me to ride and shoot before I was in fourth grade. He said they were two skills more important than algebra. Don't you think?"

Shaw didn't, but he just nodded. High school math wasn't about numbers and symbols. It was about problem solving, a life skill few people could master, and life was just a series of problems to be solved, from cradle to the grave.

"Keep it loaded and close by. Don't walk around with it, but make sure it's within reach."

The first step was to take out the drone. Until then, every move, idea, and strategy Shaw had would be telegraphed well in advance. He didn't expect the drone to be too active during daylight hours, maybe at dawn or at dusk. And it had night-vision capability. It must have, because it had followed him right across the hills to the Morgan compound in the dark, relaying his position in real-time. He had no idea it was there until it swooped in just before they captured and shot him. Like the pheasants Daisy and her father hunted, Shaw had been a sitting duck. Hunted by an almost invisible hunter. But he knew that every hunter was visible to one degree or another, you just had to know what to look for. Open sky was very different to the thick bracken pheasant typically hid in. The drone would stand out against a clear backdrop. At a distance it may register as a bird, a dot in the sky. From the dimensions of the propeller, this wasn't a micro-drone disguised as a grasshopper or dragonfly. Up close it would look like a giant flying spider, eight arms with eight propellers. But it wouldn't be like shooting pheasant or any other winged creature. This thing could turn on a dime, stop instantly in mid-air and change direction. It would be a more challenging target to hit. It defied the laws of gravity and aerodynamics. Birds flew in straight lines, arcs and curves. A drone could accelerate vertically, climb very fast then cut away at extreme angles.

"How do you hunt a difficult predator that is hidden, sneaky and cunning?" Daisy asked.

"Like everything else, surprising it is going to be the trick." Shaw replied, with a sly grin. "I have a plan. But first you have to shoot me."

****

They spent the rest of the morning working around the ranch, but not straying too far from the homestead. Business as usual, but keeping two sets of eyes attuned to the sky. Looking without looking. Shaw had shown Daisy how to do this and she was a natural.

They separated. Shaw went to the barn, loaded up with tools and continued to mend some of the fences. After that he moved to the house and did a complete circuit, checking door locks, window latches as he went, replacing, tightening, reinforcing. He wanted to make sure the place was secure, but it would never be to his standards, so he did the best he could. He did the same with the sheds and other outbuildings. The horse stables were too open, but weren't important.

Daisy hooked up a trailer to the ATV, filled it with cattle feed and did the rounds of the paddocks, dropping loads as she went. It was good to get her hands dirty again. There had been too many distractions lately and she had neglected her work. But it was good to spend a day away from the place with Ben up on the ridge, even if it brought back bad memories. And she had returned with a new sense of determination. She felt a sense of satisfaction and pride as she drove around the paddocks. Even though her cattle numbers were low, she was still very protective of what remained. As a precaution she shifted all the cattle to the closest paddocks so they would be easier to manage. In the past, all the paddocks would have been brimming with cattle and for the first time as she drove, she realized just how bare and desolate the place had become. It had lost that feel of a working ranch.

She pulled up at the next paddock. Ears turned and big dark eyes regarded her. The cattle recognized her and slowly made their way over. As they milled around her she shoveled piles of pellets. She felt safe, grounded, connected to the land. It was in her blood. But now she felt violated by something evil. She had secured the shotgun to the rear cargo rack on the ATV, covered it with a rug, and tied it down with rope.

She went from paddock to paddock, keeping her eye trained on the blue expanse of sky. But it was empty. Shaw didn't want her to stray too far from the house. He told her to stay in sight of the barn at all times.

Lunch was an outdoor affair. Some leftover roast beef and tossed greens, eaten under the shade of a cottonwood, a plaid picnic rug laid out, covering the shotgun underneath.

Hide in plain sight.

"Do you know someone called Annie?" Shaw asked.

Daisy made a face, thinking for a moment. "No, not that I can recall. Why?"

"Just something that I found," Shaw replied, wiping his hands on a napkin. He looked past Daisy to the hills in the distance, imagining the Morgan compound further still. He wondered what the old tin shed looked like in the daytime, and what else he could have found in there, if he had enough time to search it. "Callie mentioned some girl that had gone to the police about Billy Morgan, claimed that he had raped her. Was her name Annie?"

"You mean Jed, not Billy," Daisy corrected him. "There was a girl called Stacy, I think, she was a local but she didn't go to high school here, not like Callie and me. I can't recall much about the case. I only go into town when I have to, I rely on Callie keeping me up-to-date on any news or gossip."

"So this girl Stacy, according to Callie, went to the police and then it went to court, but on the day she was a no-show?"

"Callie went along as did most of the town. It became a bit of a circus. But the girl never appeared and I believe the judge had no choice but to dismiss the charges against Jed. It was in the local paper. Maybe Callie knows someone called *Annie*." Daisy slid out her cell again. "She hasn't replied to my text from last night, but I'll ask her." Shaw watched her thumbs rapidly move across the screen. "Done."

Shaw laughed.

"What?" Daisy replied.

"You may be a country girl, but you sure know how to use these gadgets," he replied, looking at the cell phone. It wasn't one of those big fancy ones that most people had glued to their hand, like their world would collapse if they let go of it for just a second.

Then Shaw had a thought.

"What's wrong?" Daisy said, the smile gone from Shaw's face, replaced with a serious look.

"Nothing," he said.

They ate and talked some more, and by mid-afternoon when the work was done, they returned to the house. Shaw wanted answers that Daisy couldn't give, but he knew where the answers could be found. He wanted to go into her father's study.

If anyone knew the answers, it was going to be a dead man.

TWENTY-EIGHT

The room was musty and smelled of old paper, dead insects, and raw leather. The afternoon light bled through the windows in a dull yellow, the shades pulled down. Daisy drew them back up, sending a cloud of dust and dead moth fragments billowing into the room. Light poured in through the sash windows, the sunlight thick with particles.

"Sorry," Daisy apologized, sweeping her hand back and forth at the haze, wrinkling her nose. "I should have come in here earlier and tidied up, but I really wasn't up to it."

Shaw just nodded. He stood in the doorway, a respectful distance, giving Daisy her space. She had taken a large brass key and opened the heavy door with the reverence of entering a vault or crypt.

It was a decent sized room, with two large sash windows that were blurred with dust and grime, and looked like they hadn't been cleaned in years. They gave easily as Daisy unlatched them and slid the frames upward, letting in much-needed fresh air.

The study was dominated by a huge old leather-topped desk, solid dark wood, thick turned legs, and ornate edging.

Shaw expected to find clutter and chaos in the room. Most men were hopeless with paperwork but kept immaculate sheds. But what greeted him as he stood in the doorway was the reflection of a man who was fastidious, organized, and meticulous, a man who demanded order in his life and was not given over to chance or speculation. Shaw was pleased with what he saw, it meant the task of finding answers would maybe be a little easier.

Two large bookcases of dark wood hugged the far wall and were filled with bound books, paper scrolls tied with ribbon, and numerous box files lined up in neat rows. An old filing cabinet, dented and rusted with age, sat in the corner. It was the same familiar shade of dove-gray that Shaw had seen many times in government offices.

The floor was polished lumber and covered with a rug that was worn and tattered at the edges. Two leather chairs sat across on the opposite side of the desk. There was a framed map of Kansas on one wall. On another wall hung a framed flag, folded thirteen times into a triangle, leaving only the blue field with stars.

Shaw didn't ask.

Behind the desk stood a button-studded leather chair that tilted slightly to one side, the leather dull and cracked from many years of faithful support. He walked into the room and went to the desk. The desk was relatively bare. Just a stack of old manila files, a pen stand with three vintage-looking fountain pens, a bronze tray with various bottles of ink, letter opener, some old tarnished picture frames displaying photos of happier times, a heavy-looking chunky telephone with a twisted cable and a large blotting pad, the paper insert yellow with age, covered in a myriad of doodles, numbers, words, lines and arrows, and cubes in various colors of ink and script. The idle thoughts of a man pouring his troubles onto paper.

There was a stack of dog-eared crinkled paper that looked like bills and old letters, and a map had been partially unrolled and pinned down by what looked like old machinery gears, the corners of which had scrolled inward toward the weights. There were more scrolls rolled up and piled on a low shelf next to the desk. Shaw could tell some of these were maps of some sort.

"What do you want to look at?" Daisy asked, coming around to where Shaw was standing looking down at the desk.

"Is it alright if I take a look?" he asked, indicating the desk. He didn't want to offend her. He wanted to search the room in full, but he knew that wasn't going to happen yet. This was her father's domain, his sanctuary, and probably the last place left that reminded her of him. The barn was a functional building full of tools and parts. However this room was a more personal space, where a man retreated at the end of the day to find solace and to think.

Daisy just nodded.

"Are you sure?" He felt like a grave-robber desecrating a site, but he needed answers.

"No, it's fine. I've been avoiding it for too long." She smiled at Shaw, thankful he was there. It would have been too much coming into her father's study alone. Too many fond memories of a man taken away from her before his time.

Shaw preferred to stand as he explored the desk. It had a single drawer on each side and he found only the typical things one would expect: pens, paper, envelopes, and a sea of loose stationery.

Shaw spread the map out further. It was a detailed survey map of the entire McAlister property, lots of lines, distances, contour markings and elevation measurements, none of which meant anything to him. There were no handwritten notes or marks on it, no clues as to why Daisy's father was looking at this particular map.

"This is our property here," Daisy leaned over and placed her finger on the map, then she traced a line up to the ridge, the contours on the map narrowing as the elevation increased. She pointed out the place where they had ridden. "This is where we were yesterday," she said.

Shaw tried to create a mental picture of where he had stood on the edge of the ravine, relative to where her finger was on the map, but it was just a bunch of lines, squiggles and shapes that represented hills, mountains and the change in inclination of the terrain. There were some dotted lines that indicated trails and roads. Give him a street map of any city and he could navigate it to any location, check building elevations for sniper positions and determine the quickest escape route to the nearest hospital. But this was like looking at the surface of Mars.

Shaw looked at Daisy. "Where would the trail around the side of the ravine go to? If I had continued along the narrow path around to the other side, where would I have come out?"

Daisy bent forward more. The front of her cotton shirt was unbuttoned, he could see the hanging curve of her breasts under the thin fabric as they swayed, the dark buds of her nipples rubbing against the inside of the shirt.

She caught him staring out of the corner of her eye. "Keep your eyes on the map, Mr. Shaw," she said without looking up.

He smiled, "I've taught you well."

"Sometimes you forget yourself, how to look without looking." Her finger followed another line on the map. "Here, I imagine this is where you would have ended up, if you had followed the path." She slid her finger farther along the map. "You would descend on the other side, see how the elevation numbers start to decrease. I think this is where the old cattle trail ends too. Maybe it joins up with that, where the old cattle yards are. As I said, there's nothing there, just some old sheds and outhouses."

He leaned his forearms on the map, trying to make sense of what he saw and what Daisy had told him. Why was her father up on an edge of the ravine, on the path where no horse could possibly go? No cattle could have strayed up there, so why was he there? What was his sudden interest in the place, and why was he camping out up there so often before his accident? Was it an accident at all?

Shaw traced the path with his own finger on the map as Daisy had done. The paper was smooth under his touch. He continued past the line and followed it to where she had pointed to. "Can you get to the same spot, if you followed the trail that runs by the barn?"

Daisy nodded. "Yes you can, but I haven't been through there in years, well before my father died. There's nothing there."

But there *was* something there. There had to be. Her father seemed to be a man who didn't do things on a whim. His life was one of careful thought, deliberate action and planning. He hadn't written any annotations on the map. He didn't want anyone else to know what he was doing up there.

He kept that information tucked away safely in his head and unfortunately he had taken it to his grave.

He was playing a game of chess, always thinking a few moves ahead. But was he playing chess against a far cleverer and more dangerous opponent?

Or maybe Shaw was reading too much into the situation. Maybe he wanted to see more than what was really there. Maybe Daisy's father went up there to be alone and think. Maybe Jim Morgan does just want the McAlister land to expand his cattle property. Maybe Daisy's father just stumbled and fell off the edge of the ravine.

Shaw had spent most of his young career linking a series of unexplained coincidences just like these ones, looking for patterns—links that would take a jumble of seemingly unrelated events and reshape them into a well-organized, intricate plan. When he had been correct in the past, he had saved lives and neutralized a threat. When he had been wrong, he had still been praised and encouraged for such foresight and intuition.

Shaw lined up the coincidences in his head: Military trained guards, night-vision cameras, aerial surveillance, high-security perimeter fencing, a skilled horseman, a family feud going back centuries, and Jim Morgan.

These weren't a series of random facts.

His intuition was telling him there was something premeditated and disturbing here.

The afternoon sun was fading, and shadows were growing from the corners in the study.

Shaw rubbed his eyes, sore from looking at the map too long.

It was time.

"Are you ready?" Shaw asked.

Daisy nodded. "Do you think the time is right?"

Shaw had no idea, he was just guessing based on what he would do. Most clandestine activities usually happened after dark, but he hoped the drone would come at dusk, while there was still enough light. "Let's see," Shaw replied. By his judgment they had about an hour of natural light left and he wanted to see if his theory was correct.

TWENTY-NINE

It took to the air fast, rising vertically from its position then climbing quickly to five hundred feet in a matter of seconds. Within two miles it dropped below the line of the surrounding hills as it tracked inbound, the rugged backdrop helping mask its approach. Then it crossed the property boundary and entered the McAlister land from behind the ridge, using it as cover, dropping further until it skimmed the forest canopy, hugging the tree line so its shape would be lost amongst the cottonwoods. When it reached the edge of the forest, it held back, hovering under some branches, using the structure of the barn as a reference point while it surveyed the terrain with its high-definition camera.

The camera zoomed in and did a slow pan of the area.

The operator of the drone sat in a small room, four miles away, with three wide-screen monitors in front of her that displayed a wide-angle panoramic view of what the drone's camera was seeing—all in crystal-clear high-definition. She had two drones at her disposal and her employer hadn't skimped on the price tag of each one after she had made her recommendation. The daytime drone that she was currently operating had been used before on previous commercial and surveillance assignments. While the commercial application of her skills was relatively mundane, she had found a lucrative market for them after returning from Afghanistan. She'd used the night drone equipped with a high-res night-vision camera to track her target last night. She was pleased with that flight and it was more interesting. The man she followed had no idea she was there, almost looking over his shoulder as he crossed the hills.

She toggled the joystick expertly with one finger, adjusting the drone's pitch slightly, her eyes never leaving the bank of monitors. The image on the three screens moved horizontally to the left in one motion as she pushed the other joystick. It was like her own head was turning looking to her left, but it was the camera on the belly of the drone that swiveled under the slight pressure from the finger of her left hand.

A few weeks back, just for fun, she had flown down the center of the horse stables just to scare the horses. She hated horses. She had watched from the cover of the trees as the blonde girl had gone into the barn, gotten into the pickup truck and had driven into town. Her employer had friends in town who had kept an eye out for the girl and reported her every movement. She used the time to do a complete reconnaissance of the ranch and all its buildings. She'd even flown up to the house and peered in every window, but they were closed with the blinds and curtains drawn shut.

The drone had thrown a propeller that day, and she was angry with that. Like Afghanistan, she didn't like leaving any trace, not until it was too late for the target and she then obliterated them off the face of the earth.

She pushed the drone forward, slowly at first, bringing it out from under the cover of the trees and toward the back wall of the barn, altering the angle of her approach, placing the barn between her and a direct line of sight to the bunkhouse structure. Sneaking up behind the barn was a tactic she had used plenty of times before when she was watching the blonde girl. She stayed well clear of the stables in case the drone spooked the horses.

Something moved to her left and she stopped the drone.

It wasn't that anything actually moved. Something altered in the distance, a gray shape past the edge of the barn, beyond the bunkhouse, but before the main house. It was hard for her to judge the depth of field from the video screen.

She saw it again, like a ghost moving, a wisp of something, then the breeze took it and it evaporated.

She knew the risk, but didn't care. There was something odd. She applied a tiny amount of pressure to the pitch and rotated the direction. The drone moved diagonally, toward and out slightly from behind the edge of the barn, into the open, exposed, twenty feet off the ground.

"What the hell?" she whispered, her eyes glued to the screens.

Something lay on the ground, to the left of the bunkhouse, on the road beyond the barn.

Smoke rose into the air.

An object? Something on fire?

Ignoring all protocols she pushed forward, creeping closer toward the object, the drone now completely out in the open and low.

A body. A man, lying on the ground, an ATV toppled on its side beside the body, smoke spiraling into the air from the vehicle.

She moved the drone closer still. The man lying on the ground occupied her left screen.

He looked dead. She zoomed the camera and panned it, the drone at twenty feet.

The front of his shirt was soaked in blood, dark red patches on his chest.

"Who the fuck shot him?" she muttered.

If only the drone operator hadn't panned the camera too far to the left, she would have still had the bunkhouse in the frame, on her right screen. She would have seen the woman come out from behind the side of the bunkhouse, the hidden side. The blonde woman who was crouching down.

She would have then seen the shotgun aimed at the drone, *at her*.

If only she hadn't been so distracted by the man's body.

"Motherfucker!" Daisy pulled the trigger, the shotgun boomed.

The drone was a sitting duck.

The shot tore off two of the drone's arms and it pitched wildly to one side. Daisy leveled the shotgun again, following the drone's erratic movements as it struggled to stay aloft. It careened toward her and she pulled the trigger again.

Four miles away in the small room, the world had tipped on its side and the three screens showed nothing but the dirt ground.

"Damn it!" the operator screamed, hitting the console with both her fists.

The screen suddenly changed. Jumpy at first as someone tilted the camera on the broken belly of the fallen drone.

A face appeared, filling all three screens at once, and the operator jumped back in fright.

It was the man, the one from last night. The one who had been lying on the ground dead with the blood-soaked shirt. He was bending down, on his knees, looking at what remained of the drone, his face huge across all three screens.

As the operator watched he smiled at the camera, *at her*. Then his face pulled back and was gone. The sole of a boot grew across all three screens, massive, its tread filling the view, crushing down on the camera lens.

The screens fizzed with static and went dark.

Shaw lifted his heel off the camera. It was smashed to pieces.

"Is it dead?" Daisy walked over. She had reloaded the shotgun.

"Yes, it's dead," he smiled, turning to her. "Nice shooting."

"Nice work playing a dead man," she returned the compliment. Daisy stood triumphantly over the remnants of the drone, its body shattered, arms scattered everywhere.

She leveled the shotgun at the drone and pulled the trigger again, obliterating what remained and blowing a small crater in the ground.

"Beers are on me," she said.

THIRTY

The next day they had made the study the 'nerve center', as Shaw termed it. After Daisy had done her rounds of the paddocks, checking on the cattle, she cleaned her father's study, attacking the dust and grime with vigor.

Shaw cleaned up the debris left by the drone, boxed it up and placed it in the barn. When he returned to the study he almost couldn't recognize it as the gloomy, dusty room he was in the day before. Daisy had removed, washed and replaced the fabric blinds, dusted, wiped down and vacuumed every surface, opened the windows and had cleaned them inside and out. There was even a vase of bright sunflowers sitting on the desk. The room was now bright, airy and ready for work.

They sat at the desk, Daisy in her father's old chair, Shaw sitting opposite her, the map spread in front of them, the shotgun propped up in the corner. Shaw didn't know if they would send another drone now that they had been discovered, but Daisy wasn't taking any chances. She had grown accustomed to having it close by. She much preferred shooting at drones than pheasant.

They had already spent an hour unfurling the other maps that were on the low shelf, but they proved to be more of the same. No notes, no directions or clues.

"So what now?" Daisy asked.

Looking at all the contour lines on the map was giving Shaw a headache. He sat back rubbing his eyes. "We need to go up there again, but not to the ravine, the other side, follow the road to where you said the old mine site is."

"But why would my father take the longer route, up along the edge of the ravine, on foot. Why leave his horse behind?"

"I don't know. Can you see that part of your land from the Morgan property? Maybe he didn't want anyone seeing him, so he always went along the ravine."

"The road travels along the boundary between our two properties, but then it cuts inland and disappears into the trees and comes out on the other side of the forest. It's secluded and you can't see it from the Morgan side."

"So let's take a look," Shaw said.

"But first I want to drop by the diner and check in on Callie."

"Why?" Shaw asked impatiently.

"I haven't heard back from her, I just want to make sure she's alright."

Daisy locked the house up tight and Shaw checked that the other buildings were secure. They met at the barn, Shaw slipped into the passenger seat and Daisy drove.

The tires hissed over the blacktop and Daisy kept the Dodge coasting at an even forty five miles per hour. The shotgun sat behind her head secured in a rear-window gun rack and the Glock was under her seat. She brought along permits for both just in case they were pulled over for a traffic stop, even though Kansas was one of the few states that allowed open carry without a permit.

They arrived at the gas station and pulled into the parking lot next to the diner. It was mid-morning, much of the breakfast crowd had gone. So much had happened that Shaw couldn't believe he was just here a few days ago minding his own business, waiting for the bus to get fixed so he could move on to Denver.

They went inside, but were told by another waitress that Callie hadn't come in again today. She had texted that she was sick, she had missed two shifts already.

"Do you know where she lives?" Shaw asked. They sat in the Dodge drinking coffee in takeout paper cups.

"I do. She lives by herself in a one-bedroom place just off Main Street." Daisy slid out her phone and texted with one hand, drinking her coffee with the other. Shaw smiled and shook his head as he took a swig, the coffee was hot, rich, and freshly brewed.

"She still hasn't replied to my other text from yesterday, or again this morning." Daisy looked puzzled at her cell phone. "It's not like her, she never has her phone off or goes anywhere without it."

"Well, let's just drive by and check in on her," Shaw conceded.

They set off again and a short time later they pulled off Main Street and drove down a side street. Shaw had the window down, his arm resting on the sill, watching the streetscape. The houses were average-looking, small-sized on blocks with neat front yards, row after row of the same houses looking mass-produced in the fifties.

Daisy eased the Dodge to the curb outside a duplex and they both got out. The front yard was small, no flowerbeds or bushes, just a rectangle of patchy short grass with a plain concrete path down the middle. The duplex was almost all gray. Gray tiled roof, gray siding, gray trim, but with white-framed windows facing the street, and four concrete steps, poured rough, with white steel railings on either side leading up to a panel wooden front door behind a screen door. A dirt driveway ran down the right side of the duplex to a small detached open garage at the rear that looked like a smaller version of the duplex itself.

The street was quiet. No cars out front, just an old sedan parked on the opposite side. Shaw automatically ticked off a mental checklist in his head. Angles behind cover, lines of sight, street and house geometry, access and exit points. It was just a typical street with affordable housing in a small country town. Maybe four or five hundred bucks a month in rent—and most houses in the street looked like cheap rentals. No pets allowed.

They walked down the path and up the steps to the front door. The screen door sagged to one side. Loose pop rivets and hinges groaned from a lifetime of opening then slamming. There was no doorbell, Daisy knocked, the sound hollow on the cheap front door.

They waited a few moments, then she knocked again.

No answer.

Somewhere over a fence a dog barked.

"Do you have a key?" Shaw asked, looking back at the street, feeling like he was being watched. Maybe just nosy neighbors, but he saw no telltale signs, no sudden movement behind curtains or blinds, no heads ducking back behind fence palings.

"No, but she usually leaves a key out around the back."

She let the screen door slam and they made their way around the side of the duplex, following the driveway. The garage structure had no door and was empty. The back yard was fenced and had the same dry patchy grass as the front. Nothing ornamental, just a few ugly bushes styled for low maintenance that looked depressing.

There was a small paved area, dull and cracked, that led to the back door. Daisy moved to a cluster of dead plants in terracotta pots and removed a key from under one.

Shaw shook his head in disbelief, not expecting something so careless and so typical.

"Does anyone else know it's there?"

"No, just me and Callie."

Through the back door they found themselves in a small kitchen. Brown linoleum in a diamond pattern, gray laminate cupboards and benches, small steel sink, washer and dryer with hookups to one side. The place was clean and tidy, but all the curtains and blinds had been drawn. No prying eyes could look in.

They stood still, listening.

Nothing, just the sound of the refrigerator compressor rattling, a few more random barks from outside.

Shaw couldn't help himself. He opened the refrigerator. No reason, just habit, search and assess mentality. A person's fridge was a window into their personality. There was minimal food, but still fresh. Quality purchases, no junk food, small batches. No pretentious bottled water from some glacier in Iceland. The milk expired three days ago and he guessed that Callie ate most meals at the dinner, before, during, or after her shift.

They searched the rest of the duplex. It was small, one bedroom, one toilet, brown carpet, cream walls with brown wooden edging, cheap furniture, some nice feminine touches to make the best of a dull, gloomy existence. But they found nothing important. Shaw resisted the compelling urge to open every drawer and cupboard, and rifle through everything including personal possessions and clothing. He had to remind himself he was here as an uninvited guest by Daisy out of concern for her friend, not because the occupant was under suspicion of committing a federal offence.

There were no signs that anything malicious had happened. It had a lived-in look and feel, but was as though Callie had closed up and gone away for a few days.

Odd, but not overly odd enough to warrant calling the police.

They stood in the kitchen again.

"I don't know," Shaw said, looking at the worried look on Daisy's face. "How does she get to work?"

"She has a car, but it's not in the driveway. An old white hatchback. Maybe she's gone to the doctor in Hays."

Daisy pulled out her cell. This time she called Callie, but it went straight to voice mail.

They left, locking the back door behind them, and Daisy put the key under the same terracotta pot, and they walked back to the Dodge. Daisy got in, but Shaw turned and took one last look at the house half-expecting a face to appear in the window.

"Come on," he said, as he slipped into the passenger side. "I want to take a look at that abandoned mine site on your property."

Daisy kicked over the engine and they headed off.

THIRTY-ONE

A call was placed, the number untraceable. It was made from an encrypted cell phone that rerouted the call first through an exchange in the Netherlands, then on to a ghost-server in the basement of a non-descript building in Istanbul, before being recoded and rerouted to a phone that sat on a polished boardroom table forty-three floors up from the street in downtown Dallas, Texas in a sleek building of glass and polished steel.

"We don't have a problem," the caller insisted.

"Our research says otherwise. The file we sent you, did you read it in full?" the man from Dallas said.

The caller didn't like being patronized. He was usually the one giving the orders, setting the agenda, telling people what to do. "Yes, I read the file, it was only mildly interesting. I don't see the man as a threat. I have spoken to him."

There was a pause on the line and the caller could sense the man from Dallas was not happy with the response.

"Our investors are concerned. There's too much money at stake to take any risks, regardless of how minor a potential threat could be."

"Your men took care of it. He won't return and if he does, he'll end up like the rest." The caller didn't like the security contractors on his property, there was no need. It seemed like overkill.

"I don't care, we have sent someone to deal with him."

The caller was starting to grow impatient, the hint of incompetence in the voice of the man from Dallas obvious. "I said we can deal with it, and we have."

"We have sent someone to deal with it, we see otherwise."

We. The faceless men from Texas who sat sheltered and protected in their ivory towers, looking at numbers on a spreadsheet, sitting in fat leather chairs and wearing five-thousand-dollar suits. The caller had contempt for them, but he needed them. Since the discovery, the caller knew this was bigger than anything he could manage on his own.

"When will he arrive?"

"*She* is already there."

"She's a woman?" the caller asked in disbelief.

"A *she* tends to be a woman," the reply sarcastic.

"What do you mean *she is already here?*" The caller was getting annoyed. He didn't like plans being made without being consulted first. He wanted to remain in control, remain the person calling all the shots.

"She's been there on the ground for a while now. Just observing, reporting back to us. Like I said, we need to protect our investment. Our backers are getting nervous, they want to know why the delays? The land from the McAlister woman should have been secured by now. They don't like delays."

The caller's head was spinning with the new information. Was he being spied on?

"What will she do?" the caller asked.

Another pause on the line, then, "Whatever is necessary. Just keep your sons in check. We don't want any unnecessary attention because of their antics."

The caller turned cold. He didn't like what the man from Dallas was inferring. He knew his sons had their own way of dealing with things, he also knew of their other perversions, but he had turned a blind eye. It was better that way. The end justifies the means, as they say. He quickly changed the subject before he said something he was going to regret.

"Is she any good?" the caller asked, still unconvinced a woman was capable of anything except bleeding and childbirth. "Is she the best you have?" The caller didn't want some amateur involved in the operation. He trusted his sons, but he didn't trust the hired help the Dallas group had insisted on sending.

"No," the man from Dallas said. "She's not our best."

The caller was growing impatient. "Why? What happened to your best man? You said this was important, a lot at stake. Why didn't you send your best person?"

"He's dead."

"So who did you send?"

There was silence down the line for a moment.

Then he replied. "We sent you the person who killed him."

The line went dead, the call ended.

The man from Dallas sat back in his chair, stared at the phone, contemplating, his fingers drumming on the polished boardroom table. He picked up the handset again then dialed another number, to a satellite phone this time. Again the call was rerouted, bounced around the globe, encrypted then sent to the recipient.

The man from Dallas was the only person who had the number, and he would be the only caller she would get.

There was no hello, greetings or pleasantries. It was all business from the woman on the end of the line. "Yes?" The voice, calm, self-assured, in control.

"Where are they?" the man from Dallas asked.

"I'm watching them now. They've just visited a house in town. Spent about twelve minutes inside, before coming out and leaving. They're heading off somewhere else."

The man from Dallas thought for a moment, his previous call left him with some doubts—not about the woman, but about the caller.

He finally spoke. "There may be another assignment after this one. Nothing major, just a quick clean-up job."

"No problem. Just tell me who and by when," the woman replied.

"I'll email you the file. This time I want the bodies to be found. Make it public, make it messy, make them suffer."

If this had been a video call, the man from Dallas would have seen the smile on her face. She really didn't do *public,* or *messy*. She much preferred private and clean assignments, her targets removed with no trace. They just disappeared.

But she did do *suffering,* on all of her assignments, even when she was told specifically not to.

"No problem," she replied. "And the man? When can I complete that assignment?"

The man from Dallas considered this, making sure the strategy was still valid. There were a lot of moving parts to this, and he didn't need the man who had appeared on the scene just a few days ago altering the schedule. Further observations by the woman had revealed that the new arrival had the potential to ruin everything. But his removal had to be just right.

The man from Dallas spoke again. "Remove him tomorrow night. No traces. Make it look like he just up and left town. Zero residual."

"Done."

"Do not forget. Under no circumstances is the McAlister woman to be harmed." The man from Dallas knew he had to manage Daisy McAlister better than Jim Morgan had. She wouldn't respond to threats nor violence. If she was harmed or even killed then lawyers would get involved and the estate could be locked up in the courts for years. Then all it would take is some smart-ass lawyer to do a little digging and uncover the real truth. The man from Dallas couldn't take that risk.

"I understand. You do not have to keep reminding me," the woman said curtly.

The man from Dallas ended the call.

THIRTY-TWO

Forty minutes later they were standing in a large clearing under the shadow of the ridge towering above them, a wall of forest pressing in all around.

They had continued along the road past the barn for two miles before cutting away from the boundary fence and heading through the forest, the track barely wide enough for the Dodge, so they parked it and went the rest of the way on foot with Daisy carrying the shotgun.

The track opened up into the clearing. To the left was a tumble of dilapidated sheds, rusted and falling apart, holes in the walls, roofs collapsed inwards, the interiors dark.

What cattle yards were once here had long been overgrown and covered by the wild vegetation. It was a mournful, desolate place and despite the afternoon sun, in the shadows where they stood, the air was cold. It didn't take long for Shaw to locate the entrance of the mine as he walked around the clearing.

The mine hole was covered with several sheets of old roofing iron, and a thin layer of dirt, leaves and forest debris. Shaw carefully slid the sheets aside. Underneath was a square hole about four feet wide. He stood back and stared into the depths. A musty, putrid odor wafted up out of the hole, a smell like stagnant water.

The inside edges and walls of the pit had been reinforced with a framework of wooden planks on all four sides. There were rungs nailed to the framework on one side that dropped away into the dark. The whole structure looked unsecure and dangerous.

"You said it was flooded a while back?" Shaw said.

"I wouldn't be going down there to check," Daisy replied, staying a few steps farther back from the edge than Shaw. Looking around, he found a large enough fragment of shale and dropped it into the hole. It seemed like an eternity until the hollow splash echoed back up.

"There's nothing here, Ben, like I said." Daisy looked around at the forest. There was something about the place she didn't like and she felt a chill, her grip tightening on the shotgun.

Shaw kept looking into the pit, as if drawn to it. It seemed to swallow all light along with his thoughts.

It must be hundreds of feet deep judging from how long it had taken the rock to reach the bottom. Finally he broke his gaze and covered the pit back up with the sheets of iron.

He did a quick search of the clearing and found a small trail on the opposite side that wound back through the trees, before vanishing into the shadows of the forest.

"That's probably the trail leading up to the mountainside and ravine," Daisy said, following his eyes.

"So you think your father spent time here?" he asked. "Why?"

"I don't know," Daisy replied.

Shaw looked around again, frustrated.

There was nothing here.

He began to walk back when his foot twisted and he almost fell. He recovered and looked down. He brushed aside a layer of scrub with his boot. There was a perfect cylindrical hole underneath, nothing large, four inches in diameter.

Shaw knelt down and felt the rim.

The sides were smooth, the shale and earth cored out.

"What is it?" Daisy stood beside him.

"It's a drill hole. Someone's drilled into the ground, like taking a core sample." He looked around. Everywhere was covered with weeds and scrub.

He started at one end of the clearing and followed a grid pattern. Daisy started at the other end and they went back and forth working from the edge of the clearing towards the center. The pace was slow and they were careful, making sure they covered the entire area.

Thirty minutes later they had found eight similar holes.

"Someone has been looking for something," Shaw said.

"Looking for what?' Daisy replied. "It's just dry rock and scrub. There's nothing here."

"What about the pit mine? What was your grandfather mining for back then?"

Daisy shrugged. "I don't know. Silver, I think. But my father wasn't interested one bit in prospecting. He told me about this place and what my grandfather had done here all those years ago, but he wasn't about to start the mine again or go digging up the countryside. His focus was on the ranch and the cattle. He didn't have time for anything else."

"Well, someone has been interested enough to drill some test holes. They look as though they were done by a machine, something recent not old. The shafts are smooth, not done by hand or by something old-fashioned."

"Well, not by my father. He wasn't interested, like I said."

It was just another puzzle with no obvious answers. "Could someone have come onto your land without you knowing?" Shaw said.

"Impossible," she said defiantly. "I would know."

"Anyone could have come here and drilled the holes. You can't see this place from the road, it's completely hidden," Shaw replied.

"But they would need machinery, tools, would have made noise. It would take a while to do. I would have noticed that.

Certainly, if someone had driven a truck with a drill mounted on it, I would have seen them coming onto my land."

Maybe Daisy's father *had* drilled them—without anyone knowing.

More questions with no answers, and Shaw didn't like it when he didn't know the answers.

As they returned to the Dodge, his mind ticked over. He wanted to get back to the house and go over Daisy's father's study again, and he didn't care if he had to pull it apart piece by piece to find the answers.

****

Daisy came from the kitchen and stood in the doorway of the study with a yellow steel wrecking bar in her hands. "Will this do?"

"Perfect," Shaw said, taking it from her. He had spent the last ten minutes trying to open the filing cabinet in the study. There was no key to be found anywhere. This made opening the cabinet even more important. Stan McAlister obviously had hidden the key and didn't want anyone else to know what was inside.

Shaw worked the beveled end of the wrecking bar into the gap near the top drawer, just under the lock, and looked at Daisy expectantly.

She nodded.

He levered the bar upward in one violent motion and the top drawer sprang out with a grating noise as the lock snapped.

The top drawer was filled with hanging files crammed in tight. Shaw ran his fingers across them, but they were mainly old bills paid and the typical paperwork for running the ranch; hardware accounts, delivery slips for fodder and cattle supplements, utility bills, equipment repairs, and cattle sales, and purchase folios. The paperwork was dated years ago, but all faithfully kept and filed away. Since taking over the ranch Daisy had set up a small office off the kitchen, in a tiny alcove where she had a table and chair, and a stack of files. She had never needed to go into the study to look for anything.

The next drawer revealed much of the same, just older invoices paid, the tops of the files yellowed and faded with age. A few silver fish and dust mites scuttled between the files as he ran his fingers over them, pulling out some to take a closer look.

As Shaw searched, Daisy went to the kitchen to make something to eat, the shotgun never far from her reach. She looked out the window near the kitchen sink as she worked, keeping a watchful eye up at the sky.

She came back to the study, carrying a large plate of sandwiches and a fresh pot of coffee, and placed them on the desk.

"Still haven't heard from Callie?" Shaw asked without turning. He was starting on the bottom drawer.

"Not a word. I don't know where she's gone."

"Has she ever gone away, maybe out of town or interstate before?" Shaw was rifling through the files. There were fewer here, not packed in as tight as the others.

"She has no other family here or close by. I think she has a cousin in Alaska. She mentioned her once." Daisy sat down and poured the coffee, making sure she had brought the cream for Shaw. She picked up a sandwich and started picking at it. They hadn't eaten since breakfast, but she had no appetite.

"What do we have here?" Shaw said, tilting his head so he could see toward the back of the cabinet drawer. He slid the hanging files toward the front and reached behind them. At the back of the drawer was a file, an inch thick, laying flat, almost hidden.

He pulled it out and stood up, rubbing his neck.

"Let me see," Daisy said.

Shaw placed the folder on the desk and opened it. "This is more like it."

The first page was an invoice from a company called Integrity Drilling LLC based in Kansas. It was addressed to Stan McAlister, three years ago, to drill several test holes. The next page was a similar invoice, but from a different company. The file contained various invoices, receipts, and documentation for soil analysis, scientific analysis of core samples, surveying, and a lot of rock and geological work that Shaw had no idea about. Just a lot of scientific jargon, numbers and explanations of work conducted by local and interstate companies and contractors.

Shaw turned to Daisy. "Do you know what all this was for?"

Daisy had a puzzled look as she picked up one of the invoices. "No idea," she said slowly. She picked up another. "Why would my father engage a geologist?"

"Maybe he was interested in prospecting after all? Maybe he wanted to open up that old mine pit of your grandfather's. You said there was silver there."

Daisy shook her head. "I said my grandfather used to prospect for silver, but my father had no interest. He said nothing at all."

Shaw could tell she was getting angry, like she had been betrayed. Her father had kept secrets from her.

Shaw pulled out an invoice and handed it to her. "Linton Geological," he said. "Let's give them a call and find out what they were doing here."

It was dated two weeks before her father died. It was for the preparation of a preliminary report and initial site assessment. It referred to a location reference that she didn't recognize, somewhere on the ranch, just a bunch of letters and a number. Linton Geological was based just out of Kansas City.

Sliding the phone on the desk toward Daisy, he said, "Call them. Tell then you're Stan McAlister's daughter and that you are cleaning up his old files, and you want to know if this invoice has been paid."

Her father's familiar scrawl across it with a date said it had been paid. More secrets. More things about her late father she didn't understand.

She picked up the phone and dialed. It was answered on the third ring.

"Hello, Astron Geological." A woman's voice, middle aged, prompt and efficient.

Daisy hesitated, then recovered. "Hello, my name is Daisy McAlister. I was after an Edward Linton please." She read the name off the invoice. Edward Linton's name was under the company name, in tiny script. He had a string of abbreviated post-nominal letters after his name that meant Linton was very qualified at what he did.

"I'm sorry, but Edward Linton no longer works here. He retired a few years back."

Daisy looked at Shaw as she spoke. "He did some work for my father, Stan McAlister, a few years ago. We have a ranch in Kansas, Ellis County. I just wanted to make sure we paid his invoice for the work."

"Yes, that would have been under Linton Geological. We bought his business back then. It's called Astron now. I'm sure it was paid, but let me check."

Daisy gave the woman the reference number and date. She could hear the woman on the other end tapping on a keyboard.

"We digitized all of the old invoices and documents," the woman explained as she typed away. "Here it is."

Daisy visualized the woman on the line staring at the digital equivalent of what she was holding in her hand, paper that was crinkled with age like old papyrus.

"It had been paid," the woman said. "There's nothing outstanding."

"Can you tell me what it was for?"

More keys clicked on the line. "I'm afraid I can't. The invoice just says for test drilling, sub-surface intrusion. Not much else." Then a pause. "Hold on, a report was commissioned as well, as part of that job number. But I don't have a copy of the final report. It was sent to your father some time ago. I just have a few file notes that were taken by Mr. Linton that were scanned and put into our system when we took over the business. The original files would have been archived and put in storage."

Daisy looked around the study. The report must be here, somewhere.

The receptionist on the line said, "Sorry I couldn't be much help. But if you get your father to contact us, I'm sure we can locate the original archived files. We can only release them to him."

"No, that's fine. Thanks for your help." Daisy hung up and explained everything to Shaw.

"So the report must be somewhere here." Shaw said.

"But where? We have turned this place completely over. There's nothing here." It was true. The filing cabinet Shaw had jimmied open was the only locked thing in the study. Every book, file, map, drawer they had pulled out and gone through. Shaw knew how to turn over a room, he had done it many times before. He had even pulled back the rug to see if there was a hidden compartment under the floorboards.

There was nothing. Short of ripping up the floor or taking a hammer to the walls, there was nowhere else to hide anything.

"Did your father have a safe-deposit box at the bank, or was there some other place on the farm he kept valuables?"

There was nothing else she could think of that would have been obvious. In the barn you could hide something small. The report could be just a few pages long. That could be easily folded and slid between boxes, or planks of lumber. There were some parts of the barn she had never gone near. There was no need.

"It would take us forever. We would have to completely search the entire ranch," she replied.

Shaw poured more coffee. He looked around the room trying to get more of a sense of Stan McAlister. He had already built up a profile of the man. Now Shaw added *secretive* to this and it made the puzzle worse.

Daisy's cell chirped. She looked at the screen and her face relaxed. "It's Callie. She says she's out of town for a while. Visiting friends. Not to worry, she'll be back in a few days." Daisy started to type a reply.

Shaw moved to the bookcases. They had already pulled out each book, looking behind them and fanning out the pages, looking for the filing cabinet key, but there was nothing there. It was pointless. He looked at his watch. It was close to 4:00 p.m.

"What now?" Daisy asked. "I need to finish up a few things with the cattle, feed and check on the horses before it gets too dark."

They agreed to split up. Daisy with shotgun in hand would finish her chores for the day, Shaw would check on the barn and see if he could find anything. They agreed to meet back at the house in an hour. Shaw warned Daisy again not to stray too far from his sight, he had no doubt she could look after herself, but there was something bigger at play that he couldn't quite figure out.

But he had a plan on how to get all the answers.

THIRTY-THREE

It was cold and the air smelled of wood smoke. The dying embers glowed a dull orange in the dark of the bunkhouse, and light flickered through the windows and across the sofa to where Shaw slept in his shirt and jeans.

It had been a restless sleep after he retired for the night following dinner with Daisy. His mind swirled with too many unanswered questions and dead ends.

Despite Daisy's request to stay with her up at the house, he preferred to go back to the bunkhouse. It spread their presence. It was just the two of them, and he didn't like the idea of being concentrated in one location. They would be any easy target. So he bid her good night, but not before she grabbed him and plunged a deep, lingering kiss on his lips, then said *thank you*.

For what, he wasn't sure.

He had done another round of the property, checking external doors and windows, before paying a visit to his friends in the stables with a few more carrots stolen when

Daisy wasn't looking. He was determined to bribe his way to acceptance from Jazz and Freddy. He then called it a night, but sleep eluded him.

After tossing and turning for nearly two hours, at 1:00 a.m. he rose, threw a blanket over himself, stoked the stove and sat and pondered the last few days, the fire and the lingering taste of Daisy keeping him warm. He eventually drifted off to sleep an hour later on the old battered sofa.

Dawn was still an hour away, but the orange glow intensified. Shaw was a light sleeper and he stirred slightly under the blanket. The orange flicker came again, this time more intense and a pungent smell rode the cold air from outside.

Then a scream pierced his sleep, not human, but still terrified.

Fear.

His mind locked into place and he woke instantly. No grogginess, no disorientation, just an immediate compulsion that something was wrong and he needed to move.

Shaw jumped up barefoot and wrenched open the door of the bunkhouse to a scene from hell, consuming his vision.

Another scream. More.

Across the yard, the horse stables were engulfed in flames.

Shaw hurdled over the porch rail, dropped to the ground and ran flat-out toward the burning stables.

Within a hundred feet, a wall of heat hit his face like a fist, hot and stinging, searing his skin and eyes. He raised his arm and looked around hopelessly for a hose, a bucket, anything.

The fire raged at the front of the stables and was eating its way along the structure, moving toward the back. Thick black smoke poured out windows that cracked in the intense heat, funnels of flame spiraled upwards into the night sky.

It was hopeless. There was no hose. The taps were at the rear of the stables in the mounting yard where the horses were washed and cleaned. Precious seconds would be lost, if he ran around the rear of the stables to reach the hose—the fire was building by the second. One hose with low pressure would be useless anyway.

Shaw spotted the water trough and ran toward it. Without stopping he rolled into the trough, completely submerging himself before jumping out, sheets of water cascading off him, his clothes drenched.

He sprinted toward the mouth of the stables, a boiling mass of heat and a million tongues of flame that curled and licked around the edges of the opening. The screams of dying horses filled his ears and a pure rage burned white hot in his head, hotter than any fire.

Save the horses his mind screamed before the fiery torrent engulfed him and he entered the furnace.

****

They buried the dead horses far from the smoldering stables so in the years to come the other horses, the survivors, couldn't smell what remained of their friends while grazing.

They used the backhoe to dig a pit, deep enough and wide enough, then the steel bucket of the backhoe to scoop up then tip the charred carcasses into the pit. They tumbled in, twisted, brittle and blackened, mouths contorted in wild fear, heinous and frozen in painful, sorrowful death.

Shaw felt a pang of sadness in his gut as he watched the macabre scene. But his sadness was a mere tremor compared to the earthquake of anger he felt splitting apart his head. Over the days he had come to understand them. They were beautiful, graceful and intelligent creatures.

The other horses, the ones that survived—Jazz among them—stood huddled, looking on nearby, unsettled, snorting, unsure of what they saw, wondering where their friends had gone, the charred smell filling their flared nostrils.

Freddy was dead, one of the unrecognizable blackened shapes that lay at the bottom of the pit. Three dead, three survived.

The curve of the sun rose, a ball of brilliant heat, fierce and uncontainable, a trillion destructive reactions. The fire truck had come from Hays, but it was too late by the time it arrived. They had lost all but three horses.

It was well after midday before they finished. Shaw sat on the steps of the porch of the bunkhouse. He felt hollow and empty, but as the smoke cleared so had his mind.

He had escaped the flames, but only just. He looked at the crumbled ribs and mound of ash that was once the stables, still smoldering. His hair, his clothes, and his skin stank of wood smoke, his face smudged with soot and charcoal, a film of grime and filth coating him. He could still feel the heat radiating off his body and face.

She had nearly died, and he had nearly died saving her. Daisy had awoken just after Shaw had and she ran straight into the burning stables to save her horses. Part of the roof would have collapsed on her if Shaw hadn't dragged her back kicking and screaming.

Daisy. Her name turned over and over in his head.

She sat on the tailgate of the ambulance while the paramedics tended to her. She had smoke inhalation, but no serious injuries. But some injuries you couldn't see. Shaw had sat with her as they strapped an oxygen mask over her nose and mouth, and she held his hand, squeezing it hard, refusing to let go, tears and raw anger in her eyes. With the mask on she couldn't speak. But no words were needed as she glared at Shaw.

What now? What are we going to do? This has gone too far.

Where he was undecided before, others by their actions had now made that decision for him.

Where he was hesitant before, happy just to let things go, to ignore, to keep walking, head down, eyes ahead, he would not hesitate now.

He knew exactly what he was going to do. He was committed. And the last time he was this committed, he had killed someone.

Taylor Giles stood beside his police cruiser, a notebook in his hand, talking to one of the firemen as the others packed up their hoses and gear into the back of the fire truck. Daisy had finished up with the paramedics. They wanted to take her to the ER, keep her overnight for observation, but she refused. She walked over to the bunkhouse and sat down beside Shaw on the steps.

She said nothing, but Shaw could feel her fury.

Finally the fire truck and the ambulance crew left, leaving only Daisy, Shaw, and Taylor Giles. He had yet to take a statement from them.

He walked over to where they were sitting. Daisy tensed, but Shaw placed a calming hand on her knee.

"Look, I'm real sorry about what happened," Giles said, nodding at Daisy. Shaw got to his feet, but Daisy remained seated, contempt in her eyes as she glared up at Giles, her face smudged with dirt and charcoal. Shaw understood, but there was a time and a place, and this was not the place to bring to the surface old feuds and past history.

"I appreciate you coming out," Shaw said, extending his hand to Taylor. Taylor's eyes narrowed as he looked at the hand, half-expecting Shaw to berate him as he had when they last met. Then he smiled, shaking Shaw's hand. "Just doing my job. Want to make sure no one was hurt."

"Three of my horses are dead!" Daisy snarled through gritted teeth.

Shaw stepped across Daisy so he stood between her and Giles. "Look, come up to the house. I'll put on some coffee and we can talk."

Giles thought about this. "Sounds good." He flipped shut his notebook and buttoned it away in his shirt pocket.

Daisy stared at Shaw in disbelief. She got up off the steps and brushed past Shaw in anger, ignoring Giles, and said, "I'm going to tend to my horses—the ones the Morgans didn't murder."

Giles stared after Daisy as she stormed off. He turned back to Shaw. "Like I said, I'm sorry about what happened."

"Come up to the house, we'll sort it out there. Daisy's hurt and upset about the horses, as you can imagine. Please don't take her words to heart. The Morgans are not to blame. She's just emotional."

Giles smiled. "Much appreciated, glad someone around here is being reasonable."

Shaw nodded and led the way.

Twenty minutes later, after Daisy had let the horses loose in a paddock for them to be free for a while, she walked back up to the house. She swung open the screen door, turned into the kitchen, and stopped.

A shattered cup was on the white tiled floor with a splatter of coffee. Taylor Giles lay next to the mess, face down, his body not moving.

Shaw stood over him and motioned at Daisy. "Grab his legs."

THIRTY-FOUR

Now was the time and the basement was the place. Shaw was going to show Taylor Giles how unreasonable he could be, if he didn't start telling the truth.

They stripped Giles down to his boxers and undershirt, and handcuffed him to a metal copper water pipe that was bracketed to the cinderblock wall. Shaw had tested the wall mounts holding the pipe and they would hold, no matter how much Giles struggled in pain.

His uniform was folded neatly on a chair a few feet away from him, and his duty belt and police radio was draped over the back of the chair. Shaw removed the handgun from its holster, stripped it apart and left it in pieces in a shoebox on the workbench. If by some miracle Giles managed to break free from his own handcuffs by chewing off his own hand, Shaw doubted he would know how to reassemble a completely broken-down Glock.

Shaw sent Daisy upstairs to get cleaned up while he watched the unconscious Giles, and then when he had gone to take a shower himself and change into a clean set of clothes, Daisy stood watch with her Winchester. They had locked all the doors and windows so the house was completely secure in case they had visitors.

Shaw returned and stood next to Daisy. He walked over to the slumped Giles and started kicking his leg.

"Come on, wake up. Wake up!" Shaw kicked him harder, then walked over to the shelves and picked up an empty paint can. He tipped out the pile of screws and washers inside it, went to the laundry sink, and filled up the can.

He threw the cold water in Giles' face and placed the can on the ground.

Giles spluttered, spitting water. His head lolled and his eyelids flashed open, his eyes slowly coming into focus. An ugly purple bruise had started to form on the corner of his mouth where Shaw had hooked him.

Giles looked confused, wondering why he was half-naked, sitting on a hard concrete floor, with both his hands handcuffed to a pipe above his head. He pulled hard, but the pipe didn't budge.

"What the hell do you think you're doing!" he yelled. "I'm a damn cop. You'll be thrown into jail for this."

Shaw glanced at Daisy.

She nodded.

Slowly Shaw pick up another chair, carried it to within just a few feet of Giles, swiveled it around and sat down on it backward so he could rest his arms on the back. It was his preferred sitting position for interrogations with a hostile subject, the most comfortable. He had once sat for six hours like this in a chair, questioning a man in the basement of a government building. Just Shaw, a chair, the man, four soundproof walls and a video camera in the corner. He didn't get up out of the chair once.

"Who said you were a cop?" Shaw asked.

Giles pulled at the handcuffs angrily. "Get these damn things off me!" he yelled again.

"Who set the stables on fire?" Shaw said, his voice low and calm, but his eyes drilled into Giles with a slow, unnerving determination.

"It wasn't me!"

"Then who was it?"

"I don't know. I'm a cop."

Shaw smiled. "You're no cop. You're a stooge for the Morgans. Billy Morgan whistles and you come running like the mutt you are."

Giles shifted his eyes from Shaw to Daisy.

"Oh, she knows about you. I've told her," Shaw replied. "Small town cop who wants to impress. New car. Jim Morgan's got you on the payroll."

"I don't know what you're talking about," Giles said defiantly.

"Sure you do," Shaw said. "Who set the stables on fire?" he said again. He could do this all day. Giles would eventually break, but he didn't have all day. Time was running out. Shaw needed to escalate things.

"Go fuck yourself!" Giles spat. "I'm a cop, you can't touch me."

"I might not." Shaw nodded over his shoulder at Daisy. "But she might. After all, you killed her horses."

"I killed nothing."

Shaw smiled. "Plenty of nice tools down here." It was an odd comment to make.

Giles looked past Shaw to the pin board above the workbench. Hacksaws, pliers, and hammers hung neatly on small hooks.

Shaw continued. "They say women are more vengeful than men, especially when it comes to the animals they own and love. They see them as part of the family, even treat them better than humans." Shaw let the words hang, keen to see the expression on Giles.

"You still can't touch me. There are laws against that."

"Laws?" Shaw leaned forward, balancing on two legs of the chair. "The same laws that Jim Morgan and his sons break every day while you turn a blind eye?"

Daisy stepped closer. "You killed my horses." She still held the Winchester low. She wasn't stupid.

"I don't care about your damn horses! Maybe you should have kept one of the dead ones. They looked well-cooked from what I saw. Make a change from all the beef you eat. Maybe they taste like chicken."

Daisy lunged at Giles, venom in her eyes, but Shaw caught her just in time and held her. He shook his head and pulled her aside.

Giles laughed. "Keep your bitch on a leash, tough-guy. Maybe all those years here alone have screwed with her head. She used to be a nice chick in high school, now she's just a nut-job, that's what they all say about her."

It took every ounce of effort for Daisy not to bring her rifle to her shoulder and put a round into Taylor Giles' head. Instead, she handed Shaw her rifle and went to the workbench. She came back with a roll of thick silver duct tape.

"Really?" Giles looked up at her. "Keep that on your bedside table in case your boyfriend here feels like a late-night—" Daisy bent down and smacked Giles hard across the mouth. She pulled a length of the duct tape, a harsh ripping sound.

Giles looked over at Shaw, blood trickling from his lips, his teeth stained red. "Hey man, did Billy tell you what he did to Daisy on the—"

Daisy slapped the tape across his mouth before Giles could finish the sentence, pressing it hard against his face, none too gentle. "Shut your mouth," she hissed. "You're just the same retard you were in high school. Just older and dumber."

"What now?" Daisy said, taking back her rifle from Shaw.

"He's not going anywhere," Shaw replied.

Giles looked at them, his eyes glowing hatred, muffled insults behind the tape.

Shaw looked around the basement then spotted something. He walked to the far corner, near the boiler, and picked up something heavy and brought it back.

As soon as Giles saw what Shaw was carrying the insults stopped, replaced with silence and abject horror in his eyes.

A cinder block is a concrete brick, eight inches by sixteen inches, used for retaining walls and building foundations. Despite it having two internal hollow sections, it was still twenty-eight pounds of hardened masonry concrete with a rough surface and sharp unbeveled edges and corners.

Shaw easily carried the cinder block in one hand. Giles started to squirm on the floor, pushing up until his back was hard against the wall, he had nowhere to go. He kicked his legs at Shaw as he approached, but it was futile.

Switching to two hands, Shaw lifted the concrete block to his chest and stood between Giles' legs. Shaw angled one corner of the block until it was directly over Giles' groin.

He raised it a little higher for effect.

"I failed physics in high school," Shaw smiled, adjusting the block in his hands as Giles wriggled. "But I know when I let go of this concrete block gravity is going to make a mess of your manhood."

Screams came from behind the duct tape, but Shaw ignored them. He looked Giles straight in the eye, his expression hard and ruthless. "I'm only going to ask you one more time before I let go of this."

Tears started to stream from the corners of Giles' eyes and it sounded like he was choking.

"Who set the stables on fire?" Shaw said.

Giles nodded, his head going up and down like he was convulsing.

"Do you want to talk?" Shaw asked.

Giles kept nodding.

Shaw lowered the block and placed it on the floor. He squatted in front of Giles and violently ripped off the tape.

"Billy Morgan!" he spluttered in a spray of tears, sweat and saliva. "It was Billy Morgan. But I had nothing to do with it, I swear."

Shaw nodded. Taylor Giles was broken. He was still a kid who was trying to act like a tough guy, another one of the Morgan minions who had been manipulated into doing the family bidding.

"What else are they planning?" Shaw asked.

"I don't know. Honestly I don't."

Shaw stood and picked up the concrete block again.

"No!" Giles screamed. "I don't know anything else."

Shaw lifted the block higher, holding it over the man's groin again. "It's not enough. Tell me more."

"Look, they are having a gathering tonight. I'm supposed to be there. That's all I know. Please," Giles begged. "That's all I know." Giles began to whimper like a child.

Shaw actually felt sorry for him. The kid was just a pawn in a bigger game. He laid down the block and squatted again in front of Giles, his face just inches from his. "What do you mean *gathering*?"

"Important people, people who help them. People from the town, county officials, some police officers, other business people and the like." Giles said, his words coming out in a sorrowful gush.

Shaw imagined the 'gathering' was some kind of community get-together of the Morgan faithful. Corrupt officials and supporters who had benefitted from Jim Morgan's dishonesty and bullying.

"Are you expected to go?" Shaw demanded.

Giles just nodded and sniveled.

Shaw tore a fresh strip of tape and plastered it across his mouth again.

"Come on," Shaw said to Daisy. He grabbed the police uniform off the chair together with the two-way radio. They left Giles in the basement and went back up the stairs. Daisy locked the basement door behind her.

THIRTY-FIVE

There were long shadows in the hallway, it would be dark in a few hours. They moved to the kitchen.

"What are you going to do?" Daisy asked.

Shaw placed the police uniform and two-way radio on the kitchen counter, then started to get undressed. "I'm going to wait until it's dark, then I'm going to pay the Morgans a visit." He put on the police shirt. It was a tight fit, Giles was smaller, but Shaw wasn't big or bulky. He managed to squeeze the buttons closed then he tucked the shirt into his jeans. There was no way the uniform pants would fit. Hopefully no one would see the ill-fitting shirt and wrong pants from a distance. He slipped the keys to the police cruiser into his own pocket.

"I want you to keep all the doors and windows locked. Go back into the basement and keep guard over him. You've got more than enough firepower and ammunition down there to defend against an army."

"I'm coming with you," Daisy said defiantly. She didn't want to be left behind. This was personal. She wanted Billy Morgan. She wanted him dead. Killing her horses was the final tipping-point. It had gone beyond being just some old family feud. It had escalated beyond anything she had expected.

Shaw shook his head. "No way. They will recognize you. At least I've got a disguise. You, they'll spot a mile away." Shaw didn't stand out, because he knew how to blend in, go unnoticed, melt into the periphery. But Daisy's face was burned on the minds of each Morgan brother. Even if she tried to disguise her appearance they would make her. These guys were sexual predators, she would attract more attention.

"I need you here to guard Giles. If he runs, he'll run straight to the Morgan compound. I can't risk that."

"But what if someone comes looking for him?"

"Then just tell them he left. Tell them he's gone to the Morgan ranch. That's where he said he was going. Plus if he doesn't turn-up, it will raise suspicion."

Shaw picked up the police radio. So far it hadn't made a sound. If a call came through from the police dispatcher he would have to somehow mask his voice and respond. The police cruiser would also have police GPS tracking. But they knew Giles had responded to the call at the McAlister ranch, so his location here was expected. Giles was also expected to be at the gathering at the Morgan's ranch, so that sat well with what Shaw was planning.

By the time Shaw left Daisy the sun had sunk below the horizon and the light was fading fast. He went down the front steps to the police cruiser. He released the trunk with the key and looked inside. Body armor, ammunition can, tool box, standard equipment you would find in the trunk of most police cars. He grabbed a police baseball cap and put it on.

Shaw shut the trunk and slid into the driver's seat. There was a shotgun upfront in a vertical rack between the front seats, a rugged-looking swivel mount laptop computer and a large side-mounted GPS screen. The cruiser would be tracked from the moment he turned the key. So he did, and the engine growled to life. He took one last look at the front of the house where Daisy stood on the porch, the glow of the lights behind her and her rifle in one hand. He nodded, did a tight turn and headed down the driveway and out onto the main road.

Shaw hunkered down over the wheel as traffic passed him by. He had the baseball cap pulled down low, the brim obscuring his face. He didn't want to draw any undue attention. Giles was well-known and spent most of his time patrolling Martha's End and the surrounding county. He was a familiar face to the locals and Shaw wasn't, but he was driving his patrol car.

****

The sky was a river of molten lead. It boiled and rolled with a threatening menace as Shaw drove. Lightning arced across the windshield, but the clouds hadn't unleashed their heaviness. Shaw had his window down, the wind in his face was cold and biting, thick with the earthy smell of approaching rain. The atmosphere prickled and hissed as the dark blanket of clouds descended around him.

It wasn't far to the Morgan property and he soon spotted the fortified entrance. He wound up the window and edged the cruiser to a stop slightly away from the security camera mounted next to the gates.

There was no intercom pad.

Good. No reason to face them.

The camera swiveled toward the cruiser and angled down.

He turned his head away, chin tucked low, like he was busy on the laptop, fingers moving, keys untouched. The camera was pointing directly at him. He could feel eyes on him, miles away, looking at his pixelated image on some screen. He leaned further back from the window, scratched the side of his face slightly longer than needed, making him less visible, obscuring the camera's view.

He rested his elbow on the inside of the window sill, drummed his fingers impatiently, and imagined a clipboard being pulled off a hook somewhere, a finger or pen nib running down a list of names, a car plate being matched. A tick made next to a name.

The gates clicked and slowly swung open. Shaw let out a huge sigh of relief.

Shaw waved at the camera, keeping his hand in front of his face as he passed. Hays County Police Officer Taylor Giles had been confirmed as a member of the Morgan community, a guest, a supporter, an ally in their treachery.

A gravel road stretched in front of Shaw only as far as the headlights could reach. The gates closed behind him and he felt a tightening of his gut. He was entering hostile territory, with the threat of being shot dead if he was discovered.

He hit the gas and the cruiser accelerated away from the gates with a throaty grumble and for the first time in a long time Shaw felt totally alone. No partner. No backup. No one to save his ass, if it all went wrong. It was a new sensation for him. But he needed to know. He wanted answers. He couldn't just move on like normal people could. He couldn't turn a blind eye like the others in Martha's End. The town was thick with injustice and he couldn't help himself. He needed to right the wrongs or do his best trying, even at the risk of his own safety.

The headlights bobbed and weaved across the barren landscape, the inside of the cruiser dark except for the glow from a multitude of display screens and instrumentation that resembled the intensive care unit of a hospital. He glanced every few seconds at the GPS screen and watched the green triangle shape of his car as it slid further along the digital line of the road, a sea of black on either side.

The screen showed nothing ahead. No other roads, intersections, structures. But he could feel something, an enormous mountain of menace in the distance ahead. The Morgan compound was there, somewhere in the abyss in front of him.

Shaw pressed the gas a little more, the tires crunched and the engine responded.

A minute later a glow rimmed the horizon ahead, and the outline of hills on either side.

Then the rain came.

No warning, no gradual patter of drops, just a violent and sudden deluge. Huge sheets of water, vertical and hard, fell on the roof of the cruiser that echoed with the beat of a thousand hammers on sheet metal.

Shaw flipped the wipers up to full, and the blades pushed deep rivers of water back and forth across the windshield, only providing milliseconds of visibility between sweeps.

He slowed the car to almost a crawl, fearful the car would be stuck in a quagmire of mud. But the wheels held their traction. The steering wheel bucked a few times as the car surged and bounced over fresh potholes. He gunned the engine some more, increasing his pace across the waterlogged landscape.

The glow on the horizon intensified and over a crest the Morgan compound appeared in a ring of blazing lights. Shaw continued downward, following the road toward the guardhouse and barrier gate.

The barrier gate had been raised. A lone figure wearing a rain poncho stood next to the entrance, assault rifle professionally held, angled downward.

The figure waved him through, and Shaw was thankful for the heavy rain that fogged the windshield, but driving a police car certainly helped.

Through the gate the road gave way to cement and he turned left into a large open parking lot. He passed rows of luxury sedans and high-end SUVs, and found a gap at the far side of the parking lot, a dark corner that suited him. He slid the cruiser between two massive pickup trucks that hid him from view. He flipped off the lights and waited a few minutes. The rain had eased and the engine hissed as it cooled.

No one approached him.

Taylor Giles knew what to do, where to go. But Shaw didn't. He had his own agenda for the evening.

He slipped out of the driver's seat, locked the car and headed toward the only place he wanted to see.

THIRTY-SIX

It only took Shaw a few moments to orientate himself relative to where he had come off the ridge previously and made it through the perimeter fence. He was just south of that location, but if he followed the fence line around to where they had caught him, he would have stood out as a stray guest, someone who wasn't supposed to be there. He didn't want to follow the main paths either. He was only wearing half a police uniform and that would have drawn attention. But he guessed correctly that there were no security cameras within the compound itself. They were on the perimeter looking outward, toward threats coming from outside. He was *inside* the fence.

He stayed away from the floodlight areas and off the paths, moving in the opposite direction from the sounds of people laughing and music playing. The ground he crossed was soggy and sunk under each step.

He wanted to locate the demountable building he had seen before, where the two men with hardhats had stood and talked. He skirted around a refueling bay with large sodium vapor lights and threaded his way between a maze of wooden pallets.

There were no workmen around, unlike the other evening. Shaw guessed they had all been sent home. They weren't part of the gathering community.

He paused at the end of a row of pallets that were stacked twenty feet high. In front of him in the distance, near the perimeter fence, he saw the shipping containers, wet and glistening, and the portable site office to one side.

Looking around, he saw no one. The site office was in darkness.

Shaw eased out from between the stack of pallets and walked casually toward the office. Better to act naturally.

Stairs and a railing led up to a small veranda. He tried the door and it was unlocked. Without pausing he slid inside and shut the door behind him.

Muted light filtered through thin venetian blinds. Shaw shut them tight and pulled out a flashlight, covered the lens with one hand and switched it on.

The office was small, two desks, filing cabinets against one wall, a large worktable in the center that was covered with sheets of paper and scrolls with rubber bands. He immediately moved to the table. It looked like a drafting table. Layers of geological maps were spread out covering the entire surface. Covering the maps was a scatter of measuring rulers, colored pens, calculators, small field notebooks and big legal pads. Shaw rifled through one. It contained pages and pages of hand written notes, figures, arrows, and calculations all in neat script that made no sense to him. He peeled back one map, the edges curled, and he looked beneath. More lines and curves. They weren't like normal maps. There were no streets, towns or common landmarks, just contour lines, numbers and odd symbols in tiny detail. These were different to the maps he and Daisy had examined in her father's study. These were like in reverse, below the surface, negative numbers, underground.

To one side on the table was a folder, no label, just plain. He opened it.

There were color charts inside and a two-page report stapled. He recognized the company logo at the top of the page. It was the same logo that he had partially seen the other night, when he watched the two men talking outside this building. The image on the side of the pickup wasn't an electricity tower as he had first thought. It was something else.

Shaw had got it wrong. Completely wrong.

Shaw looked over his shoulder at the door. It was unlocked. He quickly locked it. He bent the blinds near the door with his fingers, not too wide, just a slit to look through.

There was no activity outside. The surrounding building and sheds looked deserted. In the distance the Morgan house sat sprawling on the hill, all lights blazing, a beacon in the darkness. To one side was a broad halo of light, the clouds above illuminated on their underside. There was more movement and commotion there, but the main work area of the compound was deathly quiet.

Shaw went back to the report on the table and ran his eyes down it. It was written in layman's terms, obviously for whoever had commissioned the report. Succinct points and a conclusion. Clear and direct. There were a few numbers in a small table on the second page.

Large numbers. Huge. Beyond comprehension. He felt sick.

The numbers were worth killing for. People had killed for less. Countries had invaded others and gone to war for less.

Shaw returned to the maps. Now he knew what he was looking for and he quickly located the map he wanted. It was big, maybe three feet by two feet. The detail was astonishing. He pulled away all the maps on top of it and pushed the other equipment aside so he could see this one properly.

"Oh my god," he whispered. He took his hand off the flashlight and panned it across the surface. Almost all the map was shaded gray, like a lake.

Massive, an ocean. If the calculations in the report were right, it was gigantic.

Shaw folded the report and placed everything back on the table as best he could.

There was a steel locker against one wall with a simple latch. He opened it and shone the flashlight inside. On a hanger was a pair of utility pants, the type with multiple side pockets, and a jacket the same color, flat dark earth, a company uniform.

He quickly changed. The pants were loose, but he found a belt in the locker and a baseball cap with the same company logo as the jacket. He balled his jeans and the police shirt and threw them into the corner of the locker. He kept his boots. He shut the locker, slipped his flashlight into a side pocket along with the report. On the wall was a line of clipboards. He grabbed one and slid a few pens into the arm pocket of the jacket just for effect. Now he looked just like one of the contractors, in a uniform, clipboard and all.

He found a row of keys on a plastic key holder next to the door. They had little colored plastic tags labeled with car license plates. He selected one and looked at the manufacturer's logo on the key fob.

He smiled. "Nice."

Shaw pulled open the door. No need to scuttle about now. He was meant to be here, he looked the part. He walked down the steps, casual, like he belonged. He had a clipboard, the oldest trick in psychology. *I'm in charge. I'll ask the questions, not you. I've got a clipboard and you don't.*

Shaw walked with purpose. He was going to drive straight out of here all official, not skulk about like an intruder.

The path cut left. Shaw, clipboard under one arm, was almost tempted to whistle.

He found the cars parked neatly on an apron under a steel awning a few minutes later. He had seen them the previous evening. This part of the compound must have been allocated to the contractor company.

He pressed the key fob and orange side-lights blinked twice along the row.

"Perfect," he said.

He looked around one more time then stood on the side-step of the vehicle, opened the door and slid into the driver's seat of the Ford Super Duty truck. Two tons of polished chrome and steel.

The engine purred to life and the entire front console lit up like the cockpit of a jumbo jet.

"I might not return this," Shaw said, as he eased out of the parking lot, and drove toward the entrance gate of the compound.

THIRTY-SEVEN

Blood was in his mouth.

Some people describe the taste as coppery or metallic. But they are wrong. Blood tastes like blood, not like anything else, and if you lived in a violent world, you were all too familiar with that fact.

But right now, all that Shaw could taste was the bitterness of defeat. His head lolled to one side. He was sitting on a solitary chair, in a small room, concrete floor and concrete walls. His hands were tied behind the chair with thick black cable ties, so were his feet. Tight, really tight. They weren't taking any chances this time.

"Wake him up," a voice said, gruff and impatient. A shadow passed in front of his closed eyelids then a brutal slap across the face, stinging and teeth-jarring at the same time.

Shaw opened his eyes.

Under the harsh overhead lights Jim Morgan stood in front of him, clutching the report Shaw had taken from the office. Flanked on either side were Billy, Jed, and Rory Morgan, their expressions a mix of contempt and arrogant smugness.

"Did you really think you could just drive out of here with this?" Jim Morgan demanded, waving the report in his hand. Gone were the niceties, his controlled manner, the soothing rhetoric. It was all cold rage.

"Where's Taylor Giles? What have you done with him?" Billy Morgan stepped forward, a baton in his hand. Twelve inches of hardened rubber mallet like the kind used by riot police—or those dishing out torture.

Shaw turned his head and pain shot up his spine and neck.

He wondered how he got here, his memory just fragments of blinding light, gunshots, crunching metal and screams. Leaning against one wall was Cole, the head of security. An observer now, taking a front-row seat to the pain and suffering the Morgan brothers were about to unleash.

Shaw ignored Billy Morgan. He knew they were going to kill him.

Billy hit Shaw again, harder this time. The blow drew blood across his mouth. "I said, where is Giles? You've got his car, we found his shirt in the office you broke into," he snarled, spittle flying from his enraged mouth.

Shaw twisted his jaw. Nothing broken. "The door was unlocked. I didn't break in." Shaw looked up at Billy and smiled. "Why don't you cut me loose and then we'll see how well you go hitting me?"

"We're wasting time," Jed Morgan said. "We've got guests waiting."

Jim Morgan dismissed him with a wave. "They can wait. There's enough food and drink to keep them occupied while I deal with this."

"We can deal with this," Billy Morgan insisted.

Jim Morgan turned on his son, "You can't deal with this," he yelled. "If you had, we wouldn't be here now." He pointed at Shaw. "*He* wouldn't be here now."

Billy Morgan flinched under the wrath of his father. He wanted to prove he was capable, in control, able to show his father that he, the eldest of the three brothers was ready and capable of taking over the family business. But this stranger, this new person was a thorn in his side. He had humiliated Billy Morgan, and he seethed with resentment. He wanted to kill Shaw here and now, dispose of his body like the others. They had the barrels ready and waiting. Maybe down the mineshaft. That's where Annie had gone. Three times they had gone back there, to the old pit mine on the McAlister Ranch, just for fun to hear her moans drift up from the hole. She was beaten up pretty badly when they threw her in, but she lasted for nearly a week, slowly dying in the cold watery dark.

"What about the entertainment?" Billy Morgan said to his father. He nodded at Shaw.

Jim Morgan took a breath to calm down. He turned back to Shaw, who seemed amused by the family confrontation.

"Yes, the entertainment." Jim Morgan looked at Shaw like he was a side of beef hanging in a store window, a cold calculating expression on his face.

Shaw twisted his neck again, loosening the joints and muscles, traces of the concussion he had suffered all gone. He was fully alert and his memory restored.

Jim Morgan sensed this as he looked at him. "The pickup truck you stole is a total write off. It rolled several times, you know. Mr. Cole here and his men riddled it with bullets. You are lucky to be alive."

Shaw had nearly made it out. He had driven toward the gate, but it had been closed, the path also blocked by another pickup truck and five men with assault rifles pointing at him. Not quite the going away party Shaw was expecting.

They knew.

A drone had been flying the perimeter fence, a pre-programmed security loop. It spotted the pickup truck leaving the garage bay and tagged it as an unauthorized use of a company vehicle. It notified the security room and then tracked Shaw from above.

Shaw backed up the pickup truck and was determined to ram the fence, but they shot out the tires and he hit a drainage gully then rolled, coming to rest just a few feet short of the fence. They had dragged him unconscious out of the cab and brought him to the detention cell.

Jim Morgan motioned to Cole. "Can you give us a moment please."

Cole nodded and left the room, closing the soundproof door behind him. Now it was all just family, Jim Morgan and his three sons.

"How much do you know?" Jim Morgan demanded.
"You read the report."

"I know that you have been lying. I know that you plan to cheat Daisy McAlister out of her land."

"It's the law of the jungle, survival of the fittest. I have an opportunity and I intend to exploit it," Jim Morgan replied. "Knowledge is power, that is the only real thing of value today." Jim Morgan looked at the report again. He had read it a thousand times and still couldn't believe what was sitting on his doorstep, right under his nose, yet just a few feet from his grasp. The first survey report that he had taken from Stan McAlister was safely locked away in the safe in his study. It was the report done by Linton Geological that had first alerted Jim Morgan to what was under the McAlister ranch, the immense untold wealth that had laid there for millions of years. It was only by accident that Edward Linton, the geologist who had been hired by Stan McAlister to undertake some testing on the land, had revealed the secret to Billy Morgan.

Linton happened to be sitting at the bar in Martha's End, having a drink, Billy Morgan a few feet way. Blind luck for Billy. Jim Morgan had no interest at all in the McAlister ranch other than wanting to expand his own land holdings.

But when Billy overheard Linton tell the bartender that he was only in town for a few days, doing some work at the Stan McAlister's property, Billy's ears pricked up. Billy bought the old geologist the next few rounds of drinks and plied him for information. At first Linton didn't say much, because he didn't know much. Then on Linton's last night in Martha's End, when his work was done, Billy made it his business to have one last drink with him before leaving the next day. A few too many Jack Daniels later Edward Linton, his speech thick and slurred, revealed what he had found. The signs were there, the geology was consistent, but he couldn't say with absolute certainty until deep test drilling was undertaken. But all the signs were positive.

Billy went straight back to his father and told him. He told his father Linton would be back in a month to deliver his report in person once it was completed. It would take him that long to confirm his findings and test his samples further. Jim Morgan made his mind up. Edward Linton would never be allowed to hand his report to Stan McAlister. If he did, the McAlisters would become one of the richest family legacies for all time, right up there with the Rockefellers, while the Morgan name would shrivel into the dirt by comparison. Jim Morgan was never going to let that happen.

So when Linton turned up in town a month later telling them he had sold his business, and this was the final task he needed to do before retirement, they became suspicious. Linton was not that old, but shrewd and as tough as the rocks in the ground. After three hours of torture in the old bank building he finally told the truth. The report confirmed everything and much more. Linton said he hadn't breathed a word to anyone about what was in the report, especially Stan McAlister. He quickly sold his business and was going to convince Stan McAlister that he should come in as a business associate. A full-time geologist. His professional expertise would be needed. But he didn't get past the Morgan brothers. They took his report and gave it to their father.

After Jim Morgan had read it in full he locked it away in his safe. It was then Jim Morgan knew he had to kill Stan McAlister. The stubborn old fool had an idea of what was under his land. He would never sell, and in time would find another geologist.

Jim Morgan would never allow that to happen. It was his family dynasty, no one else's. So he agreed to meet Stan McAlister up on the ridge, neutral ground so to speak, to make him one last offer. But then Stan sneered at him, saying he would never sell, no matter the price, and Jim Morgan saw his dreams and the chance of immense family wealth vanish. So he hit Stan, dragged him semiconscious to the edge of the ridge and threw him off.

He knew with Stan gone, Daisy would be easier to deal with, not as stubborn—but he had guessed wrong. She had inherited the same dogged determination as her father. Still, Jim Morgan knew Stan McAlister hadn't told his daughter. If he had, she would have done or said something in the months after her father's death. But she never mentioned it. Stan McAlister and Edward Linton both went to their graves with the secret intact.

"It's her land, what's under it also belongs to her," Shaw said, keeping his eyes on the report that Jim Morgan held, a second report his own geologists had prepared based on the original from Linton. They had done a more extensive survey, satellite imagery and the works. It had cost a fortune, but had been worth it. If anything, Linton had been conservative, he had underestimated the quality, yield and production capacity.

"It's our land, our right!" Billy snarled as he stepped forward, fist raised to strike Shaw again.

Jim Morgan held up his hand and regarded Shaw with a shrewd stare. "So you do know what's there. You know what that ranch is sitting on, don't you." It was a statement, not a question.

Shaw stared at Jim Morgan. "You stole the information, killed people to get it, I bet. That's your style isn't it?"

"I did what I needed to do to protect my family, my family name. Something this size is too important to leave in the hands of some family of rednecks. There are other people involved now, there's too much at stake. I'm not going to let a little pissant like you spoil things."

"And Daisy? What will happen to her?" Shaw asked.

Jim Morgan didn't have to say anything, he just smiled and glanced at his three sons. "When I run out of patience with her, I'll let my boys do what needs to be done." Jim Morgan stepped forward, only a foot away from Shaw. "And I've run out of patience with you."

Morgan turned to his sons. "We had other plans for tonight's entertainment, but I think our guest will be a better and more exciting option than the girl."

He turned back to Shaw, a cruel twinkle in his eye. "We need to show our guests how we Morgans treat our enemies. Take him to the Pit."

THIRTY-EIGHT

"Ladies and gentlemen, I thank you for your patience." Jim Morgan stood at the podium under a huge open loading bay, his three sons by his side. A long banquet table stood nearby covered with grilled meats, roasted fowl, and sweet delicacies. A crowd of around sixty guests had gathered, men and women, in evening dress, drinks and food in hand.

Police officers, county officials, prominent local business owners and out of state dignitaries, all made fat and wealthy from being on the Morgan family payroll. They were the Morgan community, a network of ambitious and influential devotees who had made the Morgan family rich, and in return Jim Morgan had paid them handsomely, money that would never see the eyes of the IRS or grace a US bank account. The elected county officials had helped him get planning permission for dubious property deals and developments. The police officers present had allowed Billy, Jed, and Rory Morgan to dish out their own kind of justice in the county without so much as a parking citation. The officials from the Mayor's office had levied fines and cessation orders against business owners who competed with the Morgans, driving them eventually broke. It was a gathering of the corrupt, tainted and dishonest who had fed off the public purse so as to line their pockets with Morgan money.

Jim Morgan looked out at the sea of smiling faces. He was in his element, a preacher in the pulpit, about to deliver another sermon, his sermon, better than God's own words.

"I hope I haven't kept you waiting too long, but I'm sure you've been enjoying my hospitality in the meantime." He waved at the banquet spread. Laughter rippled through the gathering, glasses raised, nods of appreciation. He patted his hands downward, making a show of suppressing the praise. Truth was he loved every ounce of attention and praise, and he greedily sought it out at every opportunity.

"I apologize for the delay, but I have had to attend to a small disturbance."

A slight murmur of concern went up around the guests.

Jim Morgan raised his hands to hush the guests again. "It's quite alright. There's nothing to be alarmed about." Jim Morgan paused for effect, relishing this part of the gathering as he had done for all previous ones. "In fact, it has presented itself as an opportunity, not a burden. I have something very special for you this evening. Something I know you will all enjoy."

Nods went around the crowd of guests. Knowing smiles from what they had witnessed before at other gatherings.

"I have some very special entertainment planned for you all, as a special thank you for your continued support."

Jim Morgan turned to his three sons and nodded. It was a family affair. "I want to show you how we Morgans deal with disturbances. How we deal with our enemies, those who choose to go against us, those who stand in our way and not by our sides."

A hush descended over the gathering.

The crowd parted as a tight-knit group of security guards pushed through the mass of people. In the middle they firmly held on to Shaw. His hands were now chained in front to a thick leather collar around his neck like a dog. He shuffled along, his feet manacled as well. He was naked from the waist up, stripped down to just his pants and boots.

They brought Shaw up to the podium and pivoted him around to face the guests. He stood under the harsh lights, paraded like a prized bull.

And he was for sale.

The women in the audience gasped at his bare muscled chest, powerful shoulders, defined arms and sculpted torso. Some women licked their lips, lust in their eyes, while others felt heat and wetness grace their loins as their eyes lingered over such a fine young specimen. The men were different though, jealous at the sight of one so young and virile, wishing they had looked like that when they were Shaw's age.

It was going to be a public display of the Morgan wrath, and a warning to them all. Shaw was going to be made an example.

"Now, who would be a worthy opponent for this fine young man?" Jim Morgan shouted. He raised one hand, pointing above the heads of the guests.

There was movement again at the back of the gathering. A monstrous shape pushed through, huge and menacing.

Shaw watched as men and woman stepped back, giving the lumbering figure a wide berth.

The Ox appeared, a towering mass of ugliness, dwarfing all. He too was bare-chested, and for the first time Shaw could see his full shocking physique. His torso embroidered with scar-tissue and pockmarks, a history of pain and suffering both inflicted and endured, painted on a canvas of deformed flesh. He walked upright, but as Shaw watched it was like the man had missed a vital step along the evolutionary chain. Under the bright industrial lighting, his full features came into clear view. His shoulders and arms were bloated and grotesque from a lifetime of steroid abuse, veins curled like massive earthworms under his skin. His chest was a slab of concrete, thick and glistening, a fan of back muscle, forearms bowed like tree trunks, hands and fingers like the claws of an excavator, strings of saliva dripped from a twisted smile on a bludgeoned face.

The crowd roared with blood-lust as the Ox stood beside Shaw, the size comparison laughable, Shaw's head didn't even reach his shoulder. He stank of sweat, blood, and fecal matter.

Jim Morgan raised his hands to calm the crowd again. "For the newcomers to the gathering, you are in for a rare treat tonight. The bank is now live, place your bets, the odds have been set. A reserve price has also been set for those among you who wish to purchase our contender outright to do with him as you wish."

Smart phones were brought out, screens were tapped, money was wagered on the fight using a private app designed for such occasions, one of many private apps the community used to conduct its shadowy business.

Jim Morgan had set the reserve deliberately high for Shaw. He wanted the man dead in the most grotesque manner, not to be sold as a sex or torture plaything for one of the wives of the community. He wanted to put on a show tonight and not disappoint his guests.

Minutes later the guests moved out from under the covered area to a wide flat expanse. The rain had stopped, the ground was damp, but a path of wooden walkways had been laid out, lit with rows of torches.

Shaw was pushed forward by the guards, his chains clinking with each step, the Ox lumbering along by his side.

Finally they arrived at the edge of a large circular hole in the ground, twenty feet deep, with a concrete floor and smooth curved walls, perfectly round.

They had arrived at the Pit. In the middle was a massive pile of hewn logs coated with fuel. A guard lit a torch then tossed it on to the pile of wood. It caught straight away and soon roared with flames. Red-hot cinders burst then curled into the cold night sky. A handrail ran around the edge of the Pit so the guests could safely stand and watch. It was ringed with lit torches evenly spaced that cast light down into the pit. There was a ladder placed at each end, one for each contestant to descend into the Pit. Once they were pulled up, there would be no escaping.

A video camera sat on a tripod, behind it stood Rory Morgan. He pivoted the camera, filming the entourage as they approached, Shaw flanked by guards, the Ox, towering beside him. When they arrived they were separated and Shaw was taken to the opposite side. The guests quickly lined up along the rail, the women at the front, wanting the best view of the raw violence to come, some of them hoping a spray of blood from below would stain their dresses.

The Ox descended his ladder. It bowed and flexed under his weight, he had been into the Pit many times and had never lost.

The guards pulled Shaw to a standstill. One guard drew his handgun and placed the muzzle in the center of Shaw's forehead. "You decide to run, you'll be running with half your head gone." Another guard pulled a key out and removed the chains. "Move," the guard with the gun said, and pushed Shaw towards the ladder. "Try and last longer than the last person," he laughed. The other guards snickered. "Hell, we hardly had the ladder up before the Ox had smashed the poor guy's brains out against the wall. Took a day to scrub it off!" More laughter broke out among the guards.

Shaw paused at the top of the ladder and looked around. The guests jeered and screamed at him with lust in their eyes, faces twisted in the torch-light, heinous and wild.

Shaw looked down into the Pit and, one foot at a time, he began his descent into hell.

THIRTY-NINE

Daisy walked back across the yard, rifle in one hand. She checked on the horses one more time just to make sure they were settled and safe after the previous night's trauma. She cleared some space in the equipment shed and rigged up harnesses for them. She spread some hay as well on the ground, but it was a poor substitute for the stables.

She tried not to think of the dead horses, her eyes avoiding the mound of freshly turned dirt where they were buried.

She wanted to kill Billy Morgan. His entire family was the bane of her existence. She was beginning to hate this town. It was vile, corrupt, polluted. On the surface it appeared fine. Yes, it had its problems, its small town bullies, but the events of the last few days made Daisy realize the true depth of the evil surrounding her.

She didn't know who to trust anymore. The next time she drove through town, when faces turned to look at her, would they be spies for the Morgans? Part of the community? Watching her, working against her? For the first time Daisy felt like an outsider. Even the police, like Taylor Giles, were in Jim Morgan's pocket. She loved her ranch, but she now hated the town, the people, everyone.

As she walked up the porch steps she looked out into the dark, over the shadowy hills toward the Morgan compound, wondering what Shaw was doing. She feared for his safety. He could take care of himself, she knew that, but he was going up against the whole Morgan clan and their followers. He was brave, the bravest person she had even known, braver than her father. No one had stood up for her as Shaw had done.

She went to the faucet in the kitchen and poured a glass of water, then went down into the basement. Taylor Giles sat against the wall and she placed the glass of water next to his bound feet.

"I'm going to give you the water. If you so much as move or lash out at me, I'll kick you in the balls. Do you understand?"

Giles gave a nod.

Daisy placed her rifle out of his reach, squatted down and ripped off the tape. She lifted the glass to his lips and he drank it greedily. When he had finished he said nothing, just closed his eyes.

Daisy stood and gathered up her rifle. "What happened to you, Taylor? I know you were an ass in school, hanging around the Morgans and all, but I thought you would grow up, see the harm their family has done."

Giles opened his eyes. They were rimmed red and the skin around his mouth was raw. "The money," he said, his voice low. "They took an interest in me. Treated me like I was a man, part of their group."

Daisy shook her head. He was a pitiful sight, but she didn't feel one bit of sorrow for him. He was on the Morgan's side. "They used you, Taylor. Plain and simple. They knew you were weak. They knew you were training to be in law enforcement, and they saw you as another one of their implants, a spy to do their bidding."

"That's OK for you to say. I had no money. My family is poor. We don't have a big ranch like this," Giles retorted.

Daisy squatted down again, her rifle laid across her knees. "Taylor, you idiot, don't you see? The Morgans have ruined my family, sabotaged this ranch. I'm broke, I have no money. I haven't been able to pay the bills for the last three months. All thanks to the Morgans." Daisy looked away, tears in her eyes. "They're evil, evil to the core. They've driven away my workers, spied on me and now they burned down my stables and killed my horses. Why do they want my land so badly? I'm no threat to them."

"I don't know," Giles shook his head. "I didn't think they would go that far. They just wanted me to keep an eye on you and drive off any workers who came by."

"So they paid you for that? You took their money, like everyone else in this town?"

Giles just nodded, feeling ashamed.

Daisy took a deep breath.

Greed. It was always the same. It was a poison that flowed through the veins of the Morgans and they had slowly spread that same poison through the town, polluting it and its people.

Daisy's phone pinged. She stood and slipped it out of her back pocket.

Daisy, it's me, Callie. In trouble. Please help me.

Daisy typed back. *WRU?*

Moments passed, but no reply came. She looked at Giles handcuffed to the wall-pipe, and brought her gun up and leveled the muzzle at his head. "What have you done with Callie? Where is she?" she said coldly.

Giles shifted himself upright, his eyes fixed on the gun. "I don't know," he stammered. "Honest, I don't know."

Daisy stepped closer, Giles backed himself hard against the wall, turning his head away from the barrel that Daisy now pushed against his temple. "Where is she? Who has her?" she asked again, her teeth gritted.

"I don't know!" Giles screamed. "Please don't kill me," he sobbed, tears streaming down his face.

"Not good enough," Daisy hissed.

"There's a place," Giles muttered, between sobs.

Daisy's eyes narrowed. "Go on."

"A place on their property, a shed."

"What shed? Where is this shed?" Daisy's grip tightened on the rifle.

"It's a few miles inside their boundary, on the southern side, near your property," he sniveled.

"How do I find it?" Daisy replied.

"There's a gate along the boundary fence, near the road that runs on your side. The Morgans use the gate to drive onto your land."

"They drive onto my land? When?" Daisy was astonished.

Giles shifted his eyes sideways and looked up at Daisy, his head flat against the wall. "Whenever they want to. They told me they use it mainly at night, sometimes during the day, when you're not here."

Daisy's finger came inside the trigger guard and rested on the trigger. "What's in the shed? What happens there?" It took every ounce of effort for her not to pull the trigger and cover the wall with his brains.

"Tell me!" she shouted.

"They'll kill me, if I do!" Giles started sobbing again.

"I'll kill you, if you don't."

"Things. Bad things. Things they do to women. They take women there, at night."

"How do you know this?" Daisy asked, pressing the barrel of the Winchester harder against his head, willing herself to pull the trigger.

"Because I've been there," he cried. "It's a reward. A reward for being loyal."

FORTY

It was a game of cat and mouse.

If the Ox came around the bonfire one way, Shaw would circle away, keeping the distance the same. Shaw needed time to devise a plan, otherwise the contest would be over in seconds and he would be pummeled to death by the cannonball fists on the Ox.

The guests above yelled and jeered at Shaw's evasive tactics. They wanted blood and they wanted it now, but he wasn't going to oblige. The stifling heat radiated from the bonfire and bounced back off the walls, the air distorted by the flames.

Rory Morgan stood on the lip of the Pit, the video camera angled downward, recording everything, another to add to the collection. The video would be professionally edited then made available to the guests for their own private viewing on the secure website.

Shaw moved away again, his weight on the balls of his feet. The heat shimmered and for a moment he lost sight of the Ox behind the towering flames, and mild panic set in.

Then the unthinkable happened.

The flames parted and a massive shape hurtled through them.

The Ox took a running leap through the edge of the bonfire, where the wood was piled not so high. He landed in a flurry of smoke, ash and cinders right in front of Shaw and lashed out. Shaw ducked as the huge arm grazed the top of his head, the air swooshed like a tree trunk had been swung at him.

Shaw stepped forward and drove his fist into the mass of scarred flesh and ribs in the side of the Ox. It was like hitting a massive carcass of beef; dead, hard and cold. Pain ripped up Shaw's arm and shoulder. He grimaced and quickly retreated, clutching his hand and wrist in pain. The Ox was made of iron and stone. A punch that would have broken the ribs of any normal man had no effect.

The Ox smiled and advanced again, his beady eyes shifting, gauging the distance, trying to drive Shaw up against the wall. Shaw sidestepped and the Ox mirrored the movement, nimble and agile, deceptive for his size.

The man came at Shaw again, low and hunkered, all spittle and froth like a Rottweiler with rabies, beyond anger, beyond rage, beyond human.

Shaw moved, fast and low, toward the Ox not away. Shaw drove at him head on, meeting the Ox before he could react, closing the gap in a split second. Shaw realized his best form of defense was attack and he collided with the Ox, driving his shoulder and head straight into his midsection, aiming for the solar plexus just below the rib cage, a complex web of nerve endings around the diaphragm.

The Ox grunted as the air rushed out of his lungs, but he didn't go down, just staggered backward, pulling Shaw with him, his hands digging into Shaw's sides. He lifted Shaw almost vertical, head down, feet up and threw him sideways into the wall.

Shaw hit the wall hard in a tangle of arms and legs, then bounced off and he fell in a heap in the dirt.

The crowd cheered in appreciation. Finally they were starting to see some violence.

Billy Morgan looked down from the edge and smiled. The twisted body of Shaw lay unmoving and Billy was relishing the pain and suffering the Ox was inflicting on Shaw. Billy wanted it to be slow and drawn out, not a quick kill. Beat the man senseless, take him to the edge of death then pull him back from the abyss, allow him to recover just a bit then go again. Beat, recover, repeat. Billy liked that. Slowly break every limb one at a time and then finally crush his skull, but only when Billy gave the nod. These were the instructions he had whispered into the Ox's ear while they stood waiting for Shaw to descend into the Pit.

Shaw still hadn't moved, but Billy could see he was still breathing.

Good. Don't die yet on me. I have plans for you.

Billy looked around. People were cheering and engrossed in the fight, and he felt a tinge of pride. These were his people, his community, his gathering. He had formed strong ties with most of the influential people here, paving the way for when he would take over the family business.

He looked over at his father. Jim Morgan was deep in conversion with a senior county official and the Chief of Police. Soon it would be Billy talking in their ear, getting them to bend to his will, not his father's. All in good time. His father was a good businessman and Billy had been a good student, but being the next in line had made him restless. He wanted it now, he wanted the power. His father was soft though, too soft. Billy would make sure as head of the family he would be more ruthless.

Jim Morgan caught his son looking at him across the expanse of the Pit. He raised his glass and Billy nodded, and smiled back. Soon, very soon, he would put his father into the Pit with the Ox. Now that would make good viewing. He could sell tickets to that event when it happened.

Billy clapped his hands and joined with the others yelling abuse at the slumped shape of Shaw. "Get up! Get up and fight like a man!" he screamed at the top of his voice.

No one yet had fallen into the Pit by accident, but looking around Billy was keen to push a few of the people he saw off the edge. Maybe when his dogs were in the Pit.

Once, when his father was away on business, Billy and his brothers had picked up two girls hitchhiking just outside of Hays. After plying them with booze and drugs they took them to the old tin shed. The Morgan brothers called it "dessert." As like all the others they had taken there, the entire event had been recorded for future private distribution among Billy's network of friends, people who appreciated such art and had a taste for such pleasures. After Billy, Jed, and Rory had taken multiple turns, the girls were thrown unconscious into the back of the pickup truck, covered and driven back to the Morgan compound. The girls awoke in the Pit and were confronted by two of Billy's attack dogs, a vicious breed of Italian Mastiff called the Cane Corso. The dogs were specially bred by Billy. They had a sleek muscular body, a large aggressive head and powerful jaws that could chew through a human leg in seconds. Each dog weighed over 110 pounds of muscle, gristle, and teeth, the perfect four-legged killing machine. Illegal in most states, but Billy had six of them, and had put two in the Pit with the girls.

That was a special video they filmed that night in the Pit that the Morgan brothers never shared it with anyone else.

"Get up!" Billy screamed again. He could see Shaw starting to move.

The Ox was standing back waiting.

Good.

He may be a half-wit, but he listened to instructions very well.

To his right, Billy could see his brother hunched behind the camera tripod, his eye behind the viewfinder, his mouth spread in a wide grin just below the camera.

This was a far better spectacle than using the girl they had locked up for this. She would have been no sport for the Ox and the guests would have been disappointed. But Billy had other plans for her after this. Once they cleaned up the mess of what was left of Shaw, Billy and his two other brothers were going for a little dessert to conclude the evening's entertainment. And what a sweet little piece of dessert she was, locked away ready and waiting.

Blood dribbled down from a cut above Shaw's eye and his nose was bleeding, thick velvety drops fell to the dirt. He slowly got to one knee and looked up. At the sight of his bloody face the audience broke into a frenzy, a crescendo of manic screams and blood-lust cries. Grown men and women, adults, people in positions of public office and civic responsibility, reduced to a guttural mob craving senseless violence.

The Ox stood his ground, he didn't move, waiting, watching Shaw, allowing him to regain his senses and slowly get to his feet.

Shaw was shaky at first, his legs like jelly, his vision out of focus, the scene tilting left then right. Slowly his vision cleared, he expected the Ox to be on him. But the giant just stood there, ten feet away, just watching him.

It was then Shaw understood. His was to be a slow and excruciating death at the hands of the sloth, a deliberately long and drawn out exhibition to thrill the crowd and more importantly, appease the Morgan family for the intrusion he had brought upon them.

FORTY-ONE

The air was brittle and cold. Clouds rolled above, scattering then reforming across the face of the moon, threatening more rain. Lightning arced in the distance, in the direction where Daisy was heading.

She had hit Giles across the jaw with the butt of her Winchester, knocking him out cold. Then she checked the handcuffs were secure, reapplied a fresh strip of duct tape to his mouth and locked the basement door. She quickly secured the house, but left all the lights blazing. She thought about saddling up Jazz for the journey, but in the dark and with the recent deluge of rain the ground would be treacherous, and she didn't want her horse to sprain a leg or, worse still, break a bone.

She donned a heavy, waterproof hooded anorak, grabbed a flashlight and with her Winchester set off down the road past the barn and along the shared boundary fence. She had never shot anything at night, but she knew she needed a weapon. Her phone was in her back pocket and she still hadn't heard back from Callie.

Her mind swirled as she hurried along the road, the comforting lights of the house shrinking in the distance behind her, the dark and unknown in front of her.

She was in a foul mood as she trudged along the road, her flashlight sweeping low, her mood worse than the storms brewing again in the distance. She knew where the old access gate was, but she was seething that the Morgans were using it to drive on to her property like they owned the place. First spying on her with their drone and now this. God knows what they had done while she was away in town or at night when she was asleep.

She soon came to the old gate and immediately regretted not having chained and locked it before. At least then, if it had been removed or tampered with, she would have known. She slid through the rails and took her bearings. She needed to follow a straight line about a mile or so out from the gate and the shed should be on her right. That's what Giles had said.

The clouds cleared for a moment and the moon cast a watery glow across the terrain. In the distance the faint outline of low hills cut across the horizon. Beyond them lay the Morgan compound.

Daisy set off, trudging across the sodden ground that was rutted with pools of water and muddy from the downpour. She pulled her jacket around her and found comfort in the feel of her rifle in her hand.

A few times she lost her footing when her feet sunk unexpectedly into a large puddle, but she kept going, sloshing through until she reached solid ground. She paused and took her bearings again. She couldn't see the fence line behind her, but she could just make out the lights of her house. It looked infinitely small and distant, and she suddenly felt so alone in the dark.

She turned and pressed on, determined to find Callie and put an end to this madness.

****

The Ox still hadn't moved and Shaw used a few more precious seconds to shake off the mild concussion he suffered and assess his injuries. His shoulder ached deep to the bone. It had taken the full impact when he hit the wall, but thankfully there were no broken bones, yet. The feeling was returning to his wrist and he massaged it as he carefully watched the Ox.

Then the Ox hunkered down again and rushed at Shaw, his face wild, hands balled, bone-hard knuckles. Shaw waited until the last moment then pivoted hard, just managing to avoid the freight-train as it swept past him.

The crowd cheered, enjoying the bullfighter move.

The Ox skidded and turned as Shaw leapt up and forward, throwing a flying elbow at his face, catching a cheekbone and opening up a deep gash. Crimson poured down, hot and wet.

The Ox lashed out in anger, a wild swing. Shaw stepped inside, brought his arm up, stopping the bone-jarring blow before it reached its full momentum. Pain bloomed in Shaw's forearm, the blow almost breaking it. He quickly retreated away from the giant. But he had to keep going, moving and delivering strikes as best he could, letting his adrenaline and his own fear numb the pain.

When your opponent outweighs you, is bigger and stronger, the anatomical weak points become your only hope: the eyes, throat, groin, joints of the limbs, those soft tissue areas where nerve-endings bunch together.

Shaw stepped back in, bringing his knee up aiming for the groin, praying it would connect. He extended his hip and drove it straight up between the Ox's legs and deep into the pelvic bone.

The Ox screamed, an inhuman shriek, and collapsed forward on top of Shaw, driving him downward under his own massive weight into the dirt. His hands grasped Shaw around his neck for balance then started to squeeze.

He had Shaw's throat in a vice and was slowly squeezing the life out of him. The Ox got to his feet, lifting Shaw off the ground by his throat, his feet dangling. Shaw clawed desperately at the Ox's hands, but they were iron-clamped.

The Ox looked up at Billy Morgan, who gave a subtle shake of his head.

The Ox turned in rage and flung Shaw through the air.

Shaw cart-wheeled then clipped the edge of the bonfire, before tumbling across the dirt, a plume of cinders and a scatter of burning logs in his wake. Shaw fell awkwardly on his ankle and a twist of sharp pain shot up his shin and leg.

The Ox grunted and slowly lumbered toward him. Shaw struggled to his feet, his ankle screaming in agony as soon as he placed weight on it. He gritted his teeth, trying to ignore the pain as he hobbled backward. He picked up a small half-burning log in his hand, one end glowed orange, the embers crackling and hissing.

The crowd roared, the end was coming, money at minimal odds would be won.

The Ox pushed forward, closing the gap, forcing Shaw closer to the wall, cutting off his angles of escape. In desperation Shaw lunged forward, swinging the burning end of the log at the Ox's head. The Ox easily battered it away with a meaty hand, and the log burst into charred smoking fragments.

Shaw limped backward and felt the wall behind him.

The Ox loomed in his vision, blocking out everything, hands extended, drooling face grinning.

Shaw tried to slide along the wall, dragging his ankle through the dirt, but the Ox cut off his movement. Shaw threw another punch, sluggish and obvious. It was feeble and he knew it.

The Ox caught Shaw's fist in midair, swallowing it up in his massive hand like a catcher's mitt, fingers closed around it, and he began to crush Shaw's hand.

The pain was immense and Shaw dropped to one knee, struggling to pull his hand out. The Ox leaned over him, his head inches from his face. Shaw made a fist with his free hand and swung a hook into the side of the Ox's head repeatedly hitting it, but the Ox just kept smiling, and squeezed harder. Each successive punch from Shaw faded in intensity until it was reduced to a pitiful slap.

The Ox drew his other hand back, his fist a mass of hardened bone, calloused knuckle and scarred flesh.

Shaw struggled to break free. He was about to get punched by a human pile driver, a one-punch kill. Helpless, he brought his arm up across his face, protecting his head, but he knew even if he could block the first punch, his forearm would surely shatter and the second punch would find its mark.

The punch drove through the air straight into Shaw's shoulder, not his face, dislocating it. Shaw collapsed onto his back in pain, his shoulder hideously deformed by the dislocation.

The Ox looked down at the crippled man and felt no remorse. He wished he could have killed him the other night in the parking lot, except the woman with the gun had turned up. She had spoiled everything. But Billy had told him that if he followed exactly his instructions tonight, then he would get a treat, a special reward. He had pulled him aside before he went into the Pit and said that he had a woman for him, a nice woman that he would like. Billy said he could have her all to himself.

The Ox never had a woman before.

Never.

He had seen the videos though that Billy and his brothers had shown him, so he knew what to do. He was happy they had shown him the videos. Now he knew what to do once they gave him the woman, how to treat her right, just like how Billy and his brothers had treated the girls on the videos.

Billy also said that he and his brothers were going to get her from the big metal box and take her to that special place after he killed the man. They would take him there too. Then he would star in his own video, just like Billy.

He liked that a lot. Maybe even more than killing this man now.

The Ox raised his arms and yelled.

The crowd yelled back.

He glanced up at Billy again.

Billy smiled, but this time gave a tiny nod.
Now.

FORTY-TWO

The Ox grabbed Shaw by the ankle, the injured one, and dragged him toward the bonfire. He was going to crush his spine first then throw him into the bonfire to slowly burn. What a sight it would be. It was a special request from Billy and the Ox didn't want to disappoint Billy. The Ox wanted his treat.

Letting go of the ankle, he grabbed Shaw under the arms in a bear hug, and lifted him off the ground, his body limp and lifeless, and began to squeeze him.

Shaw couldn't breathe. Pain tore across his chest and back. His lungs burned, starved of air. He could feel acute pain pierce his vertebrae like metal spears being inserted.

Kill him. Kill him now! Voices screamed at Shaw, his vision started to fray at the edges, darken then collapse inward. The pain was devouring him, he could feel his spine bending.

Kill him! The voice again. His voice, telling him what to do, the only option available.

Shaw gritted his teeth, swallowing the pain and brought his hands up. He grabbed each side of the massive head in front of him and drove his thumbs as hard and as deep as he could into each eye socket.

The Ox shook his head violently, but Shaw held on, driving his thumbs harder, deeper into the eye sockets, in and behind the orbs. The iron grip around Shaw's chest faltered, and Shaw gulped in a breath of air, and poured on what strength he had left, puncturing the soft gelatinous orb of each eyeball until they popped out in a vitreous dribble of fluid, membrane and a ribbon of optic nerve.

The Ox screamed and let go of Shaw. He clutched his empty eye sockets, each eye a saggy mush in the dirt at his feet, two hollow pits in his face, blood streaming down his cheeks.

Shaw staggered to his feet, heaving precious air into his lungs.

The Ox teetered in front of him. Blind and in agony, clawing at the hollow pits where his eyes had been. Shaw crouched and sprung forward off his good leg, driving his head into the giant's gut. The Ox stumbled backward and lost his footing, his heels catching on the loose logs near the edge of the bonfire, and he tumbled into the thermal flames and red-hot embers.

The crowd went silent, stunned, confused, in disbelief.

Shaw staggered back and watched as the flames engulfed the man thrashing about, his struggles burying him deeper under the mass of burning logs, his body catching fire like a human torch. Flames rippled across his flesh, melting his shape, his struggles lessening as the fire consumed him.

Then all movement stopped, and black smoke billowed from the charred, frozen shape in the center of the bonfire.

Then cheers went up, slowly at first, then growing into one roar from the guests.

It was an unfair fight, the guests knew that, but what they loved more was an underdog. And Shaw was the underdog. He had won the crowd.

He raised his good arm acknowledging them, like a gladiator, they cheered even louder. He needed them, if he was going to live the next five minutes.

Shaw looked at Billy Morgan above, his face cold in silent loathing. Billy returned Shaw's look of hatred with a faint smile, the smile told Shaw his victory was going to be short-lived.

Shaw looked back at the bonfire, a blackened and twisted shape at its center, a husk of carbon and bone.

A ladder was lowered, Shaw hobbled toward it. He gripped the first rung with his good hand and slowly hauled himself up, one painful step at a time, leaving behind the hellish nightmare of the Pit. Two arms pulled him up when he reached the final rung and they dragged him onto the concrete edge. Two security guards held him upright, taking his weight as the crowd pressed around him, hands on him, patting his back, his arms, his head, shouts of praise, garish smiles.

The crowd parted and Jim Morgan approached, a fake smile on his face hiding his obvious disappointment, his three sons in tow. It wasn't expected to turn out like this. Shaw was supposed to die.

Jim Morgan reached Shaw, leaned in and spoke into his ear. To all it looked like congratulations. "You have bought yourself a short reprieve, but my sons will finish the job."

Jim Morgan stepped back and smiled at the crowd. He couldn't kill Shaw here and now, but his sons soon would, more privately, away from prying eyes. He raised both hands to hush the guests. "Ladies and gentlemen. What a display of courage and fighting spirit," he said, each word forced and tasting like acid on his tongue. "I'm sure you agree a worthy winner. Now, tonight's gathering is far from over and neither is my hospitality. Please make your way back to the covered area and enjoy yourself with more food and drink."

The crowd drifted back to the banquet.

When it was just Shaw and his three sons, Jim Morgan turned to them. "Get rid of him," he hissed. "I don't care how or where, just do it now and do it quietly. I want no traces." And with that Jim Morgan stormed off in a fury to attend to his jubilant guests.

The two security guards held Shaw between them, he was almost unconscious with pain. Billy Morgan turned to them. "Get him patched up quickly." Billy lifted Shaw's drooping head. "I don't want to make it too easy for him." Billy laughed.

"What have you done with Callie?" Shaw croaked.

Billy smiled. "You've probably walked right past her a few times and not even known. The first time when you were an uninvited guest, and again tonight as well."

Shaw tried to remember back, but his mind was crowded with pain and his entire shoulder and arm was on fire. Then it came to him. He knew where Callie was, where they had put her.

"But don't worry," Billy continued. "Once we're done with you, she's going to get the royal treatment from us." Billy turned to his two brothers. "Isn't that right boys?" Jed and Rory both sniggered childishly.

Rory licked the stubble on his lower lip, grabbed his crotch and said, "Yeah, we're going to treat her real nice. Had her saved for the Ox, but since he's toast we're going to have to teach her a lesson ourselves."

The guards dragged Shaw away to the medical shed. Billy slapped his brothers on their backs. He was disappointed that the Ox was dead, and that he wasn't going to see Shaw's head pulled from his body, but it presented a new opportunity he was going to relish. "Saddle up boys, we're going hunting!"

FORTY-THREE

Three ATVs were lined up just beyond the perimeter fence, motors idling, the headlights and light bars cutting through the darkness revealing the rocky and barren terrain. Each ATV had a GoPro attached to the side of the roll-cage. The Morgan brothers weren't into extreme sports. They were into extreme hunting, the human kind.

Billy, Jed, and Rory leaned casually against the ATVs, each of them holding an assault rifle fitted with a night vision scope. Shaw stood shivering in front of them, still just in his pants and boots, his hands bound with a cable tie.

They had pumped some pain-killers into his shoulder and his swollen ankle making it easier for him to run, but they hadn't reset his dislocated shoulder. One arm hung limp by his side, the drugs only taking the edge off the pain. Shaw felt more lucid, but the drugs would soon wear off and the bone-numbing pain would return.

Billy stepped up to Shaw, unsheathed a large hunting knife and sliced the strip of plastic between his wrists.

"We're going to give you a twenty-minute head start. If you make it to the McAlister boundary fence, you're home free. You came this way the other evening, so you should know how to get back there."

Shaw didn't believe Billy for a minute, but he stood patiently and listened. Jim Morgan wanted him killed immediately. Billy Morgan wanted some fun.

The way the Morgans were kitted-up Shaw knew they had done this before, hunted people for sport on their land in some perverse game they liked to play. At least he wasn't in the Pit and he wasn't restrained anymore. "And after twenty-minutes?"

"Then we'll come after you." Billy nodded at the outline of the hills. "We need to go around, so it will take us longer, whereas you can climb over them. You'll have a decent head start."

There was no head start in Shaw's mind. He only had the use of one arm, his ankle was injured and he was going to be run down by three men with assault rifles and driving ATVs.

"Will you let Callie go, if I make it?"

"You can have the slut, for all I care, and Daisy too," Billy said. He had no intention of releasing Callie. She was as good as dead. As for Daisy, as soon as they had taken care of Shaw they were going to slip up to her house and do her as well. About time too. Billy's father said that she was off-limits, but Billy didn't care anymore. He had to step up to the plate, as they say, start making his own moves. He couldn't live in the shadow of his father forever.

Billy checked the luminous dial on his watch. "You've got twenty minutes."

Shaw took off as fast as his injured ankle would allow.

The Morgan brothers watched the hobbling figure of Shaw until the dark swallowed him up.

Billy pulled something out from behind the driver's seat of his ATV—the balled-up jeans they had found in the locker after they had captured Shaw.

Billy slipped a walkie-talkie from his belt and spoke into it. "Bring the dogs."

****

A cold drizzle began to fall and the moon disappeared behind a veil of cloud. As a child, Daisy had laid awake at night in her tiny bed with the covers pulled up tightly under her chin as she stared out of her bedroom window at the storms rolling toward the ranch. She would count the seconds between lightning and the eventual rumble of distant thunder. If the seconds got less and less, she knew the storm was coming toward her, and she would pull the covers a little tighter around her.

She did the same now as she trudged over the sodden ground. The cold air carried the musty smell of rain.

Another storm was approaching, and she was walking straight toward it.

She had stopped once or twice with her heart in her mouth when the silhouette of some mantis-like creature loomed out of the darkness. It squatted, watching her, waiting to pounce. But it turned out to be the rusted-out carcass of an old abandoned farm tractor or plow that was half-buried in the low scrub.

Daisy turned on her flashlight and continued across a section of marsh dotted with thin reeds, her boots making sucking noises in soft mud, insects clicking around her. It was getting colder. Patches of mist seeped from the ground and hovered around her ankles as she moved, like boney white fingers trying to pull her back.

Then the ground flattened and became more solid where the earth had sucked up the rain from the last downpour. The texture was rough dirt littered with stones that crunched under her boots. She passed rows of shallow furrows covered in a fine layer of mist. The clouds cleared for the briefest of moments widening her visibility, Daisy realized that she was in an old field that had long since grown its last harvest, the ground sandy and coarse like all the nutrients had been sucked out of it. She pressed on, following a straight line. As best as she could tell, she was still heading in the right direction.

The lightning grew more frequent and the intervals to the thunder less.

FORTY-FOUR

The three beams of the ATV headlights converged on the body. It lay twisted, disfigured, a shallow furrow in the ground behind it, the dirt pushed up in front like it had been moving at speed then had plowed head-first into the ground.

Billy Morgan climbed out of his ATV, the engine idling. Jed and Rory got out of their vehicles but kept their distance, rifles in their hands, scanning the dark that pressed in around them where the headlights didn't reach.

Billy squatted down beside the dog's corpse and placed his palm on the rib cage.

It was still warm.

"Jesus Billy, what's going on?" Jed said, as he looked at the ghastly sight.

Billy said nothing, just kept looking down at the body, seething. The Ox they could replace, there were plenty of dim-witted men they could train-up. He was expendable.

But the dogs, his dogs, he loved beyond measure. They were harder to replace. He had raised them since pups, loved and cared for them, treated them better than most humans. When they hurt, he hurt.

And now his insides were torn at the sight in front of him.

The huge dog laid dead, a fist-sized hole of flesh, fur and shattered ribs blown outwards in its side from where the bullet exited. The dog may have survived for a few minutes after being shot, but just to make sure, someone had also cut its throat for good measure. A viscous pool of blood spread from underneath its head that was almost severed from the body.

Rory looked over Billy's shoulder at the dog, his voice unsure and fidgety, "How the hell did he get a knife? He had no knife!"

Billy stood up and looked at Rory. "Forget the knife, you dumb idiot! The dog has been shot. He must have stashed or buried a weapon somewhere around here when he came over the other night, just as a back-up."

Clever bastard, Billy thought.

It was freezing, but Billy's blood boiled with anger. The odds were starting to tip against them.

"Find him and kill him!" he screamed, his breath like steam in the cold air.

Billy ran back to his ATV, jumped in and stamped on the gas. The big tires skidded then gripped, the ATV lurching forward. Jed and Rory quickly jumped in their vehicles and tore after Billy, their headlights bouncing and slewing through the night.

****

Shaw ran for his life, one arm dangling, the other pumping wildly, urging him forward. The drugs were dwindling, the pain spreading in waves. He fell, gathered himself and stumbled on, the limping stride of an injured gazelle.

Something was chasing him through the darkness from behind. Something big, he could feel it, the displacement of air as it bore down on him. It wasn't a vehicle. There were no headlights. It was something else. Something much worse than the Morgans in their ATVs was closing in on Shaw as he staggered forward.

He could see the tin shed up ahead and he angled toward it.

It was close, almost on him, he could hear its snarl, but Shaw kept on.

A shape shot out of the darkness, four large paws churning up the dirt in a rhythmic beat, before becoming airborne. Over one hundred pounds of muscle, sinew, bone and teeth careened into the back of Shaw, barreling him over.

The Italian mastiff peeled sideways then rounded back on Shaw as he lay on the ground. The worst thing Shaw could do was to bring his arms up, extending them, giving the dog something clean and easy to latch its crushing jaws onto. Instead he curled into a ball protecting his throat, head and belly, the soft areas that attack dogs want to rip into.

The dog closed in and Shaw tensed for the onslaught of being torn to pieces.

Blood splattered across Shaw in a warm spray, then nothing.

Shaw looked up. The dog was a few feet away, slumped in death, steam rising from its body, it twitched once then stopped.

Shaw kicked away from the animal, looking around, confused.

Three ATVs burst out of the night and skidded to a halt in a spray of dirt and rocks a few feet from Shaw, the glare of the driving lights blinding him.

Billy Morgan almost fell out of his ATV as it skidded to a halt, such was his ferocity of wanting to reach Shaw and kill him. A bullet was too good for him. He was going to beat Shaw to death with his bare hands.

Billy stumbled upright then sprinted past the body of his second dog. The sight of its mutilated shape pushed Billy over the edge, a white-hot nail of rage drove right into his brain. Most of the dog's head was gone, ripped apart. From the neck up it was a twisted bloody bouquet of skull, furry mush, partial jawbone, pink gums and canine teeth.

"You bastard!" Billy screamed. He started kicking into Shaw as he lay on the ground, sinking his boots in. Jed and Rory rushed forward and joined the melee, soon all three churned up the dirt in a violent frenzy, feet and legs back and forth.

Shaw balled-up again, covering himself as best he could, protecting his head, face, ribs, and groin. His forearms, elbows, back, knees and shins bearing the brunt of the onslaught as he curled into the fetal position.

Thirty seconds later Billy yelled, "Enough!" His voice hoarse from exertion, his face coated in sweat, tears and dribble, eyes wild with rage.

Rory sunk in one last kick for good measure then backed off with Jed.

Shaw's nose was bleeding and a nasty gash had opened above one eye where a boot got through his defenses. He rolled onto his back and gulped in air. It was like he had been beaten by a sledgehammer. He ached all over, but thankfully nothing was broken. Bruises would heal and eventually vanish. Broken limbs took a little longer.

Jed collected his rifle from his ATV and came back to Shaw.

"No," Billy said, as he looked at the bloody and beaten shape of Shaw. "He deserves a more painful death."

Billy looked around, but couldn't see any gun that Shaw had used. It didn't matter, his mind was focused elsewhere.

He had an idea.

He unsheathed his hunting knife from his belt. "I'm going to skin him alive like a deer. Hang him up and peel him open like a carcass." He gave a manic laugh like he had gone completely insane.

"Yeah, just like that bitch Annie," Jed sniggered.

Rory moved closer. "Yeah, but we did her first, took turns in the shed," he said, nodding toward the tin shed that was lit up by the headlights.

Shaw looked up.

Annie? The girl whose silver identity bracelet he had found.

"Pity we can't fuck him first like we did her," Rory sniveled, disappointment written across his face.

"Don't forget, we've still got that other whore locked up safe and sound in the shipping container," Jed replied. "Ox won't be needing her anymore."

"Shut up, the pair of you!" Billy growled. He held up the hunting knife. Ten inches of serrated steel glinted in the headlights. "He'll get fucked alright," Billy said quietly, as he regarded the razor-sharp beveled length of the knife.

Shaw looked at the knife and slowly gathered himself, tensing each muscle, ready to fight no matter what. But his eyes shifted back to the dead dog.

"Annie?" he said. It was worth a chance, to prolong the conversation. The one thing he knew was that murderous bullies always liked to brag about their conquests, their sick achievements. They got off on it. And Billy Morgan was no different.

Billy tilted his head as he looked at Shaw. It made no difference to him. He was going to skin and flay open Shaw anyway. The man was going to die. And Billy liked to reveal to his victims some of the pain and suffering they were about to endure. He enjoyed seeing the fear in their eyes. But for some reason this man had no fear. He just regarded Billy with a calm stare.

"Tell me about Annie," Shaw said, raising his hands submissively, like he had given up, he was their prisoner now.

"Bitch ran too," Billy lowered the knife, but still held it by his side. "Thought she was fast, but not fast enough." He paused, thinking back to Annie, shuffling through the catalogue of images in his mind, trying to recollect that particular girl. There had been so many. "Didn't use dogs that night," Billy continued, his voice distant. "No need." Billy pointed at the shed with the knife. "Told her if she got to the shed then we would let her go." Billy looked at Jed and Rory, and gave a demented smile.

"Bitch didn't know me and Jed were waiting for her in the shed," Rory laughed. "Should've seen the look on her face when Billy finally caught up with her and she ran inside and saw us in there too."

"Squealed like a pig that girl," Jed added. "Thought she had won. Thought she was home free." Jed turned and looked at Shaw, the eyes of a sadistic killer. "But we never let them go once we have 'em."

For three hours they had Annie Turnball in a hellish nightmare inside the old tin shed. Three hours of wonderful video footage. Annie was special. Her video was Rory's favorite. It was the one he had shown the Ox so he would know what to do when his chance came. The Morgan brothers had taken their time with Annie.

"So what did you do with her?" Shaw turned to Jed.

"She's deep. Real deep. In hell, I suppose," Jed replied.

For a moment Shaw thought Jed was just fantasizing. Then he realized what Jed had meant, where Annie was, her body. And the others too.

Real deep.

Billy looked at Shaw. "Don't worry. You'll soon be joining her. In hell, that is." Billy raised the knife again. He always wanted to gut and skin a person. He and his brothers had done it with deer and the like. But not a human. That would be neat. Ever since he watched some TV show on cable, some medieval fantasy series, he had wanted to do it. The show had plenty of tits, ass, and killing. He liked the show, because all the evil people seemed to get away with anything and all the goody-two-shoes were killed off.

Billy liked that. He wished he could be in a TV show like that. There was one character in the TV show, some evil dude who lived in a big old castle. Killed his parents so he could rule the family throne. Nice guy. Had hunting dogs as well. That's when Billy decided to get the dogs, big hunting dogs so he could hunt people too, like the evil dude on the TV show. The dude on the TV show even skinned people, flayed them open. Billy liked that a lot, it was like the dude on the show and he were kindred spirits.

"When we're done with you, we're going to pay old Daisy a little visit," Billy said to Shaw.

"Bring her back here, to the shed. Got another video camera all set up for that one," Rory added.

Billy slipped out a cell phone from his pocket with his other hand and held it up for Shaw to see. "I'll just let Daisy know Callie is coming too."

Shaw looked at the phone in Billy's hand as he thumbed a text message. He realized it must be Callie's cell phone. Billy had taken her phone and was sending fake texts to Daisy, leading her on.

"You know I had her back in high school," Billy said without looking up. "Prom night, senior year."

Shaw could feel his anger rise. He thought as much. The way Daisy had reacted to Billy. The comments made by Taylor Giles in the basement.

"Little whore wouldn't put out, so I had to make her see my way of things," he laughed as he tapped on the screen. "She soon learned, after I roughed her up a bit. She had it coming, you know." Billy looked up and shared an evil smile with Jed and Rory. They both chuckled.

"Some call it rape. I call it a lesson in discipline." All three Morgan brothers laughed. "Now it's Jed and Rory's turn to teach Daisy McAlister some discipline. I'm just going to watch while they do her. You know? Keep it in the family like. I like to share everything with my brothers."

Billy sent the text and pocketed the phone.

They moved toward Shaw, their backs to the ATVs, their shadows falling across Shaw as he pushed away from them along the ground.

"Jed, Rory hold him down," Billy said, bringing up the hunting knife. "I need to cut away his pants first."

Shaw heard it first, a suppressed puff, a faint expulsion of sound like a spitball through a drinking straw.

The high-velocity bullet went into the back of Billy's right shoulder, punching a neat dime-sized hole through his anterior deltoid. It went in clean, but came out messy. The .338 Lapua Magnum round was overkill, but she preferred it that way. Better to shoot once, be certain, leave a mess.

Billy took another step before he realized that most of his front shoulder was gone.

He dropped the knife, but stayed upright and did what any normal person would.

He turned around and looked behind him.

It had the desired effect.

Jed and Rory turned as well, to the only direction the shot could possibly have come from.

They were perfectly lit, standing dumb as deer in the headlights.

Three more suppressed shots, left to right, an easy natural sweeping arc, hitting them each dead center, bridge of the nose, precision shooting.

Head shots. Dead kill. No chance.

Jed, Rory and Billy dropped like puppets with their strings cut.

Shaw could only look on in disbelief. In a split second the Morgan family tree had been pruned. Permanently.

The darkness behind the ATVs moved and the silhouette of a woman materialized like a wraith.

Shaw raised his hand, shading the glare from the headlights.

She walked around the front of the three ATVs and the light hit her in full. She was tall, lithe, and moved with grace and supreme confidence, maintaining her feminine poise in a world where men typically did what she had just done.

All black tactical clothing. Black gloves, boots, blackened face, raven black shoulder-length hair tied in a ponytail for practical reasons. Black compact sniper rifle in her hands, a German-made DSR-1, lightweight, with silencer and night-vision scope.

Shaw just gaped at her.

Two obliterated attack dogs, three dead Morgan brothers, the reason standing in front of him.

What the hell, he was going to die anyway.

Shaw said, "Halloween is still a few months away." He grimaced as he got to one knee, hands raised. It hurt even to breathe, let alone talk.

The woman didn't smile. Two emerald green eyes stared at him from black camouflage face paint. She looked down at the bodies of Billy, Jed and Rory Morgan. She kept the muzzle of her rifle trained on Shaw without having to look at him. If she could hit a dog running flat-out in the dark, across undulating ground at three hundred yards, then killing a man on the ground ten feet away wouldn't be an issue. She just needed to flex her index finger a millimeter and Shaw would be added to the body-count.

Shaw knew she wouldn't answer the first obvious question, so he asked the second obvious question that came to mind.

"Why?"

She looked back at Shaw, battered and beaten.

Her eyes narrowed like she was deciding how much to say. "The girl. They weren't supposed to touch the girl."

The woman had crept up behind the three Morgan brothers while Billy was telling Shaw everything. She had heard it all. They were told not to harm the girl, just spook her a bit. But they had taken it too far and the woman had orders to make sure no harm came to Daisy McAlister. She had to intervene. They were dumb-ass murdering rapists that she would have killed for free anyway.

The dogs were a separate matter. She had been watching the Morgan compound from a distance and had seen Shaw being led outside the fence to where the three Morgan brothers were standing with their ATVs. She had watched them let Shaw go and then the dogs were brought and soon after they were released after him. He had no chance. She retreated back toward the McAlister ranch but kept an eye on proceedings. While she was tracking Shaw through her night vision scope as he stumbled across landscape, she could see that one of the attack dogs was closing in on him. As she watched, the dog suddenly stopped, sniffed the air then turned its head toward where she lay perched on a small rocky ledge.

She didn't know they were going to use dogs. If she had, she would have washed three times with a fragrance-free soap and not worn any deodorant or body-spray. Maybe even set up a bait decoy to draw the dog in.

The dog must have picked up the faint trace of her, and was deciding whether or not to follow the new, stronger scent. So she put a bullet in its side before the dog made up its mind.

She hated attack dogs. They were vile, vicious creatures bred for killing. So she cut its throat as well just to make sure the thing was dead. That gave her some pleasure, made it more personal with the dog's owner.

The woman lowered her rifle slightly. "I don't have to provide proof-of-kill," she said, looking at Shaw. "It's not a requirement for you."

Shaw was perplexed.

"I don't like what happened here," she continued. "It's none of my business. I don't ask questions. But you are part of my business. I was paid to make you disappear."

Shaw felt a tightening of his gut and raised his hands a little higher. "Who paid you to kill me?"

The woman shook her head. "You don't seem to understand. I was paid to make you *disappear*. That's what I do. So disappear."

Shaw cocked his head questioningly, but she answered him before he could ask.

"You have twenty-four hours to leave, disappear, never come back. Return to the McAlister ranch if you must, but do not set foot again on the Morgan property. It will be taken care of."

There was a backup plan. Her employer always had a backup plan. Jim Morgan had his chance to resolve this, but he couldn't control his three sons. So her employer had no choice but to instruct her to intervene.

She looked down at the three corpses. "I'll tell them I started early on my next assignment." She looked at Shaw. "The girl will be safe. But you won't be, if you're not gone in twenty-four hours. Leave town. If you return, I will kill you. I have a reputation to keep." She had never failed an assignment, but she looked at Shaw with a mutual respect. She had seen his file. Like all her assignments, she was always given a meticulously researched dossier on all her targets.

Her hand went behind her waist, unclipped a trauma pouch and tossed it to him. "Don't go to a doctor or local hospital. It will raise suspicion. You will find everything you need in that to recover quickly. I have a spare."

The trauma pack landed just in front of Shaw. It contained everything to treat wounds ranging from a simple infected laceration to a full chest gunshot. Antibiotics, insulin, adrenalin hyperemic, halo seals, CAT tourniquet, including special military-grade steroids to aid a fast recovery.

"But first," she said. She slung her rifle over her shoulder, stepped forward, and bent down. Taking Shaw's hand in her own she said, "Lay flat on the ground." Shaw did as he was told. He knew what she was going to do

"Thank you," he said. There was no time to inject anything into his shoulder, he was just going to have to bear the imminent shock.

"Don't thank me. It's purely business and your business here is concluded. Leave and don't return." She stood up, placed her foot on his shoulder, pushed her weight down on it and slowly rotated the arm to the angle she wanted.

She gave a nod to Shaw. "Ready?"

He took a deep breath, closed his eyes and nodded.

FORTY-FIVE

The heavens opened and the rain fell in cold, solid sheets. Daisy's phoned pinged, but she didn't hear it over the downpour. Someone was coming toward her, a shape through the curtain of rain.

She raised her rifle and took aim, her finger on the trigger. The sky flared with lightning.

There was a loud crack and thunder exploded overhead.

Then Shaw hobbled out of the darkness toward her.

She lowered her rifle when she recognized it was him, slung it over her shoulder and started running, catching him just as he was about to fall.

"Christ, what happened?" she yelled.

Shaw put his arm around her shoulders, grateful to take the weight off his swollen ankle. "We need to keep going," he grimaced in pain. "Get away from here . . . back home."

She shone the flashlight on him. He felt ice-cold, his body shivering, his face drawn. Streams of water cascaded off his head, turning pink from a deep cut above his eye, before running down his chest and bare torso, his skin pale, bruised, drawn tight, his ribs showing.

Daisy pulled off her anorak, wrapped it around his shoulders and held him close.

Shaw went to sit down, but Daisy dragged him upright again. "No!" Daisy screamed. "You need to keep moving, I need to get you back to the house or you're going to die of exposure."

"Callie," he mumbled. "Your phone, it's not her."

Daisy tried to make sense of what Shaw was saying, but the rain beat down with such ferocity that she had to yell as another flare of lightning cut across the sky, and a clap of thunder boomed directly overhead.

"Callie, what about her? Where is she? Does Billy have her?" Daisy was desperate, wanting answers.

Shaw was disorientated, he looked around wildly. He had gone another mile thinking he could make it without any meds, but the cold overhauled him and now hypothermia was setting in.

"Here," he said, thrusting the small nylon pouch into her hands. "Open it," he slurred. He was chilled to the bone. The rain had brought a sudden drop in temperature. His teeth started to chatter.

Daisy took the pouch, unzipped it. It opened up like a clam. It was packed on each side with an array of medical supplies: small bandages, auto injector pens, field dressings, foil packets, shears, all held neatly in place in layered pockets and Velcro bands.

"Quickly." Shaw fumbled through the contents, his fingers almost numb, and found what he was looking for: an auto injector. He removed the pen-shaped object, pulled off the safety release with his teeth, spat it away and pressed the end hard against his thigh and pressed the button releasing the spring-loaded syringe.

He felt an instant surge of warmth and energy coursing through his body.

He gave the spent injector to Daisy to put back in the pouch, he didn't want to discard it—he wanted to leave behind no trace of himself or any evidence.

Shaw took a deep breath and felt his energy reserves kick in from the meds.

They still had a distance to go to get back to the ranch, but Shaw knew he could make it with Daisy's help.

"Your phone, I need your phone," Shaw said. "We need to save Callie."

"Where is she?" Daisy said distraughtly. She pulled out her phone, saw the last text, and deleted it.

The rain started to ease, the storm moving away.

"You need to make a phone call. I'll tell you the number. Tell the person who answers that you have a message from Ben Shaw. Say my name. Tell them the address of the Morgan ranch. They'll know what to do. Tell them it's urgent. They need to contact the sheriff department, not the Hays local police. Tell them people are dead and more will die." Shaw spoke rapidly while Daisy dialed the number. "Tell them there's a woman held hostage in a shipping container on the Morgan property."

Daisy looked at Shaw in horror.

"It's OK, she'll be safe for the moment," Shaw said. But he didn't tell her it was because the three Morgan brothers were dead, or that she and Callie were going to be the brother's next victims had they lived.

Daisy made the call, following Shaw's instructions.

A woman answered after two rings. At first the woman on the line seemed confused, then Daisy told her a line, like a code, that the woman understood, to verify the caller. Daisy told the woman the information, stressed the urgency and ended the call when she was done.

"Let's go," he said, leaning on her again.

Daisy took his arm, steadied him, and they set off in the direction of the ranch.

****

The Ellis County Sheriff officers were the first to arrive, a convoy of five squad cars from Hays. Lights blazing in the predawn darkness they descended on the Morgan Ranch and were none too happy about being greeted at the entrance by a private security force armed with automatic weapons.

Since the sheriff's department had a county-wide jurisdiction compared to the local police, the Hays police officers who were among the guests could do nothing but stand aside and watch as the sheriff's deputies made their way to the shipping containers and demanded that they be opened.

Jim Morgan was all smiles and very accommodating—until they unlocked the third shipping container.

Then all hell broke loose.

Inside they found a young woman, Callie Wilson, a waitress from the local diner at the gas station who had been missing for three days. She was chained to the inside wall and was left with nothing more than a water bottle and a steel bucket to urinate into.

The entire Morgan property was immediately placed in lockdown. No one was allowed to leave including the mayor and several high-ranking state and county officials. Paramedics were called and then, forty minutes later, the FBI rolled in from the closest field office and things got a whole lot worse for Jim Morgan and his guests.

Callie Wilson was relatively unscathed except for mild dehydration, but she was bundled into the back of an ambulance and taken to the local hospital.

Computers, laptops, and external hard drives were seized that would later reveal that Jim Morgan and a number of his guests were involved in an extensive underground network of political corruption, money laundering, tax fraud, and business extortion.

Just after 9:00 a.m. a second team of FBI investigators found a large collection of hard drives hidden in the living quarters of Billy Morgan in the sprawling Morgan home. The FBI estimated in total the drives contained over five hundred hours of high definition recordings showing more than forty women being violently raped, tortured then murdered over a number of years. All three Morgan brothers were featured in most of the videos together with local police officers and county officials, most of them married with children.

Forensic testing of the computers would later also reveal an entire online community who had access to a secure "members only" website run by Billy, Jed, and Rory Morgan, where live video streaming was conducted on pay-per-view basis. Special live requests were being sent by the members for a certain fee during the live streaming of victims all in real-time.

A thorough search of the Morgan compound failed to locate the three Morgan brothers: Billy, Jed, and Rory. However a wider search of the property was made and three bodies were discovered in an old tin shed where three ATVs had also been found. The bodies had been trussed up to a rafter, and each had been killed by a single head-shot. Upon closer inspection the FBI found that the genitals of each brother had been removed and stuffed into their own mouths.

Based on the information provided in the phone call by Daisy McAlister, a second contingent of sheriff deputies arrived at the McAlister ranch by mid-morning. Daisy had simply relayed what she had been told to say by Shaw, that another area of interest was the old pit mine that was located on the McAlister property.

When the FBI came up to the McAlister home, Daisy greeted them and invited them inside. She escorted them down into the basement where Taylor Giles was still handcuffed. He was promptly taken into custody when Daisy told the agents that he was one of Jim Morgan's corrupt associates who also took part in the systematic rape of young women abducted by Jim Morgan's three sons.

Taylor Giles was subsequently identified in three of the rape videos taken as evidence by the FBI.

The FBI agents thanked Daisy, but said that they would be returning the next day to question her and search her property as part of the widening investigation. She thanked them as well and said she would fully co-operate with any search and investigation. She told the FBI that it was just her, on her lonesome on the ranch, as it had been for years.

Later the police would search the old pit mine where they would make the gruesome discovery of three bodies of women in various stages of decomposition at the bottom of the mine. Post-mortems and DNA tests revealed that one was a young woman called Annie Turnball from Michigan, who had gone missing six months ago.

In the weeks that followed the raid on the Morgan compound, the FBI would descend on all business locations and property holdings of the Morgan family across the entire state to conduct a thorough forensic examination of all their business dealings going back more than twenty years. Bank accounts would be frozen, assets would be bonded, and all property would be seized pending a full federal investigation.

The old bank building in Martha's End was one of the locations identified by the sheriff department after viewing the videos on the hard drives, and the building was raided. Inside the vault room they found twelve barrels of acid containing the remains of other victims of the Morgan brothers. One of the barrels contained the partially liquefied body of an Edward Linton, a geologist who had gone missing several years ago after selling his business.

FORTY-SIX

It was well past noon when Shaw woke in the upstairs guest bedroom. The window was drawn up and a light breeze ruffled the edges of the net curtain. Daisy carefully helped him sit up in bed, propping some large pillows behind him.

On the bedside table sat the open trauma pouch, several auto injector spent cartridges, and a glass of water. When they got back to the ranch before dawn, she took Shaw into the shower. They stood together under the scalding hot water, Shaw naked and Daisy fully clothed until he warmed up and had stopped shaking.

She dressed him in some of her father's old clothes then helped him into bed. He told her which meds to give him and she injected him with another dose of painkillers, antibiotics, and steroids. He fell into a deep sleep and was oblivious when the FBI first turned up at the front door hours later.

After Shaw was settled, she set down a breakfast tray and watched him eat hungrily. Shaw had made an amazing recovery. His face was still bruised, but his ankle and shoulder were on the mend thanks to the painkillers and other drugs. While he ate, Daisy filled him in on what had happened.

While she prepared breakfast she had turned on the television. Across all local channels it was being reported that an army of federal and state law enforcement agencies had descended on the private property of one of the wealthiest businessmen in the state of Kansas. A few of the national affiliates stations were also starting to air the breaking story. It had been rumored that several bodies had also been found on the property, and that a number of county officials and local police officers, including the mayor, were being detained by the FBI at the scene.

"What happens now?" Daisy asked. She sat at the foot of the bed and watched Shaw as he finished eating.

"It will run its course. It will take months before the full investigation is finished. How's Callie?"

"She's doing fine, she called me from the hospital. She'll be out in a few days. She said she owes you her life."

Shaw looked out the window. It was a bright clear day, a new day. He wished he could have figured out sooner that Billy Morgan had taken Callie. He felt bad knowing that she was in that shipping container for days right under his nose and he never knew. He turned back to Daisy. "I did nothing. She owes me nothing."

He looked at her and felt real sorrow for what had happened to her, for what Billy Morgan had done back in high school. "Daisy, I'm so sorry."

Daisy paused for a moment, searching his face, seeing what he now knew. She fought back tears, not wanting to relive the memories of that horrible night. "Is he dead?" It was all she could say.

"All three of them are dead," he replied. "And there will be others. The Morgan brothers were a bunch of murderous rapists. The police will find other bodies, their victims. I think they will find some down the old pit mine. They came onto your land, but I think they just used the mine as a place to dump the bodies, nowhere else I think on your land." Shaw only hoped but he didn't tell Daisy that.

Daisy just nodded, not wanting to know the details, content to know they were dead.

Shaw went on and told her everything he knew or had worked out so far. Daisy said nothing, listening. The shadows had moved far across the room by the time he had finished.

"The report by Edward Linton will be returned to you," Shaw said. "It was addressed to your father, it belonged to him and as next-of-kin it now belongs to you. The police will locate it when they go through everything, I imagine. You don't really need it anymore." Shaw had told Daisy about the second report Jim Morgan had commissioned, the one Shaw took from the site office. Daisy could also just as easily engage someone else to investigate, but she knew now what was under her land.

"How big are we talking? The discovery," she asked.

Shaw tried to remember the figures on the report. There were terms like *source rock, hydrocarbon reserves, oil reservoirs*. But on the last page the true scale of the oil field was revealed together with likely production capacities.

"Daisy, we're talking of an oil field being the biggest find in history here. Billions of barrels, high-grade quality, billions of dollars. Enough for America to be totally self-sufficient just on your oil field for more than a hundred years."

My oil, my oil field, Daisy liked the sound of that.

She smiled, "Maybe I can pay some of the bills now."

"Are you crazy? You can buy all of Europe and more."

"Why would I want Europe? I have everything I want right here." But Daisy's life was not going to be the same again, ever.

"Jim Morgan killed your father because of it." Shaw said. "Your father had an idea of what was under his land and the Morgans found out."

Daisy knew that Jim Morgan had killed her father. She knew when she saw her father dead at the bottom of the ravine on that frightful day. Call it gut instinct or a woman's intuition. She just couldn't prove it.

"The FBI will be back. They'll search here, the ranch, this house," Daisy said. By now she had figured out that he had some sort of loose connection with the authorities, a connection that he didn't want to reveal or discuss. The woman who answered the phone wanted to know where Shaw was, she was persistent. But Daisy just passed on the information and hung up.

"Are you in some kind of trouble?" Daisy asked. She wanted to know more, but was also respectful of his privacy.

Shaw smiled, "No. It's nothing like that. It's just that there are things about my past that I want to leave be." His expression became suddenly serious, he was running out of time.

Twenty-four hours. That's what the woman last night had said. A clear threat. He didn't want any harm to come to Daisy or Callie.

"I have to go," he said.

Daisy just nodded. She understood. She had dreaded this moment, the moment she knew would eventually come—when he would tell her he was leaving.

"When?" she asked, wishing the answer would be days not hours. But she knew Shaw wanted to be gone before the FBI agents returned.

"In a few hours," he replied.

Daisy felt crushed. During the last few days she had felt such joy and excitement just being around Shaw. But she knew it had to end. She had never felt so alive as she had in those intimate moments they had spent together, moments that had changed her as woman.

Daisy took a deep breath, "Then we still have time."

FORTY-SEVEN

It was slow, tender. They took their time. There was no rush. The last bus leaving town was still four hours away.

Daisy had to be careful, wounds had to heal. But they held hands, with her on top, her hips moving slow and rhythmic, with him deep inside her, her eyes never leaving his as she moved up and down, long and slow along his entire length. A late afternoon breeze came through the window, the sun slowly setting, a golden hue across their nakedness.

It was different than the other times she had been with him. It had more meaning, more emotion, more connection, not just physically, but that too.

His gentleness with her made her even more turned on, and it showed. She had never been so wet before, she was almost embarrassed. There was a moment of awkwardness in her eyes and she blushed slightly. That's when he reached up and pulled her face toward his, and kissed her. A deep, long and tender kiss that went on forever.

With a newfound confidence she tilted back from him, pivoted her hips forward, arched her back, placed her hands behind her on his knees.

She opened herself up more to him, revealing everything.

He moved deeper inside her, she tilted back farther, bringing her feet under her, pushing back and forth with her legs. The sensation was more intense. Then taking one of his hands, she guided his fingers between the juncture of where they came together, at her apex where her skin formed a tiny hood, like the pollinia of a beautiful orchid, her petals thick and engorged.

She took the pad of his thumb and guided it to where she wanted him to rub with each thrust in to her, small circular swirls, around and around, over the small erect nodule that had now shed its hood and was hard and swollen.

I'm the boss, she thought, before her own heat consumed her.

****

She watched the pickup truck, the Dodge, the one she had seen many times before. It pulled up in the dirt parking lot, kicking up a plume of dust before coming to a stop. It wasn't really a parking lot, just a vacant plot of dirt boxed between two abandoned buildings that was dimly lit by a single light pole. Apart from the Dodge, the parking lot empty.

Two people got out: a man carrying a backpack and the girl.

She was safe.

The woman watching was happy, if that was at all possible for her.

After completing the assignment on the ranch, she had packed up her equipment and withdrew to the small township. There was too much activity on the property now to stay, but they would find no trace of her other than the three bodies.

She adjusted the focus on the binoculars, watching her last assignment walk to the sidewalk, the girl following. He was doing as he was told, a few hours earlier than the deadline she had given him as well.

Good.

She liked a man who did what he was told. When they didn't, she made them disappear.

Permanently.

A few minutes later the Greyhound bus slid out of the darkness, its long silver shape dulled with road grime and exhaust dust. It pulled up just past where the man and the girl stood. The doors hissed open revealing a gloomy interior, tired faces leaned against the long bank of windows along its length.

The man and girl embraced, no kiss, just a lingering hug, more like friends than lovers, the girl holding on for a moment longer. They parted and the man stepped up onto the bus. The doors hissed closed and the bus lumbered off with a deep mechanical groan.

The girl waited until the bus was gone, then she drifted back to the Dodge, twirling her hair. No sadness, but an obvious glow of contentment in the way she walked.

She opened the door, then paused. She turned around and looked in the direction of the woman with the binoculars, hidden amongst the bushes, across the street.

The girl stared straight at her.

The woman shifted further back among the leaves and branches.

The girl turned and slid into the driver's seat of the Dodge and started the engine. With a turn of the wheel, and a skid of dirt, the girl was gone.

The woman lowered her binoculars. She knew she hadn't been seen, but it was still an eerie feeling.

Twice now.

The woman withdrew back through the bushes, returned to her car, and placed her binoculars in the trunk where the rest of her gear was neatly stored. She got in and started the engine.

On the passenger seat was a tablet device. She called up a file and punched a new address into the car's GPS. She hit the gas, drove back along the short road, onto the main road and toward her next assignment.

She was glad to be leaving this small town. All her assignments here were complete.

It was nice town, with a few less bad people in it now.

THE END.

IF YOU ENJOYED THIS BOOK

★★★★★

Thank you for investing your time and money in me. I hope you enjoyed my book and it allowed you to escape from your world for a few minutes, for a few hours or even for a few days.

I would really appreciate it if you could post an honest review on any of the publishing platforms that you use. It would mean a lot to me personally, as I read every review that I get and you would be helping me become a better author. By posting a review, it will also allow other readers to discover me, and the worlds that I build. Hopefully they too can escape from their reality for just a few moments each day.

For news about me, new books and exclusive material then please:

- Follow me on Facebook: JK Ellem on Facebook
- Follow me on Instagram: @ellemjk

- Subscribe to my Youtube Channel
- Follow me on Goodreads
- Visit my Website: www.jkellem.com

About the Author

JK Ellem was born in London and spent his formative years preferring to read books and comics rather than doing his homework.

He is the innovative author of cutting-edge popular adult thriller fiction. He likes writing thrillers that are unpredictable, have multiple layers and sub-plots that tend to lead his readers down the wrong path with twists and turns that they cannot see coming. He writes in the genres of crime, mystery, suspense and psychological thrillers.

JK is obsessed with improving his craft and loves honest feedback from his fans. His idea of success is to be stopped in the street by a supermodel in a remote European village where no one speaks English and asked to autograph one of his books and to take a quick selfie.

He has a fantastic dry sense of humor that tends to get him into trouble a lot with his wife and three children.

He splits his time between the US, the UK and Australia.

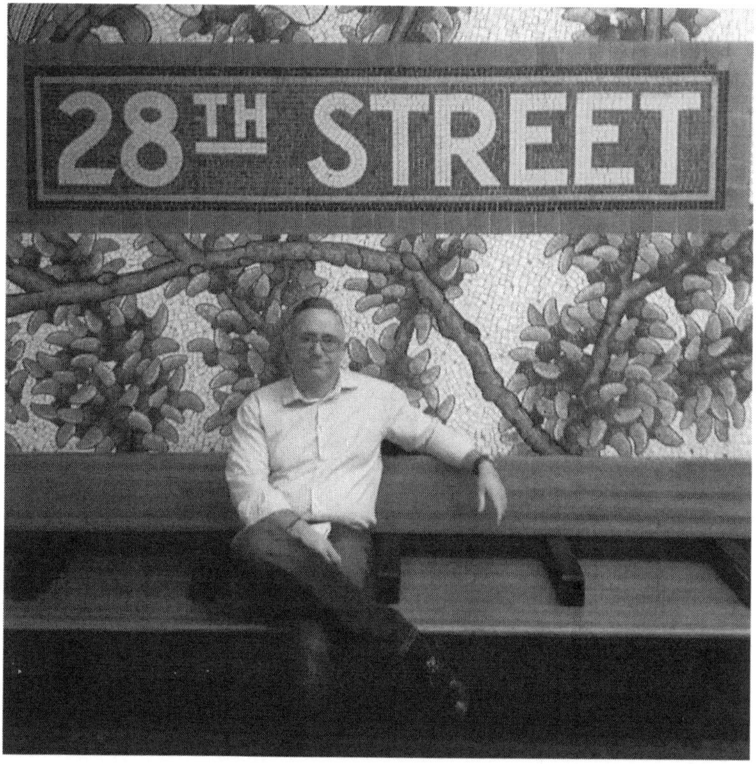
28TH STREET

Printed in Great Britain
by Amazon